The meat locker door clanged shut

It had locked, like the storeroom and huge garage-style doors of the warehouse. If there was some way Joy could make the crates around her fall and not get herself crushed in the process, she could climb to the windows near the ceiling, crawl through, hang by her hands and then drop.

She tugged on one crate and it tumbled. Others followed with hollow, pounding sounds, like artillery fire. She used the crates as a staircase, then opened one of the windows.

A snorting, blowing noise sounded in the silence. It seemed human . . . and nearby. Joy froze. Perched across from her sat a little man with the face of a gargoyle. A creature straight from hell. And he was staring right at her.

ABOUT THE AUTHOR

Vickie York has served as a commissioned officer in both the U.S. Army and U.S. Air Force. After an assignment to the Defense Language Institute in Monterey, California, where *School for Spies* is set, Vickie served as an intelligence officer for the rest of her military career. She was awarded a Bronze Star for service during the Vietnam conflict. Beginning with the publication of *The Pestilence Plot* in 1982, in hardcover, her novels have been based on her intelligence expertise. Vickie has traveled extensively and now makes her home in Tacoma, Washington, where she was born. She enjoys riding ferries on Puget Sound with special friends, singing in the church choir and taking long walks with her German shepherd.

Books by Vickie York

HARLEQUIN INTRIGUE

School for Spies

Vickie York

Harlequin Books

TORONTO • NEW YORK • LONDON
AMSTERDAM • PARIS • SYDNEY • HAMBURG
STOCKHOLM • ATHENS • TOKYO • MILAN

For my brother, Douglas

Acknowledgments
Major Diane M. Dempsey and
Petty Officer B. R. Brown
Public Affairs Office, Defense Language Institute
Dr. Alma B. Kelly, Pathologist

Harlequin Intrigue edition published January 1992

ISBN 0-373-22178-9

SCHOOL FOR SPIES

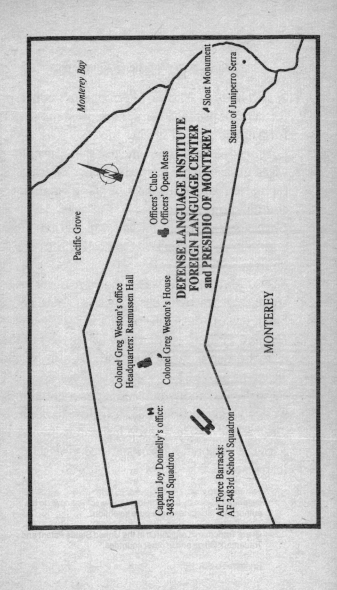

Monterey Bay

Pacific Grove

Officers' Club:
Officers' Open Mess

Colonel Greg Weston's office
Headquarters: Rasmussen Hall

Colonel Greg Weston's House

**DEFENSE LANGUAGE INSTITUTE
FOREIGN LANGUAGE CENTER
and PRESIDIO OF MONTEREY**

Sloat Monument

Statue of Juniperro Serra

MONTEREY

Captain Joy Donnelly's office:
3483rd Squadron

Air Force Barracks:
AF 3483rd School Squadron

CAST OF CHARACTERS

Joy Donnelly—The air force captain's concern for her troops made her a target, and the search for truth could cost her her life.

Gregory Weston—The "mustang" army colonel was a devastatingly attractive man...with a reputation for ruthlessness. It was a volatile combination.

Chris Tuck—The airman knew more than most, and someone was anxious to keep him from talking.

Santos Mueller—He was well aware of his students' extracurricular activities...and he had a few off-duty jobs of his own.

Barbara Philpott—The sergeant's loyalty to the army bordered on the fanatical. How far would she go to prove it?

"Eye"—The anonymous newspaper columnist was suddenly hitting *much* too close to home.

Julio Ramon—He was too intimately involved with the personal lives of some of his instructors.

Chapter One

Tuesday Night

A man's voice hissed at Joy Donnelly from the blackness behind the junipers. A harsh whisper, the sound was blotted out almost immediately by the distant bellow of the foghorn at the end of Lighthouse Avenue. She couldn't make out the words.

Joy froze in her tracks. With a bag of groceries in each arm and her house key buried in the depths of her shoulder bag, there was no way she could get inside quickly. Her defenses down, she was at the mercy of the unknown intruder.

Settle down, she told herself, fighting her panic. *Wouldn't our stalwart commandant gloat if he knew I was on the verge of collapse at hearing somebody's voice from behind the bushes?*

The thought gave her courage. The commandant, a hard-nosed army colonel named Greg Weston, seemed convinced she didn't have any gumption. Well, she'd show him.

The voice spoke again, louder this time, strained almost to breaking in its effort to be soft and yet heard.

"Psst! Captain Donnelly! Over here!"

Every nerve in Joy's body collapsed with relief. The intruder had used her military rank. That meant he was probably in her outfit.

"Who is it?" she demanded in her best squadron-commander's voice. "Come out where I can get a look at you."

"I can't," he whispered in the same urgent tone.

The hollow bellow of the foghorn drowned out his voice again. Joy strained to catch his words.

"It's Airman Tuck, ma'am. If I come from behind this bush somebody might see me."

Joy let out her breath in a long sigh. She might have known. Airman Tuck was on the verge of washing out of the Defense Language Institute's Spanish program. In addition to his academic problems, he seemed determined to get himself into serious trouble. His last scrape had involved a free-for-all with several other airmen in Joy's Air Force Student Squadron. Now this. Didn't he realize coming to her house at eleven o'clock at night was out of line?

She peered into the blackness, trying to locate him. "Get away from those bushes so I can see you," she ordered.

There was a barely discernible movement near one of the largest junipers. An instant later, through the wispy fog, she recognized the airman's squarish face. The rest of his small, wiry frame was almost invisible, covered in dark clothing that blended with the shrubbery behind him.

"I've got to talk to you right now, Captain, where nobody can hear us." His words were halting, his voice unsteady.

Exasperated, Joy walked the short distance to the porch and set down her groceries. Then she retraced her steps, her rubber soled running shoes crunching on the weedy lawn.

As soon as she got a whiff of the liquor on his breath, she had a pretty good idea what was behind Airman Tuck's unexpected appearance.

If this doesn't take the cake! she thought. *Only Airman Tuck would come calling on his squadron commander uninvited, three sheets to the wind, and in the middle of the night. If the commandant finds out, he'll be all the more convinced I'm too easy on my troops.*

"Report to my office at 0730 tomorrow morning," she ordered crisply. "Sergeant Blakeman and I will discuss whatever's bothering you then. Your story had better be good, Airman Tuck." She paused for emphasis. "It had better be very, very good."

Even in the darkness, his face looked a couple of shades whiter than before she'd spoken. She'd obviously shaken him.

"But it's a matter of life and death," he croaked.

"Since you had time to stop for a few drinks on your way here, I rather doubt that," Joy said.

"I'm not drunk, Captain, if that's what you think." His attempt to sound reassuring failed when his voice broke. "It took more drinks than I'd figured on to warm up that policewoman."

Joy curbed her curiosity. There was no way she'd let him entice her into an extended conversation on the front lawn.

"Tomorrow morning, Airman Tuck," she said, starting toward the porch.

In a last-ditch effort to convince her, he left the shelter of the junipers and padded along behind her.

"Please, Captain," he pleaded. "You've got to help me. I don't know who else I can go to."

This time Joy caught the panic in his voice. It added a sharp edge of urgency to his plea.

He seemed to sense that her resolve was weakening. "It's truly a matter of life or death, Captain. I'm not exaggerating."

Perhaps she'd been wrong about his motives. He was out of line in coming, but maybe she should hear what he had to say.

Joy stopped walking, and he darted back behind the shrubbery.

Was she guilty of coddling her troops, as the commandant claimed? She pictured Colonel Weston's prominent jaw, rugged features, and the black eye patch that gave him a certain rakish look. Well, no matter how much he looked like an adventurer, he certainly didn't operate like one. In her eight years in the Air Force, Joy had never run into a more by-the-book, dogmatic officer. He was Army, not Air Force, of course. What Greg Weston needed was a tour of duty with a flying outfit. If that didn't loosen him up, nothing would.

Annoyed with herself for letting her attention wander, she turned to face the young airman. In spite of what the commandant might say about his unexpected midnight visit, Joy simply couldn't postpone discussing the man's problem until tomorrow morning—not when he seemed so upset.

"It's about Maria Cardoza," he whispered, speaking quickly so that Joy would be forced to hear him out. "She didn't drown accidentally, Captain. Somebody killed her."

Joy felt a tug on the arm of her sweatshirt as he tried to pull her into the bushes with him. She jerked away.

"I'm sorry," he apologized, "but we can't let anybody see us together. Whoever did it is already after me. If he thinks I've told you what I know, he'll be after you, too."

His voice broke, and he was silent for a moment. Fear oozed from him like a stain.

A shudder crawled down Joy's spine. She resisted the impulse to look over her shoulder.

"Go on," she prodded.

The airman took a deep breath. "Of course there's no way for him to figure out exactly what I've been looking for. Just knowing I'm snooping around's been enough to get him after me."

Joy's eyes narrowed as she remembered the incident. The head of the Spanish Department had gone to Miss Cardoza's home when she failed to report for work. He'd found her body in her backyard swimming pool and called the police. As far as Joy knew, the authorities considered the drowning accidental.

"What was your connection to Maria Cardoza, Airman Tuck?"

As she asked the question, Joy recalled that the woman had been a teacher. Small, with a voluptuous figure, she'd radiated the high-intensity alertness of a hunting falcon.

"Was Ms. Cardoza your instructor?" Joy asked softly, almost certain she'd been. No wonder Airman Tuck was upset. Since classes at the Defense Language Institute were small, limited to ten or less, students got to know their teachers very well in a short time.

"Please step behind this bush, Captain," he pleaded. The panic in his voice turned it to falsetto. "That light-colored running outfit you've got on sticks out like a sore thumb."

Joy didn't move. His fear was getting through to her, but she didn't intend to show it. Neither did she intend to let him tell her what to do. She kept her voice calm, her words reassuring. "There's nobody watching us, Airman Tuck. What makes you think there is?"

"Somebody's been following me. If he was on my tail tonight, he knows I spent the last two hours buying drinks for an off-duty policewoman, and that I probably found out what I wanted to know."

"Which is what?" She forced herself to be patient.

"That Maria wasn't wearing the crystal I gave her when she was found in her pool."

Joy didn't let herself get sidetracked by asking questions about "the crystal." Assuming it was some kind of jewelry, she said, "Maybe she took it off when she went swimming."

"She *never* took it off. Even in the shower."

"You seem awfully sure of that."

"I'm absolutely positive."

So that's how it was. He knew her intimately.

Was it possible that Airman Tuck himself was involved in her accident? Weren't the ones most closely involved with the victim the logical suspects in a suspicious death? Joy stepped backward, away from the junipers concealing him.

As though he could read her thoughts, the airman said, "You're probably wondering why I don't go straight to the police." His voice broke. "If I say anything, I'm afraid they'll think I did it. I was with her that night. We'd had an argument. It's just not fair that the last words I said to her were so nasty. She must have been killed sometime after I came back to the barracks."

He seemed on the verge of breaking down completely. It was so out of character for the cocky young airman that Joy put her hand on his arm to steady him. Under his wool sweater, he was trembling.

"You've got to help me, Captain," he went on. "I sure as hell don't want to risk going to jail, but I can't just stand aside and let whoever murdered Maria get away scot-free. If you won't help me, I'll set a trap for the bloody bastard."

"With yourself as bait, I suppose?"

He didn't answer—as though afraid that saying anything more might give Joy enough information to interfere with his plans.

She kept her voice calm. "Come into the house, and we'll talk about this, Airman Tuck. I want you to start from the beginning and tell me everything that's happened."

"We can't, ma'am." The panicky edge returned to his voice. "With all those lights on, somebody'll see us."

"Even if we're being watched right now—which I doubt—nobody will see you. My roommate's out for the evening, and I'll go in and switch the lights off. You can slip inside in the dark."

"Not until I look around." He turned to scrutinize the empty street. Nothing moved in the darkness. "I came to you because I trust you, Captain," he pleaded, his face a chalky blur behind the junipers. "Please don't tell anybody about me and Maria."

"Of course I won't tell anybody. At least not until we've had a chance to talk." She put some authority into her voice to give him the security of knowing somebody competent was in charge. "Now, I'll see you inside in about five minutes."

She started for the door before he could protest.

On the porch, Joy fished her house key out of her shoulder bag, opened the door, and picked up the two sacks of groceries.

Inside, she put the groceries on the kitchen counter and returned to the living room, turning off lights as she went. She'd left most of them on when she went to the store an hour or so ago.

When all was dark, she opened the front door and stood just inside, watching and listening.

From the next block came the dull roar of a motorcycle engine. The foghorn blared again, covering the fading sound of its motor.

For at least five minutes, Joy waited alone in the darkness by the half-open door, searching the shadows for some sign of movement.

There was none.

Apparently the young airman had lost his nerve.

Wednesday Morning

GREGORY WESTON fingered the black patch on his right eye and cursed the freak accident that had forced him, in the prime of his army career, to take a mothball job like this.

Being commandant of the Defense Language Institute might be a command position, but it was no place for a tough airborne-infantry soldier. A glorified desk job—that's all it was. With any luck he'd be out of here in a month or so. A new special forces training center was opening up in Florida, and Greg was almost positive he'd be chosen to command it.

His intercom buzzed. His secretary, Sergeant Barbara Philpott, made his morning even more dismal by announcing the arrival of Colonel Erick Spellman and Captain Joy Donnelly.

"They want to see you about an urgent matter involving an airman in Captain Donnelly's squadron, sir," said his sergeant. With her horse face, straight brown hair and imposing bulk, Sergeant Philpott was no beauty, but her loyalty more than made up for her lack of good looks.

"I'll see them in a few minutes," Greg said to the squawk box. With the switch off, Greg snorted loudly to himself. So Captain Donnelly had another "urgent matter" involving her airmen. Only last week she'd objected to the physical training program he'd just approved for all enlisted personnel E-4 and below. Somehow she'd managed to get the senior medic at neighboring Fort Ord to back her up. Rather than take the matter to higher authority, he'd modified the exercises.

Greg rubbed a hand over the rough skin on his cheek. Out of habit he rose and shaved early, long before the central California winter sunrise. By 0830 his beard had grown enough so that he could feel it.

Too bad I didn't get rid of her when I had the chance, he thought, settling back in his chair and putting his feet on the desk. The air force assignment people had sent him a copy of her service record before she arrived. He'd objected to her on the grounds that she was too young and too junior for the slot, which called for a major. In fact, the man she'd replaced was an O-4 in his mid-forties. She was an O-3, a captain, and only twenty-nine.

The assignment people insisted she had the necessary experience, pointing out that she was on the promotion list for major below the zone. Greg was well aware that only the best officers were selected for early promotion. Reluctantly, he'd okayed Captain Donnelly's assignment.

As soon as he saw her, he knew he'd made a serious mistake.

An older, less distracting woman would have been highly preferable to the all-American girl who had reported to him three months ago, her well-tailored blue air force service uniform emphasizing her aura of superb physical fitness.

Judas Priest, he'd thought, giving her a head-to-toe once-over. *She looks closer to twenty than twenty-nine.*

Her dark red hair, her girl-next-door smile topped by freckles across the nose, her vigorous, well-proportioned body—combine all that with a few hundred eager young troops and the commandant's got big trouble. Or so Greg thought at the time, disturbed by his own reaction. Highly disciplined, he was able to control his momentary lapse almost immediately, but it bothered him anyway. If she affected him like this, what would she do to the men in her squadron?

As things turned out, she had no discipline problems with her troops. Instead, most of her difficulties seemed to stem from Greg himself. Sparks flew when she didn't agree with one of his regulations for the military students attending the school. Which was most of the time.

Frowning more sternly than usual, he took his feet off his desk, straightened in his chair, and spoke into his intercom.

"Sergeant Philpott, please send in Colonel Spellman and Captain Donnelly."

Half standing, he nodded toward two empty chairs beside his desk as they came into his office, Captain Donnelly first, followed by a smiling Erick Spellman.

Spellman didn't wait to sit down before he started talking. A round little man, almost completely bald, he was five years older than Greg but looked three times that. As he talked, Greg listened with one ear, most of his attention focused on Captain Donnelly.

She looked different, somehow. Usually there was a kind of positive sauciness to her as she ripped into one or another of his regulations.

Not this morning.

Her usual smile was gone, too, and there were faint circles under her eyes. Her burnished red hair didn't seem to catch the light the way it usually did. This morning every one of her twenty-nine years was showing. It gave her an interesting maturity he hadn't noticed before.

Maybe the matter *was* urgent this time, he thought, tuning in to his second in command.

"As soon as Joy—Captain Donnelly—mentioned that the Cardoza's woman's death might not be accidental, I brought her straight to you, sir. The airman didn't return her call last night, and she couldn't locate him in the barracks this morning or in his eight-o'clock class. Since the young man's in the air force, she did the right thing coming to me first."

As though Captain Joy Donnelly needed anybody to make excuses for her, Greg thought, leaning across his desk.

He stared at her. She stared back at him without smiling, her chin lifted slightly.

"It's your turn, Captain," he said, his frown deepening. "Let's hear your version of why one of your airmen was hiding in your bushes at eleven o'clock last night."

JOY EXAMINED the granitelike face of the man across the desk from her. His black eye patch, instead of detracting from his appearance, seemed to enhance it. Too bad the real man was so different from the image he projected. If it weren't for his perpetual frown, he'd be almost good-looking.

He was going to be even more hard-nosed than usual, she thought, irritated with herself for stopping at Erick Spellman's office instead of reporting directly to Colonel Weston. She'd wanted to clarify her position before she approached the commandant. Spellman was the logical choice. The air force colonel was a good-natured man who was easy to talk to even if he didn't have much backbone.

As soon as she saw the commandant's frown, she realized she'd made a mistake. Not only was he frowning, the dark shadow evident on his chin and cheeks was a sure sign he'd gotten up early. By this time of the morning he was probably feeling as congenial as a hungry bear.

Darn. She should have known she'd never win points with the commandant by showing up in his office with another senior officer in tow.

The surgeon from Fort Ord had been a necessity to prove her point about the PT program.

Colonel Spellman was anything but, and now it was too late to do much about it.

The commandant's expression—and his frown—didn't change as she repeated essentially the same story Spellman had just told. As with the assistant commandant, she omitted her suspicion that instructor and student were having an illicit relationship. Somehow not saying anything seemed less a breach of the young man's confidence, even though Joy's almost word-for-word report of her conversation with him last night could leave her two listeners with no other conclusion.

When she was finished, the commandant drummed his fingers on the desk. "Is that all, Captain?"

"Yes, sir." Joy could tell that he wasn't pleased with her answer by the way his one eye narrowed. How a man with a perpetual frown and five-o'clock shadow at nine in the morning could still be so darn attractive, Joy couldn't fathom. What she did know was that he was the most disagreeable man she'd ever worked for. But then, she'd never had an army boss before. If they were all like him, she hoped she'd never again be assigned to a combined service organization.

"Maybe I'm missing something," he said, "but it seems to me that you've left out a key bit of information." He paused, waiting.

"The airman's name," he prodded. "Surely you know the name of your source."

"I'm sorry, sir, but I can't tell you who it is without talking to him first."

A flash of anger crossed his face, and Joy tensed in her chair. The commandant was furious, and a man like him was dangerous when he was furious. *Here it comes,* she thought. *He's going to order me to tell him, and when I don't he'll do something awful to my career.*

"I need to know who he is, Captain. The man's made serious accusations that, no matter how unfounded, may very well reflect on this school and the Presidio. I'm going to insist that you tell me his name."

Joy Donnelly knew a direct order when she heard one. If she didn't speak up, the commandant could take disciplinary action through the military judicial system. She had no doubt he'd do it. The way she had him sized up, he was a tough jungle fighter with a heart the size of a pinhead who would crucify his own grandmother if she stepped one inch out of line.

Hadn't he tried to get rid of her before she arrived? Friends in personnel headquarters at Randolph Air Force Base had passed her that interesting bit of information.

Wouldn't he gloat over the chance to prove himself right if she defied his direct order?

He was waiting for her answer.

What in the name of heaven was she going to tell him?

Chapter Two

Greg didn't like asking one of his people to break a promise but there was no alternative. He had to know which airman was making wild accusations about Maria Cardoza. Whether true or not, the story—if it became public knowledge, could affect operations at the Defense Language Institute. As the school's commander, he was compelled to prevent anything from interfering with his organization's mission. The story would have to be checked out and put to rest ASAP.

Greg cursed to himself. Unless he missed his guess, Joy Donnelly was about to back him into another damned-if-I-do, damned-if-I-don't corner. The thought gave him that heated, out-of-control feeling he associated with her. When she was around, it was as though a cog in one of his well-oiled internal wheels had slipped out of its track.

Damn! He'd known it was going to be a bad day from the minute he crawled out of the sack at 0500 this morning and took his first look at the clammy fog outside his bedroom window.

To his surprise, she turned to Erick Spellman.

"Would you mind leaving me alone with the commandant, Colonel?" she asked.

Understanding—and a vague expression of relief—flowed across Spellman's face.

"Of course not. You're making the right decision," he told Joy, so eager to leave that he almost tipped his chair over.

Obviously Spellman thought Captain Donnelly was going to do what Greg wanted. Greg was sure she wasn't. If getting rid of Spellman meant privacy, it also meant there wouldn't be any witnesses when she defied his direct order.

He noticed that she waited until Colonel Spellman closed the door behind himself before she said anything.

"I'm sure you wouldn't want me to reveal a confidence, Colonel Weston." Her smile and congenial tone couldn't hide the determination in her voice.

Greg realized she'd never break her word even if it meant jeopardizing her career. He had to give her credit for the stand she'd taken, even if it seemed to him that her dedication was misplaced. Since the airman had disappeared without giving her a chance to hear him out, her obligation to him—if indeed there had been any obligation in the first place—was nullified.

At that moment, Greg realized something else. He didn't want to force her to back down, even if he could. There must be some other way to find out who the airman was.

He cleared his throat. "Now that I think about it, there's no reason for you to break your promise, Joy." Her first name slipped out before he could catch it. He hurried on, hoping she hadn't noticed. "I'm sure I can come up with your airman's name in less time than it would take me to force it out of you."

IF JOY HADN'T HEARD IT with her own ears, she would never have believed it. The commandant had called her by her first name!

Even though it wasn't unusual for a military boss to call his staff members by their first names, in her three months at the Defense Language Institute she'd never heard Colonel Weston do it. Not with anybody, not even Colonel Spellman, the assistant commandant, or the chief of staff, a navy captain. Had it been a mere slip of the tongue or was he trying to disarm her?

Be careful, ma'am, she thought, studying the six rows of ribbons on his chest. Five bronze stars for valor, a silver star, numerous service ribbons—the man's record was legendary.

She lifted her gaze to find him staring at her. An unexplained shiver ran down her spine. Was it her imagination, or had the face above the military decorations lost its stern edge?

"All I'm asking for is a few minutes to talk to him, sir," she said, testing the waters.

"I thought you said he didn't report to his morning class. How do you expect to find him so soon?" he eyed her quizzically. "Or maybe you've got some idea where he's gone?"

Up until that moment the notion of tracking down Airman Tuck herself hadn't occurred to Joy. As soon as the commandant suggested it, though, she knew what she had to do—find the frightened young man and let him say his piece without any pressure. It was the only way to remedy last night's mistake.

She had a good idea where to start looking.

The man opposite her leaned forward, his elbows on his desk, his one eye focused on her as though reading her thoughts.

What a shame he's a mustang colonel, she thought, admiring the aquiline curve of his nose. Mustang officers who come up through the ranks rarely, if ever, made general. Greg Weston would probably never have the chance to be a top-level army leader. It would be the Army's—and the country's—loss.

He repeated his question. "Do you have some idea where your airman's gone? If you do, lets hear it. We need to talk to him ASAP."

Joy took a deep breath. There was something about the commandant, especially when he stared at her like this, that left her quivery and unsure of herself. But there was no way she was going to tell him where she thought Airman Tuck had gone. Or that she planned to go after him. This was her problem. She'd solve it her way.

She felt a trickle of sweat run down her back. "When I said I needed a few minutes to talk to the airman, I meant when he returned to the dormitory, sir." It wasn't a lie. Going after him was an afterthought. She watched the commandant closely.

He leaned back in his chair. "Since that may be a while," he said, "then I guess I'll have to figure out who he is on my own."

Joy thought she heard a hint of conditional surrender in Colonel Weston's words. Relieved to be off the hook, she stood to go. The sooner she was on her way, the sooner Airman Tuck would be back in the squadron dormitory where he belonged.

But no. She'd guessed wrong, as she always seemed to do with this unpredictable man. He motioned her back to her chair. "Stick around, Captain. Once I've figured out who your airman is, we'll need to decide what to do about him."

Joy sat down, her face clouded with uneasiness. Whatever Greg Weston was up to would be sure to complicate an already difficult situation.

The commandant pressed the button on his intercom. "Sergeant Philpott, would you come in here with your book, please?"

The enlisted woman marched into the room, her green service uniform devoid of creases, her brass gleaming, her low-heeled service shoes spit-polished to a mirrorlike sheen. From the frankly critical look she cast at Joy, it was obvious that Sergeant Philpott looked down her nose at what she considered the Air Force's more relaxed uniform standards. Not for her the prepolished silver on Joy's uniform or Joy's patent leather pumps.

"You know Captain Donnelly, Sergeant?" Greg asked.

"Yes, sir. Good morning, ma'am."

The required smile and greeting. Everything done according to the book. Joy could see why she got along so well with the commandant.

Sitting on the chair Erick Spellman had vacated, Sergeant Philpott positioned her notebook on one crossed knee.

"Call the Spanish Department and get a list of the airmen who were assigned to Maria Cardoza's class," the commandant began. "Not the army, navy, civilian or officer personnel, Sergeant Philpott. Just the airmen."

Having instantly surmised that the man concerned about Maria Cardoza's death had been assigned to her class of ten students, the commandant proceeded to narrow the eligibles.

"Once you've got the names—there shouldn't be more than two or three, maybe only one—get the department to check and see which of them didn't get to class on time this morning. If he's come in since, have him report to me on the double."

When Sergeant Philpott had left, the commandant turned to Joy. "After we find your airman, you can talk to him alone for a few minutes first if that will relieve your conscience."

"Thanks, I will," she responded, surprised at the offer. Maybe the commandant wasn't quite as intractable as she'd thought. For the next few minutes she sat silently, watching Greg flip through some papers on his desk, until Sergeant Philpott reentered the office.

"There were three airmen in Ms. Cardoza's class," she said, studying her notebook. "One of them failed to report for duty this morning: Airman Christopher L. Tuck. As a matter of fact, Airman Tuck has been listed on the morning report as AWOL."

Sergeant Philpott glanced sideways at Joy as she announced this information. Joy could tell what she was thinking. Obviously, if an airman was absent without leave, it was the squadron commander's fault. In well-run units with high morale, people didn't go AWOL.

Joy was inclined to ignore Barbara Philpott's dirty looks as another sign of the army enlisted woman's prejudice against the air force, but there seemed to be something more than simple disdain in her hostile glance. Was it possible that Sergeant Philpott had a secret grudge of some sort against Joy? Her curiosity roused, she made a mental note to keep a closer eye on the woman, then turned her attention back to her airman's disappearance.

"I've got to call the squadron and tell Sergeant Blakeman to check the hospitals and police stations," Joy said, standing up. "Airman Tuck may need our help."

"Use my phone," the commandant said, to her surprise. "It's worth a try, even though Sergeant Philpott is probably right, and he's simply gone AWOL."

While Joy was dialing her first sergeant, the commandant focused on his secretary. "Thanks for the quick answers, Sergeant. Coordinate with Captain Donnelly's sergeant regarding the calls to the hospitals. Be sure you contact the civilian facilities, too."

"Yes, sir," Barbara Philpott said. Her words were so crisp and her manner so military that Joy could almost hear the click of metal-tapped heels when the enlisted woman started toward the door.

"If you want to make some of the calls yourself from my phone, feel free," Colonel Weston said. "The telephone books are in the top drawer of the cabinet in the corner."

Joy's eyes widened at his offer. It hinted at concern for the young airman. Could there be a modicum of warmth and understanding lurking behind the commandant's black eye patch? It was a dangerous thought. She couldn't afford to drop her defenses before a stiff-necked, by-the-book officer like Greg Weston. There was no telling how far he might go with a few inches of rope.

Half an hour later, all the hospitals and police stations in a fifty-mile radius of the Monterey Peninsula had been contacted with negative results.

The commandant looked up from his paperwork as Joy stood to go.

"Thanks for the use of your phone, sir," she said.

He came around his desk toward her.

Joy wasn't a petite woman, but when Greg Weston was near her, she felt strangely small and delicate. It wasn't so much that he was a terribly huge man as that he had the kind of presence that filled the space around him.

"Call me as soon as Tuck turns up," he said, walking to the door with her.

Joy said she would and made a hasty exit before the sudden weakness in her knees got any worse. What was there about the commandant that evoked so many unpredictable responses? She'd handled difficult commanders before. Why was Greg Weston different from the others?

IN HER SMALL OFFICE, Joy flipped through her list of organization addresses to Maria Cardoza's name. The list hadn't been revised since the instructor's death last week, so her rural number was still included in the directory. Joy jotted it down on a piece of paper. Then she called the Monterey Visitors' Bureau to find out exactly where the house was located. It was deep in the Carmel Valley, a woman volunteer told her, at least ten miles past the village and twenty beyond the expensive gated communities and golf courses close to Carmel.

That's where Airman Tuck was. Joy felt it in her bones.

In the commandant's office she'd remembered what the young man said about setting a trap that the "bloody bastard can't ignore" and had known instinctively that there was only one place for such a trap to be set. With any luck she'd be able to find him and correct the wrong she'd done him.

A few minutes later she was heading south in hazy sunshine on the W. R. Holman Highway. The haze, less noticeable on California's Highway 1, disappeared completely almost as soon as she swung east on the Carmel Valley Road. With the cooling fog gone, the inside of her Firebird got warmer, and she rolled down her window part way.

Her road map lay on the seat beside her. She'd circled the approximate location of the house Maria Cardoza had been renting. There should be no difficulty finding it.

The road narrowed from four lanes to two. On one side, cattle and horses grazed on pasture land watered by the Carmel River. On the other, clumps of ancient scrub oak dotted rocky ground rising steeply from the valley floor. Luxurious homes perched high on the surrounding hill-tops.

Ten miles beyond the village, she found a gravel road blocked by a wooden gate. She got out of the car and opened the gate, then closed it behind her after driving through. The road wound gradually upward through dry hills. In her rear view mirror, she noticed a cloud of dust marking her passage. Finally, she reached the house.

With its gray paint peeling and screens hanging loose from some of its windows, it looked like something out of a John Steinbeck novel. The roof was flat and the casement windows high and small, giving the house the appearance of a big railroad car. The impression was enhanced by a small garage attached, cabooselike, to one end. A two-by-four nailed diagonally across the front door held a printed sign.

Joy climbed out of her car and walked up cracked flagstones to the porch to read it. Under the No Entry announcement were the scribbled name and telephone number of Deputy Sheriff Amanda Hawkins. Joy fished around in her black leather service shoulder bag for a pad of paper and a pencil to jot down the information. Deputy Hawkins had to be the policewoman Chris Tuck had mentioned.

"Airman Tuck," Joy called, "I know you're here. Come out and let's talk."

Silence. The place looked sealed, but probably wasn't since the front door was the only exterior entrance that was blocked.

Joy glanced around her, searching for movement in the patches of mesquite under the scrub oaks that shaded the house and above-ground pool where Maria had drowned.

Nothing stirred. The stillness was unnerving. She stared at the two-by-four across the door, and a shiver ran down her back. Suddenly, something about the way it looked nailed shut, with the printed warning at its center, made her think of a plague house, boarded up to keep the contagion from spreading.

What was she doing here anyhow, snooping around on private property that had been declared off-limits by the police? Maybe there was a grain of truth in what the commandant claimed. Maybe Captain Joy Donnelly *was* a tad overprotective of her airmen.

Suddenly the sun felt hot on her back and head. She took off her gabardine service blouse and flight cap and carried them to the front seat of the Firebird. It did no good. In her short-sleeved shirt, she found herself perspiring and shivering at the same time.

Why would a single woman want to live way out in the boonies like this? Joy wondered, shrugging off her nervousness. She knew the answer as soon as she caught a glimpse of the view from the far side of the porch. From it's lofty perch, the house overlooked miles of undulating hillside.

On her instructor's salary, Maria Cardoza could never have afforded to rent a house on the Monterey Peninsula with this sort of view. Housing costs there were among the most expensive in the country. Or perhaps something about the Carmel Valley had reminded her of her native Spain.

Joy took a satisfying breath of the clear air. As far as she could see, the countryside was devoid of human habitation. Then she noticed settling dust on the opposite hillside. Squinting, she could barely make out a road, probably leading to a house like this one, hidden from sight on the far side of the hill.

She started toward the back of Maria's cottage. L-shaped, it was larger than it looked from the road. At the far end of the porch, drawn draperies covered sliding glass doors that probably led to the master bedroom.

The pool rose about four feet above the ground, an ugly blue vinyl liner in an oxidized metal frame painted white. Stretched across it was a faded blue pool cover, loose at one end, where the liner joined a curved wooden deck. A hose extending down the hill was attached to a spigot at the base.

Someone—probably the police or the house's owner—had drained the pool after the accident.

Joy walked around the pool's metal frame a couple of times, searching the dry ground for any clue to Airman Tuck's whereabouts. She had no doubt he'd been on the premises since Maria Cardoza died. That was undoubtedly how he'd gotten the policewoman's name—the same way Joy herself had.

But he didn't seem to be here now.

Feeling a little foolish, she called him again. As she called, she glanced at the bushy growth on the opposite hillside, looking for any movement.

A flash of light near the road on the hill across from the house caught her eye. As she watched, it disappeared, only to flash again a moment later.

The sun was reflecting on something, she thought. That was all it could be. Not from the windows of a car, either. She'd have been able to spot a vehicle.

Then she realized what it was. Someone was watching her through binoculars from the hill opposite.

Joy's heart leaped into her throat. She fought the urge to run. Willing her racing heart to be still, she forced herself to stay where she was. She didn't have time for irrational fears. One of her people was in trouble. The only way to help him was to come up with logical, clearheaded answers; not to flee, panic stricken, at the first sign of trouble.

Besides, hasty flight would only alert the unseen watcher that she knew he or she was there.

Who could it be?

From everything she'd heard and read, the police considered Maria's death an accident. They'd be unlikely to waste people for a twenty-four-hour surveillance.

Could the watcher be Maria Cardoza's murderer? Chris Tuck seemed convinced that Maria had not died accidentally. If he was right, could her killer be watching the house?

The thought brought back the panicky feeling Joy thought was under control. There was nothing scarier than someone watching you that you can't see, she thought. If

Airman Tuck was right, the murderer had been watching *him*. No wonder he was so scared. And now the same murderer might be observing her.

Joy gave herself a swift mental kick. Talk about imagining things. It should be obvious to her who was over there.

Chris Tuck, of course.

She should have known he'd be too smart to hang around close to Maria's house. But how did he plan to set a trap for Maria's murderer by watching her house through binoculars? It was the first question she'd ask him.

In her uniform and pumps she couldn't very well go chasing across the canyon after him, but, remembering the road she'd seen on the opposite hillside, she could probably drive there. Returning to her car, she checked the map. It showed an access route to the neighboring hill from a crossroad intersecting with the Carmel Valley Road. Without bothering to put on her uniform blouse or flight cap she headed toward the intersection.

She reached the narrow graveled track before she expected it. Like the road to Maria's it was protected by a gate. On the other side, it wound through the rocky canyon for what seemed an eternity. Finally, she reached an old abandoned quarry. Grass was growing in gouged sections of sandstone worn smooth over the years.

She stopped the car, got out, and looked around, trying to ignore the eerie emptiness of the place. Unseen eyes seemed to be watching from the canyon walls. Shivering, she got back into the car and locked the door while she studied the map.

Apparently this road, not marked on the map, came to a dead end at the quarry on the canyon floor. There was no way to cut across. She'd have to go back the way she'd come.

There was no harm done, she thought. A few minutes wouldn't make any difference.

Ten minutes later she turned right again. Judging from the slowly settling dust, another car had passed only minutes before, going in the opposite direction.

There was no question this was the road she'd been hunting for. It wound upward for several miles along the hillside. Looking south through her window, she could see Maria's mountain. She slowed, searching for a glimpse of her house.

There it was! From this distance the ramshackle cottage, with its sparkly sand-and-tar roof, shimmered in the noon sun like a beautiful jewel.

She drove on, looking for a parked vehicle that would betray Airman Tuck's location. She saw nothing but rocks, mesquite, and scrub oak.

When the road curved and she lost sight of the house, she retraced her route; then, reaching the downhill side, turned again. By the time she'd driven back and forth twice along that section of road, she'd spotted the most likely place to observe Maria's house. It was on a flat strip of land extending twenty to thirty yards from the road and permitting a virtually unobstructed view of the place.

She parked the car off to one side under some scrub oaks and picked her way through the underbrush until she found the best vantage point. Here the ground was relatively free of growth, but a watcher could remain hidden in the mesquite. Surely this was where Airman Tuck had stationed himself. What had he been watching and waiting for?

She glanced around looking for signs of a long vigil. If he'd spent even a few hours here, surely there would be trampled brush, scraps of paper, some other indications of his presence.

Except for a couple of weathered paper cups that had probably been there for days, there was nothing to show that anyone had lingered in the vicinity. Even so, Joy was positive he'd been watching her from this very spot only minutes ago.

Had his motorcycle raised the dust she'd seen on her way in? she wondered. Was it just a coincidence that she'd barely missed him or had he somehow guessed what she intended and deliberately avoided her? And if so, why, when he'd been so determined to talk to her last night? These were questions that could be answered only by Chris Tuck himself. She had to find him before he got into serious trouble.

Aggravated by her wrong turn and the delay it caused, she poked through the underbrush, hoping to turn up something—anything—that would tell her he'd been here. For almost half an hour she inched her way, step by slow step, around the area, her eyes to the ground.

She's almost reached her car when she found the clue she'd been looking for.

There in the dust near her left rear tire was a silver circle about the size of a half-dollar, with the capital letters *U.S.* on its raised surface. She picked it up.

In the palm of her hand was a silver service insignia, the type worn on both lapels by enlisted air force personnel. As far as Joy was concerned, it was proof positive that Chris Tuck had been here.

Chapter Three

Joy examined the small circle of metal. The clutches used to secure the two pins in back to the uniform lapel were still in place, firmly fastened to the ends of the pins. The insignia hadn't come loose and fallen off accidentally or the clutches would be missing.

Since Airman Tuck hadn't been wearing his uniform last night and, according to the squadron's first sergeant, hadn't returned to the dormitory to change, he must have been carrying the insignia with him. Did that mean he intended to change into uniform at Maria's? Joy didn't doubt that he had keys to all the doors and would use the house if he felt like it, in spite of the police warning posted on the front door. She would have given a month's pay to take a quick look inside but had too much respect for the law to consider breaking in.

Wrapping the insignia in a tissue, Joy put it in her shoulder bag. If he'd had it in a pocket, why had it dropped out here? A hole, perhaps? She searched the ground around the car for other items he might have lost but found nothing.

The next step was finding out why he'd left in such a hurry and where he'd gone. Was it possible that he was on his way to Maria's house to intercept Joy herself?

That wasn't likely, she thought. If he'd wanted to catch her, he wouldn't have watched her for fifteen minutes.

Nonetheless, she returned to Maria's house. The yard, with its ugly aboveground pool, was as deserted as before.

Joy wanted to believe the insignia she'd found indicated that the young man was okay, that he'd been watching her from across the canyon only minutes ago. Stubbornly she tried to ignore the fact that he had no logical reason for being there.

But try as she might to believe he was all right, she couldn't forget the sheer terror in his voice when he told her he was being followed. He was in serious trouble. She could feel it in her bones.

The sign on the front door caught her attention again. Deputy Sheriff Amanda Hawkins, whose scribbled name appeared below the No Entry announcement, had probably talked to Airman Tuck for at least an hour the night he disappeared. Maybe she could give Joy an idea where he'd gone.

IN HER MID-THIRTIES, almost as broad as she was tall, Deputy Sheriff Amanda Hawkins had a moon face like the cartoon character Smiley with a grin to match. Her wavy brown hair was cut short, and she was wearing a tan short-sleeved uniform shirt tucked into pants the same color. Joy caught something cherubic in her round face and pink cheeks in spite of the service revolver in the black leather holster hanging at her side. She came around her desk when Joy entered her small office.

"I'm Joy Donnelly from the Defense Language Institute, Deputy Hawkins," Joy said, extending her hand.

It was gripped in a bone-crunching clench. Joy got the strong impression that the bulk under the policewoman's uniform was muscle, not flab. Deputy Hawkins was looking less cherubic by the second.

"What can the Carmel Valley Deputy Sheriff's Office do for you, Captain?" she asked. She had a wide-open grin, but her alert eyes were busy checking every silver button and insignia on Joy's flight cap and uniform blouse.

Joy felt like shaking her hand in the air to get the circulation going again. Instead she adjusted the strap on her shoulder bag.

"I'm the commander of the Air Force Student Squadron at the Presidio," she explained, choosing her words with care. It was too soon to reveal Airman Tuck's confidences to the authorities, and she didn't want Deputy Hawkins to suspect she was hiding anything.

"One of my airmen, Christopher Tuck, is missing. He told someone he'd spent some time with you last night. I was hoping he might have said something that would give me a clue as to what's happened to him."

Joy watched the deputy's face closely as she spoke, certain she was correct in assuming Amanda Hawkins was the policewoman Airman Tuck had referred to last night.

"So the kid's gone AWOL," Deputy Hawkins said, obviously recognizing Airman Tuck's name. "I'm surprised to hear that. He was pretty tight when I put him in a cab last night. Thought he'd sleep like a baby once his head hit the barracks pillow."

Joy smiled encouragingly. Maybe this wasn't going to be as difficult as she'd feared. "He never made it back to the dorm," she said. Joy always referred to the squadron barracks as a dormitory because she thought it sounded more homelike.

"If you put him in a cab," she went on, "he only took it to wherever he'd parked his motorcycle."

Amanda Hawkins gave her a penetrating look that made Joy wish she hadn't said anything about a motorcycle.

"Maybe we'd better talk about this," the deputy said. "Unfortunately, I've got an appointment in Carmel in half an hour. Instead of waiting until tomorrow to get together, how about dinner tonight at the place where I ran into your airman last night? An evening sharing information might be profitable for both of us."

Joy wasn't sure she liked the idea of "sharing information" about Airman Tuck with Deputy Sheriff Hawkins, but the chance to pump the policewoman in an informal setting was too good to pass up. They agreed to meet at the Foghorn Inn in Monterey at eight o'clock that night.

WHEN JOY RETURNED to the squadron orderly room, her first sergeant stood up and handed her a couple of yellow telephone memos.

"Colonel Weston wants you to call him, Captain," he said. A balding, black non-commissioned officer, Sergeant Blakeman was the senior enlisted man on Joy's staff of five enlisted people and two officers.

Joy glanced at the messages. "The commandant called twice?"

"Three times. I didn't bother to write the last one down."

"Thanks, Sergeant. I gather there's been no news of Airman Tuck?"

He shook his head. "I've talked to some of his buddies, and none of them has any idea where he's gone."

"Be sure you tell me about anything that develops, anything at all. If somebody so much as mentions his name, I want to know it."

Sergeant Blakeman rubbed his chin with his hand. "Then you'll want to know the Spanish Department called to ask about him. Tuck's new instructor's upset that he's gone AWOL."

Joy's eyes narrowed. "Did his instructor call personally?"

"No, ma'am. But the secretary said the instructor was the one who wanted her to find out."

The seed of an idea began to germinate. Maybe Airman Tuck's new language instructor could give her some idea where he'd gone.

"Did she mention the instructor's name?"

He shook his head. "No, but if you want it, I'll have it for you in two minutes."

Here was a hot lead begging to be checked out. What was the best way to do it? Joy made a quick decision.

"Arrange an appointment for me with the instructor, would you, Sergeant Blakeman? The sooner the better—1500 hours if possible."

"In your office, ma'am?"

She nodded. "Yes. Be sure the instructor knows this meeting's important and takes precedence over routine school business."

Leaving her office door ajar, Joy hung her flight cap and uniform blouse on the coat rack beside the door. Then she sat down in the executive chair behind her desk.

Like the rest of the furniture in the small room, the chair was government-issue gray metal. Joy had brightened the walls with some framed posters of California's scenic spots—Yosemite's El Capitan on one wall, the rugged central coast and southern high desert on others. The window behind her was open a crack, and she caught the faint smell of eucalyptus in the cool, moist air as she bent to put her shoulder bag in her bottom desk drawer.

Before she reached for the telephone receiver, she cleared her throat and took a couple of deep breaths. When Sergeant Philpott put her through to the commandant, she didn't want to sound as shaky as she felt.

That was what she got for going without lunch, she told herself, ignoring the fact that she hadn't felt at all shaky until Sergeant Blakeman told her the commandant wanted her to call him.

She dialed his number with mixed feelings of anticipation and dread.

"Colonel Weston," came a growl at the other end of the line.

For the space of a heartbeat, Joy was speechless. The commandant never answered his own telephone. There were three secretaries in his outer office to do that: Sergeant Philpott and two civilians.

When Joy found her voice, she spoke with all the confidence she could muster. "I'm returning your call, sir."

As soon as the words were out of her mouth she realized she hadn't identified herself. Feeling like a schoolgirl, she blurted, "It's—"

"I know who it is," he said brusquely. "Can you come to my office right now? We need to get our heads together and track down your missing airman before he damages the mission of this organization with his unfounded allegations."

"I've arranged a 1500 appointment with Airman Tuck's new instructor," Joy began, watching Sergeant Blakeman enter her open door and approach her desk. She caught his eye. He nodded and put a piece of paper on her desk with SANTOS MUELLER printed across it in capital letters.

Covering the telephone receiver with one hand, she pointed at the name with the other.

"Are you sure that's right, Sergeant Blakeman? Mueller doesn't sound like a Spanish instructor's name."

He nodded. "That's what I thought, too, Captain, so I double-checked it."

"His name is Santos Mueller," Joy said into the phone. "I think it's important to talk to him on the off chance he might be able to give me a clue as to where Airman Tuck is. If it's okay with you, sir, I'll report to your office after he leaves."

"I've got an even better idea," the commandant said. "I'll arrange for Mr. Mueller to meet us here at headquarters after his class, and both of us can pick his brains."

"You don't have to bother, sir," Joy said. She didn't want the commandant listening when she talked to Chris Tuck's instructor. Mueller would probably be more forthright with her alone. Not only that, she'd die of nerves with the commandant hanging over her shoulder. Anytime Colonel Weston was in her vicinity, her intellectual and emotional waters grew uncharacteristically muddy.

"I'll find out if he knows anything and follow up on it, sir," she added.

There was an uncomfortable silence. When the commandant spoke, his voice was deceptively soft.

"Perhaps I didn't make myself clear, Captain Donnelly."

His enunciation was much more precise than before. Joy stiffened in her chair. Was he going to chew her out for implying the commandant was too busy to bother with a missing trooper?

"Your idea about talking to Tuck's new instructor is outstanding," he went on, his voice surprisingly mild considering his clipped words. "Maybe Mr. Mueller's observed something in the past week that'll be useful to us." He paused. "I want to hear what he has to say."

Joy could almost hear the line under that last sentence. Tension tightened her spine. Airman Tuck's disappearance was her problem. She wanted to solve it her own way.

"Do you want me in your office at three o'clock, too?" she asked, careful not to let her aggravation show in her voice.

"Why don't you come right now?" he said. "That'll give us a few minutes to compare notes before Mr. Mueller joins us."

As she hung up the phone, Joy knew that the commandant intended to become involved in her search for Airman Christopher L. Tuck. Whether he would be a help or a hindrance she had no idea. The one thing she was absolutely sure of was that in the past two minutes her life had become infinitely more complicated.

"LET'S BE COMFORTABLE," the commandant said, guiding Joy to a sofa against the wall opposite his desk.

There was something different about the way Colonel Weston looked this afternoon. It took Joy a moment to realize that he was clean shaven, with no trace of the familiar darkness on his jaw. He shaved twice a day, she thought and felt her cheeks flush as she imagined him in his robe, his face lathered with shaving cream, the black band holding his eye patch pushed up.

She sat down at one end of the sofa, putting her flight cap and shoulder bag on the cushion beside her. Like the rest of the furniture in the commandant's suite, the sofa was upholstered in army blue, a color somewhere between navy and royal. Joy had heard that Barbara Philpott had the offices redecorated at the colonel's expense when she was first assigned.

The commandant sat down at the other end. He was wearing his black uniform sweater over his light green open-necked shirt. Even with the eagles on his shoulders, he looked vaguely collegiate, not as severe as he usually did in his more businesslike service blouse. That, combined with his fresh shave, gave him a surprisingly boyish appearance. Joy's chest tightened. He was so attractive that her breath caught in her throat. Forcing herself to breath naturally, she tried to concentrate on Airman Tuck's disappearance.

"You share quarters with Major Easely?" he began.

"Yes, sir," Joy said, mystified. The question seemed unrelated to Airman Tuck's disappearance. "She owns the house. I pay rent and share expenses."

"You're aware, of course, that she's the DLI Public Affairs Officer."

Now Joy saw what he was getting at. Public affairs officers dealt with the media. The less the press knew about the allegations Airman Tuck had made, the better it would be for the reputation of the Defense Language Institute. As commander, the reputation of his organization was Colonel Weston's primary consideration.

"I don't intend to discuss Airman Tuck's confidences with her," she said. "Or with anybody except, possibly, the authorities."

"Good!" he said, but his frown belied the word. "If Major Easely knows nothing about Airman Tuck, she won't have to beat around the bush if she's questioned. As far as the authorities are concerned, we'd better hold off on telling them, too."

Joy hesitated, keenly aware of the lingering fragrance of after-shave in the air. "I can understand keeping it from the press," she said, "but surely we should report what he said to the police."

"It's the one thing we can't do," he growled. "Unless we want your name and the name of this school plastered all over the evening news."

He wanted to cover the whole thing up! Joy sat bolt upright on the army-blue sofa.

"Airman Tuck is missing," she said. "Maybe something's happened to him. The least we can do is tell the authorities he thought somebody was after him."

"This thing has all the earmarks of a nasty scandal," the commandant returned. "It's exactly the sort of juicy story that attracts a lot of attention. If we say anything to the police, the press will know about it ten minutes later."

"I'm sorry, but I can't go along with that, sir," she said, defiance in her tone. "If Airman Tuck doesn't turn up in the next day or two, the authorities will have to be notified. My airman is more important than the reputation of this school."

He leaned toward her. "Of course he is."

He sounded surprised that she'd brought it up.

"I'm just as concerned about this young man as you are, Captain Donnelly. Believe me, I am." His voice rang with sincerity.

In spite of his apparent concern, Joy suspected that he was humoring her to keep her from going to the police—that he'd already made up his mind there was nothing to Airman Tuck's fears. She swallowed her irritation.

"Even more than you," he went on, his voice softer, "as school commander, I want to find out how much truth there is to his allegations. But there's no reason to go rushing to the police with that cock-and-bull story he told you. Let's ask a few questions on our own, first."

"If we find out anything to indicate he's in danger, you've got to agree to go to the authorities," she said firmly.

"That was always understood," he said.

From his complacent expression, Joy could see that he never expected to have to take that step because he was certain Airman Tuck was okay. With all her heart, she hoped he was right. At the first sign he wasn't, she intended to report Chris Tuck's disappearance to the police, no matter how much Colonel Weston objected.

GREG SAW THE DOUBT on Joy's face and moved closer to her on the couch. Even though he knew she'd do what he asked, he wanted her to understand his position as school commander. For some reason, it seemed important that she realize how dedicated he was to his command and all its people, including her missing airman.

A little surprised at himself for bothering to explain, he said, "If there's one thing this school doesn't need right now, it's more newspaper headlines. When the media tried to connect the DLI to those traitors at the National Security Agency, it was bad enough. A murder would be the last straw the do-gooders in Congress need to close our operation down. You can just bet those fool reporters would find some way to tie in the Cardoza woman's so-called murder with espionage at NSA."

From the way Joy straightened her shoulders, Greg could tell he'd hit a responsive chord. Damn, but she was an attractive woman with that red hair and those rosy Irish cheeks.

"The newspapers didn't actually say DLI had anything to do with the military people caught selling secrets," Joy said thoughtfully. "Just mentioned they'd gotten their language training here before being assigned to NSA. I've got to agree, though, that it didn't seem fair to put the school in the headlines."

"You're damn right it wasn't fair," Greg growled. He backed up his stern tone with a frown. "There's always somebody wanting to interfere with the Institute's mission because we train language experts for NSA, and they object to the government's eavesdropping. As far as they're concerned, it's irrelevant that we're able to prevent hijackings and assassinations because the National Security Agency is keeping an ear on what the world's saying. We can't give these people a murder as an excuse to close us down."

"You won't get any argument from me," she said quickly, "as long as Airman Tuck doesn't get sacrificed in the meantime."

The bitterness in her words disturbed him. "Nobody's going to be sacrificed, not while I'm commander of this or-

ganization. But until we find out more about his allegations, I have to protect the school from a media spotlight
that might be distracting and harmful."

Her green eyes flashed, but she nodded.

Greg resisted the urge to belabor the point. It would only
irritate her. He sought Joy Donnelly's cooperation and understanding—not her opposition.

"Santos Mueller is meeting us at the club at three
o'clock," he said, changing the subject. "We might get
more out of him in an informal setting. Before we talk to
him, I want you to know that he and I share a common interest. Skeet shooting."

Her expression changed from bitterness to alert interest.

"I see you have an expert marksman's badge," he said,
glancing at the single row of ribbons on the left side of her
blouse. For a moment he swallowed an unwanted observation of her femininity. He'd have to keep his thoughts in line
if he wanted to get this mess straightened out.

"Have you done any shooting recently?" he asked.

She shook her head. "It's been years since I held a rifle,
Colonel."

"As long as there's nobody around, let's be on a first-
name basis, Joy," he said. He could tell from her startled
look that he'd surprised the hell out of her by suggesting it.
*Good! No harm letting her know the commandant has a few
surprises left in him.*

"You don't object to firing a weapon?"

"I guess not. I hadn't given it much thought."

"Then you wouldn't mind going with Santos and me to
the skeet range next Saturday?"

"I don't understand…. Aren't we meeting him at the club
at 1500 hours?"

"Let me explain," Greg said. "This afternoon Sergeant
Philpott learned something interesting. Santos Mueller
specifically asked that Airman Tuck be assigned to his class
after Maria Cardoza's death."

Across from him, Joy's eyes widened. "That's very significant, Greg. It means Mr. Mueller's got more than a casual interest in our man."

He noticed that she'd used his first name with no hesitation. Without thinking about it, had she perhaps been calling him by his first name in her thoughts?

He couldn't tell, and it was off the point. Immediately, he returned to Santos Mueller.

"It might mean he's got more than a casual interest. Or it might mean he simply needed another airman to balance his group. I must admit it seemed somewhat suspicious to me—suspicious enough for the two of us to get together with him next Saturday. Too bad we have to wait 'till then, but this can't seem contrived or we'll never find out anything. Santos is a good-natured man who talks a lot without saying much. It seems to me we'll get more out of him at the skeet range than we will this afternoon at the club."

"Are you going to ask him why he did it? Asked for Airman Tuck, I mean."

Greg knew she was excited from her quick, breathless words and the way she was leaning toward him.

He shook his head. "Not today. Maybe Saturday, depending on what's developed by then." He glanced at his watch. Noting that it was almost three o'clock, he stood up.

"One more thing before we go," he said as they started toward the door. "The Spanish Department's having a cocktail party at the chairman's house tomorrow night. If you're free, I'd like you to go with me. It'll give you a chance to talk to the instructors and their spouses. Maybe you'll be able to find out if Tuck's stories are circulating in the department."

When he glanced at her, she looked flabbergasted.

"It's a good place to start checking out what your airman told you," he said, to convince her.

She needed no convincing. "Of course I'm free. What a marvelous opportunity."

Her eyes were still wide, but Greg sensed that her astonishment had turned to anticipation.

When they reached the door of the outer office, Greg remembered that he hadn't told Sergeant Philpott where he
was going. He swung around quickly and caught a look of
such utter hatred on the enlisted woman's face that it
dumbfounded him.

Was it directed at him or at Joy or at both of them?

What possible reason could his loyal sergeant have for
such feelings? Surely she couldn't be jealous of him and Joy.
Sergeant Philpott was too levelheaded to let a schoolgirl
crush interfere with duty.

Or was she?

Chapter Four

During the short ride to the Officers' Club in Greg's Jeep Cherokee, Joy considered telling him about the insignia she'd found across the canyon from Maria Cardoza's house. They arrived before she'd made up her mind, and so she said nothing.

Neither did she mention her dinner date that night with Amanda Hawkins. Since she had no intention of revealing anything significant to the deputy sheriff, there was no reason to tell Greg about it. Besides, this was her investigation, and she intended to do it her way.

Her took her arm when they stepped under the canopy-covered portico leading to the main entrance of the building. They walked together up the stairs.

Santos Mueller was waiting for them inside the lobby. A big beefy man whose muscle was turning to fat, he had a prominent nose, blue eyes so light they looked bleached, and straight brown hair. Joy remembered seeing him at the club a number of times but had never associated him with the Romance Language Division. He looked more Northern European than Latin, like an aging Arnold Schwarzenegger. As tall as Greg, he was much heavier. The well-cut brown suit he was wearing couldn't quite camouflage the flab around his midsection.

He shook Greg's hand and bowed to Joy warmly.

"Ah, *Comandante,* my friend." His expression was warm, almost buddy-buddy. "I trust that the purpose of this urgent summons is not to convey bad news."

Joy was glad Greg had told her about shooting skeet with the instructor. Otherwise, she might have misinterpreted his familiar tone.

"Good to see you, Santos," Greg said. "As you've probably guessed, Captain Donnelly and I were hoping you might be able to shed some light on Airman Tuck's whereabouts."

"Yes, I'd just received the invitation for a meeting with her when I was told of the change in plans." He beamed at Joy showing big, very white teeth that were too perfect to be real.

Greg turned to Joy. "Have you two met?"

"Not formally."

"Captain Donnelly, Mr. Santos Mueller," Greg said.

Joy extended her hand. Instead of shaking it, the beefy instructor bent over, and his thick lips nibbled at her knuckles, his breath warming the back of her hand.

"Ah, Captain Donnelly," he said, staring at her with his bleached hypnotic eyes. "I wonder if those airmen of yours know how fortunate they are to have a beautiful lady looking out for them."

While he spoke, he was still holding her hand, caressing the top of her fingers with his thumb. Trying not to appear obvious, Joy withdrew it. Mueller was making her uncomfortable.

Greg, watching them intently, seemed to disapprove of Santos's cavalier gesture. With a frown, he turned toward the dining room.

"Thanks for the compliment, Mr. Mueller," Joy said, following Greg. "But I rather doubt my airmen consider themselves that lucky. Especially when I enforce the commandant's regulations regarding proper maintenance of their quarters."

"Ah, the restrictions of military life," Santos said. He had a flat nasal voice that grated on her nerves.

Greg led them across the dining room, cheerful with its yellow upholstered furniture. Windows overlooked a grassy parade ground. In the distance, Monterey Bay sparkled under hazy February sunshine.

As they passed occupied tables, several instructors smiled and spoke to Greg. To each, he said something in a different foreign language. Joy recognized the sounds of a Romance language and the sing-song cadence of an Oriental tongue.

Amazed, she watched their faces. The people loved him! she thought. It was the first time Joy had seen him mixing with instructors, and she couldn't help but be impressed by the reception he was getting.

She recalled some of the stories she'd heard about Greg Weston: thirteen hostages rescued from armed terrorists without losing a single member of his team . . . a coup attempt in an African democracy foiled by government troops he'd trained . . . an air drop into Central America to assist local troops in containing a mob-supported drug overlord.

Most of his exploits had involved close contact with the locals, she realized suddenly.

No wonder he seemed at home with these people, she thought. He'd spent most of his service career working in foreign countries. He knows how they think.

Joy's eyes narrowed. Too bad he wasn't as interested in his own people. She sat down in the chair Greg held for her, and then watched while he seated himself with his back to the brightly lit window. Her heart skipped a beat when he caught her staring at him. How could a man with his adventurous reputation be such an overbearing, by-the-book commander? she wondered.

After their waitress brought coffee, sweet rolls, and—for Joy—a chicken salad sandwich, Santos lathered butter on a lemon Danish and poured cream and sugar into his coffee.

"So you're looking for Airman Tuck," he said, before either Joy or Greg had introduced the subject. Taking a small bite of his roll and a sip of his coffee, he stared shrewdly at Joy.

"It's no mystery where that foolish young puppy of yours has gone, Captain Joy. I can tell you exactly where to find him."

Joy struggled to hide her shock. Beside her, Greg had stiffened. She resisted the urge to catch his eye.

"Out with it, amigo," he barked, before Joy could find her voice. "What's happened to Captain Donnelly's airman?"

The big man shrugged his shoulders. "Of course I'm just guessing, *Comandante,* but there's only one place a love-sick young pup like him would go."

Joy leaned back in her chair, glad Greg had warned her what to expect. As he'd said, Santos Mueller was a talker. From "knowing exactly" where Airman Tuck was, he'd gone to "just guessing." She watched him sip his coffee, delighting in their attention.

"Where the hell is he?" Greg demanded.

Setting his cup down, the instructor twisted his head to one side and leaned closer. "Maria Cardoza's house in the Carmel Valley." His voice was conspiratorial.

So, Joy thought, someone else suspected Airman Tuck was at Maria's place. Apparently their affair was common knowledge.

"Why would he go there, Mr. Mueller?" she asked. Let the man tell what he knew. Maybe she'd learn something.

"Ah, it was an affair of the heart, Captain Joy."

"Everybody calls me Joy, Santos," she corrected. Ordinarily used by juniors to show friendly respect to much older senior officers, "Captain Joy" sounded ludicrous from the middle-aged instructor.

For a tense moment she thought he was going to grab her hand again in another cavalier gesture, so she took a quick bite of her chicken sandwich.

"Answer Captain Donnelly's question, amigo," Greg ordered. "Why the hell would Airman Tuck go to the Cardoza woman's house?"

Gratefully Joy noticed that Greg seemed eager to get the instructor's attention off her.

"Señorita Cardoza and Airman Tuck were, shall we say, *involved*."

"Involved? You mean they had a relationship?" Joy asked.

Santos looked down at his coffee cup. "I'm afraid so, Captain."

"Are you certain of that, Santos?" Greg interjected. "Surely Miss Cardoza knew about the school's nonfraternization policy between instructors and students?"

Santos shrugged again. "She was discreet, but it is difficult to keep that sort of thing hidden. She was tutoring him privately almost every night. Some of her other students complained. One thing led to another...."

"If you knew about it, then everybody in the Spanish Department knew about it," Joy said.

"It was, shall we say, an open secret."

Greg's face had darkened. "Why the hell didn't you say something to me Santos? If I'd known, I could have put a stop to it before it got to the open-secret stage where it affects everybody's morale."

"I make no excuses for my silence," Santos said and then proceeded to do exactly that. "But I didn't want to be the one to cost Maria Cardoza her position."

Greg took a deep breath. "That was something I needed to know, Santos. Next time try trusting me, *amigo*."

The big man managed to achieve the woebegone attitude of a chastised St. Bernard. "This will never happen again, *Comandante*."

Joy took a deep breath. The instructor's posturing annoyed her.

"Even if they were having an affair," she asked, "why should he go to her house now that she's dead?"

"He was, shall we say, *shattered* by her death, Captain. In his condition, it was the only place he could find solace. Part of her remained there..."

"What do you mean by 'his condition'?" Greg interrupted.

Joy heard the authority in his voice.

"I don't like to say this, *Comandante,*" Santos began hesitantly.

"For God's sake, get to the point, man. The airman may be in serious trouble."

Grudgingly, Joy applauded Greg's words. He finally sounded ready to concede that there might be something to Chris Tuck's fears.

Santos sighed, deep in his chest. "Very well, *Comandante,* Captain." He glanced from Joy to Greg. "Since Señorita Cardoza's accident, Airman Tuck drinks all the time. Ask his friends in the squadron about the liquor. Her death was a terrible thing, and he took it very badly."

Joy didn't have to catch Greg's eye to know he was thinking the same thing she was. Christopher Tuck had been intoxicated last night when she'd seen him. Was that because he'd been trying to get information from a police officer, as he said? Or was it part of the alcoholic pattern Santos Mueller was describing?

Joy had to find out the answers. They represented the difference between a drunken airman's vague ramblings and a young man afraid for his life.

Wednesday Night

WHEN JOY ARRIVED at the Foghorn Inn, Deputy Sheriff Hawkins was already enjoying her first rum and Coke at the table she'd reserved for them. Her lavender blouse with its Peter Pan collar made her face look even rounder and her cheeks even pinker than her uniform did.

Joy sat down without offering her hand. One bone-crunching clench that day had been enough.

"Good to see you again, Deputy Hawkins," she said.

"Amanda, please," the policewoman said, grinning widely. In spite of her congeniality, Joy noticed that—as they had that afternoon—Amanda's alert eyes were busy checking every silver stud in her denim pants and jacket.

"Agreed," she said. "I'm Joy." She glanced around. Weathered wood, knotted ropes, and polished brass were everywhere in the place's five or six eating areas. At the far end of the room, a shiny staircase wound to the ceiling.

"You look about ready for another drink," Joy said, glancing around for a cocktail waitress. She ordered a Scotch and water in a tall glass for herself. Amanda ordered another rum and Coke.

"How many people are in your organization, Joy?" the deputy asked, after the usual comments about the traffic and the weather.

The question sounded aimless, but Joy suspected there was a point to it.

"Including the marrieds living off post, four hundred thirty-seven," she answered.

Amanda put both elbows on the table and leaned toward her. "That's a lot of people. Do you go to this much trouble with every person who turns up AWOL? Or is Airman Tuck a special case?"

"Nobody's gone AWOL in the three months I've had the squadron," Joy said. Even though the query insinuated favoritism, she didn't want to seem defensive. "Since he's the first, I suppose he *is* sort of a special case."

Amanda sipped her drink. "In the office you mentioned that he said he'd spent the evening with me. Since you're the one who showed up asking questions, I'm guessing the someone he told must have been you. Am I right, Joy?"

Amanda's alert eyes were watching her intently. Joy had the disturbing feeling that she was stepping into quicksand, but she didn't see how she could avoid confirming the obvious.

"Yes, he stopped by my house in Pacific Grove after he left you."

The deputy raised a knowing eyebrow. "Is that sort of thing customary, Joy? I don't know much about how the Air Force operates, but in my line of work nobody stops by a lady's house in the middle of the night without an invitation."

Amanda Hawkins was staring at her with the same penetrating look Joy had noticed that afternoon.

"It's not customary," Joy said, anxious to dispel any notions of impropriety. "As soon as I saw he'd been drinking, I told him to go back to the dormitory, and I'd talk to him first thing in the morning."

An innocent, angelic smile appeared on the round face opposite her. "Then he didn't say anything to you about why he'd come to see you? Other than that he'd just talked to me?"

Luckily the waitress arrived to take their dinner orders, and Joy had a few seconds to organize her thoughts before she answered.

"I thought maybe you could give me a clue as to what was bothering him," Joy said, after the waitress left. "I've been in the Air Force more than eight years now. This is the first time anybody's showed up at my house the way he did. He must have thought it was pretty serious."

"Why don't you level with me, Joy? It's got something to do with the Cardoza woman's death, doesn't it?" Amanda leaned forward expectantly.

Joy sucked in a huge mouthful of air. For one giddy moment she was tempted to tell the whole story to the policewoman. What a relief it would be to talk about her fears to someone sympathetic, someone in a position to follow up the vague allegations Airman Tuck had made.

The moment passed. She'd given him her word not to talk about his relationship with Maria—and she'd as good as promised Greg she wouldn't tell the story to the police without more to go on.

"I'm afraid it's my fault Airman Tuck didn't say much," Joy said. "I sent him away before he told me anything more than that he'd talked to you. I've been kicking myself ever since for not dragging him in the house for some coffee."

The policewoman relaxed in her chair and started her third rum and Coke. Joy stirred her drink with a lighthouse swizzle stick but didn't sip it.

"Of course you do know about the kid's affair with the Cardoza woman?" Amanda asked.

This lady had a real talent for startling her listeners, Joy decided. The policewoman was probably making an educated guess based on Chris Tuck's interest in Maria's accident.

"I've heard some gossip," Joy said carefully. "But I'm not sure whether to believe it or not. Ms. Cardoza was at least fifteen years older than Airman Tuck."

The policewoman's round face lit up with delight. "If you think that makes a difference, you haven't been watching TV lately," she said. "I was pleasantly surprised when the kid acted so interested in me. He had a certain way about him—lots of energy but sensitive, too, the way older men are." She sighed. "It didn't take me long to figure out what the score was. As soon as he found out I was connected to the Carmel Valley Sheriff's Office, Maria Cardoza was all he could talk about. Wanted to know everything about her accident."

Joy nodded but didn't say anything, hoping the liquor would oil her companion's tongue. It was probably a fond hope. After three rum and Cokes, Amanda Hawkins seemed as sober as when Joy had joined her at the table.

Unfortunately the waitress appeared with their dinners, and Joy wasn't able to get back on the subject of Maria until they were almost through eating. Midway through dessert, she asked if there was anything the young man had said that made Amanda suspect they were having an affair.

"He kept talking about a crystal Ms. Cardoza wore all the time," Amanda said. "The only way he could have known that was if he'd spent a lot of time with her. He tried not to let on, but I could see how upset he was that it was missing."

Joy's ears pricked up.

The other woman nodded. "It was a real beauty—a natural transparent quartz crystal with the phantom image of a six-pointed star inside. Why do you suppose he was so interested in it?"

"He probably gave it to her," Joy said, without hesitation. It was the obvious answer. "Maybe he wanted it back."

"You might be right," Amanda returned. "He kept asking if we'd found it when we searched the house."

"You didn't?"

"No. What do you suppose could have happened to it?" In spite of the liquor she'd put away, the policewoman's eyes were as bright as ever.

"Obviously she took it off before she went in the pool," Joy said. *Or somebody took it off her before she was drowned, figuring nobody would wear a big piece of jewelry while swimming.* An icy breath swept down Joy's back, in spite of the green wool turtleneck sweater she was wearing under her denim jacket.

Amanda Hawkins was watching her with wide, round cat's eyes. "So what happened to it? It wasn't anywhere around the pool area."

The murderer slipped it into his pocket and took it with him. That is what happened to it. Joy could almost see the scene in her mind.

For the deputy sheriff's benefit, she shrugged her shoulders. "Maybe it fell in the bushes. Your people couldn't possibly have sifted through every inch of dirt around there."

The waiting cat pounced. "You've been out to her house, then?"

Joy was trapped. Backed into a corner, she had to lie to get out gracefully.

"No, but I know how dusty it is in the eastern end of the valley," she said. Though she kept her voice nonchalant, she wasn't sure Amanda Hawkins believed her. "If something fell in the dirt out there, it could easily disappear."

"Our people are pretty thorough," she said.

"Even on accident cases?" Joy said, suddenly realizing that she was being baited. "C'mon now, Amanda. There are any number of reasonable explanations for what Maria Cardoza might have done with that crystal."

"The kid said she always wore it on a gold chain around her neck."

Joy frowned, hoping her expression looked as dubious as Amanda Hawkins's. "That's what she told him. Maybe she was snowing him."

For the first time that night, the deputy showed a bit of the influence. She giggled, but—by this time—Joy knew better than to lower her guard.

"The truth, the truth, my kingdom for the truth," Amanda said, her giggle disappearing as quickly as it had come.

She suspects I was lying about being at Maria's house, Joy thought. She forced herself to smile across the table. *What am I getting myself into, lying to a police officer like a hardened criminal?*

A few minutes later when Joy signaled for the check, Amanda announced that she'd already taken care of it.

"It's charged to the taxpayers," she said cheerfully. "We spent most of the night talking about official business, didn't we?"

Hearing the subject of their meeting referred to as "official business," Joy felt as though she'd played into the deputy sheriff's hands. After Greg's insistence that she not go to the police, he would have to be told about tonight's meeting first thing tomorrow morning—on the off chance that Amanda might call him with some question about the AWOL airman from the Defense Language Institute.

Remembering Greg's willingness to share information about Santos, Joy felt annoyed with herself for not confiding in him. She walked out of the Foghorn Inn with the strong impression that she'd gotten more than she'd bargained for from her meeting with Deputy Sheriff Amanda Hawkins.

OUTSIDE THE RESTAURANT, a damp fog muffled lights and sounds, turning the nearly deserted Monterey street into a ghost walk.

When Joy reached her car in the adjacent parking lot, she switched on the Firebird's defrosting system to clear mist from the windshield. A few minutes later, her seat belt fastened and the doors locked, she pulled out into the street.

Since the Foghorn Inn was set by itself on a low hill overlooking the harbor, the road leading to it had no traffic other than that headed for the restaurant. Several cars passed her going uphill in the opposite direction, but there was no one behind her. At least not at first.

She doubted she'd have noticed the lights except for the fog. About halfway down the hill, she glimpsed another vehicle's lights in her rear view mirror, reflecting through the fog on the curve behind her. She was driving slowly, waiting for it to catch up to her, but it never came in sight, even when she stopped for the traffic signal at the base of the hill.

A crawly feeling crept down her spine.

Hadn't Airman Tuck insisted someone was following him? The thought gave her the creeps. As she turned the corner, Joy jabbed at the Firebird's automatic lock to make certain both doors were secured. Her reflexive motion, although vaguely reassuring, did nothing to quiet her anxious thoughts.

Chris Tuck talked to Deputy Sheriff Hawkins at the Foghorn Inn just before he disappeared. And now Joy herself had done exactly the same thing. Intensely aware of every breath she took, she peered into her rearview mirror, trying to penetrate the fog shrouding the streetlights along the empty street.

A block and a half away, a nondescript van came around the same corner she had. Then, blinker flashing, it prepared to turn again at the next intersection. The one directly behind her.

Braking the Firebird to a jerky stop in the middle of the street, she put the transmission in Park and twisted around in her seat to read the name painted on the side of the van before it swung around the corner. It was an impossible task in the murky fog. The vehicle lumbered out of sight before she got a good look at it.

For another second or two, her heart pounding, she waited where she was. The van had been following her. She was sure of it.

Behind her, a low-slung sports car entered the street from another direction. Its driver honked self-righteously as he veered into the opposite lane to pass. In a moment, he too, had disappeared.

If that van was following me, it's gone now she thought, breathing deeply to quiet her pounding heart. *And they've probably figured out I'm suspicious—just the way Airman Tuck was suspicious that somebody was following him.*

Stopping in the middle of the street wasn't a very smart thing to do, she decided.

When she shifted into Drive, her hand was trembling.

Chapter Five

Thursday Morning

Even though it was only seven-fifteen, Barbara Philpott was already on duty in Greg's front office when Joy arrived. Like a watchdog sensing a threat to its master, she gave Joy the noncom's equivalent of a warning growl.

"The colonel's inside, but he doesn't like to be bothered before 0800, ma'am," she said, still seated behind her desk. "He keeps his door locked and doesn't turn his squawk box on until then. You'll have to come back." Her tone was supercilious, her expression smug.

Most of the time Joy could ignore the woman's subtle put-downs, chalking them up to army pride. Not this morning.

After spending half the night awake, planning how she was going to tell Greg about last night's meeting with Amanda Hawkins, Joy intended to see him immediately.

She pulled out the chair next to Sergeant Philpott's desk and sat down.

"Don't you think we've carried this Army versus Air Force rivalry far enough?" Joy asked.

The secretary refused to meet Joy's gaze. "I don't know what you mean, ma'am."

"I sense that there's a problem between us," Joy went on. "I thought it was connected with your understandable loyalty to the Army. If that's not the problem, I'd like to know what it is."

Barbara Philpott's spine was so rigid, she looked carved in stone. When she spoke, her tone was harsh.

"It's not my place to comment on your ethics, Captain."

"*My ethics!*" Joy's voice rose in surprise. "You'll have to explain yourself, please."

Sergeant Philpott folded her arms across her chest and stared straight at Joy, her eyes baleful.

"Since you've asked, it's your involvement in the Spanish instructor's death that's been bothering me, ma'am. It's not ethical. If you don't stop what you're doing, it's going to hurt the school, the colonel, but most of all, it's going to hurt you."

The words, along with the woman's hostile expression, sounded vaguely threatening. Joy let her breath out in a long sigh. "How is what I'm doing going to hurt me, Sergeant?"

The secretary looked away from Joy's penetrating gaze. A red flush colored her neck. She cleared her throat. "I meant your career, of course, ma'am. If you ruin this school by making a big deal out of the Cardoza woman's accident, your career will be ruined right along with it."

An instant ago, Joy could have sworn there was something sinister behind Sergeant Philpott's words. Now she chided herself for her suspicions. The woman was simply being loyal to her boss. Hadn't Greg said essentially the same thing—that media attention could hurt the school? And, by implication, Joy's career?

"I appreciate your telling me this, Sergeant Philpott, but my career isn't your problem."

"I realize that ma'am. You did ask."

Joy had hoped that their talk might clear the air between them, but the secretary's expression seemed even more hostile than before.

"Now, will you please tell Colonel Weston I'm here," Joy said. "He's capable of deciding for himself if he wants to see one of the officers on his staff—no matter what time it is."

"I'll let him know you're waiting, ma'am." Sergeant Philpott stood up.

During the few seconds it took the secretary to get to Greg's door, Joy glanced down at her desk. An appointment calendar was open to the current week. Even though Joy was looking at it upside down, she recognized the number of her unit, the Air Force Student Squadron, on one of the entries.

Curious, she turned so she could read it. According to the entry, the assistant commandant had scheduled a meeting at her dormitory for three o'clock tomorrow afternoon.

Joy could not remember being informed about Colonel Spellman's visit. As squadron commander, she should have been.

She made a mental note to check into the matter when she returned to the orderly room. It would also be interesting to find out why Sergeant Philpott had entered the appointment on her calendar when Colonel Spellman had his own secretary to keep track of his meetings.

Greg appeared at his office door as soon as Sergeant Philpott announced that Captain Donnelly was waiting to see him.

"More problems at the 3483rd, Captain?" he asked, stepping backward against the open door to let her enter.

"You might say that, sir." Joy turned toward Sergeant Philpott. "Thanks, Sergeant. I appreciate your comments."

After Greg shut the door, he smiled. "Was she giving you a hard time?"

"Not at all." Joy glanced at the heavy mahogany door to see if it really could be locked, as Sergeant Philpott said. A polished brass key extended from an old-fashioned lock below the knob. "Incidentally, Greg, how much have you told her about Airman Tuck's suspicions that Maria Cardoza was murdered?"

"Nothing," he said. "Why do you ask?"

"Because she just informed me that I'd ruin the school and my career if I focused undesirable attention on Maria's death."

Joy studied his face. He looked vaguely amused at her revelation.

"I'm sure you straightened her out in short order," he said, smiling. Then, sobering, he added, "Even though she was out of line by mentioning it, it was rather clever of her to figure out the media threat from what went on yesterday."

"I don't see how she could have, Greg. All she knew was that we were hunting for Airman Tuck."

Joy paused as another thought struck her. "You don't suppose she listens in on your office conversations through her squawk box?"

He scowled. "Not possible. I never leave my box open when I'm not using it." His expression lightened. "And even if I did, I trust the woman implicitly. She's privy to all the business conducted in this headquarters. I've never had a more loyal—or closemouthed—secretary."

Joy didn't share Greg's high opinion of Barbara Philpott, but resisted the urge to argue since she had nothing but her gut feeling to go on.

"One other thing, Greg," she said, "does Sergeant Philpott keep a record of Colonel Spellman's appointments?"

"Not that I know of." He stared at her quizzically. "But I suppose it's possible that the secretaries maintain double records to remind each other of important meetings."

"I noticed an appointment for Colonel Spellman on Sergeant Philpott's calendar and wondered about it," Joy explained, feeling a little foolish for being so suspicious. "But that's not the reason I wanted to see you."

"We might as well sit down while we talk," he said, guiding her to the sofa.

Again this morning Greg was clean shaven. That was because it was so early, Joy thought, angry at herself for the maddening glow that warmed her cheeks. Why should the mental image of Greg Weston shaving provoke such an embarrassing reaction?

"Yesterday we agreed this wasn't the right time to tell the authorities what Airman Tuck said to me just before he disappeared," she began after they sat down.

Greg was at the other end of the sofa. He nodded and leaned forward, his head turned to one side like a fellow conspirator.

Encouraged, she hurried on. "Let me start by assuring you that I've said absolutely nothing to the police about what Airman Tuck told me Tuesday night."

My God! She's gone to the cops! Greg struggled to keep his alarm from showing. The last thing he wanted was to lose control and break the fragile bond of trust developing between them. "Okay, whom did you talk to? What did you say?"

Joy took a deep breath. Compared to his usual frown, Greg looked downright pleasant. But that didn't mean he was going to like what she had to tell him.

"Last night I had dinner with Amanda Hawkins from the Carmel Valley Sheriff's Office. She was the policewoman Airman Tuck spent Tuesday evening with."

More concerned than ever, Greg stood up and walked to his desk, sitting on one corner. "Yesterday you told me you didn't know who she was," he said, careful to keep his voice calm. He didn't want to make her feel trapped, as though he were trying to pin her down.

Joy leaned forward, anxious to explain. "Airman Tuck didn't mention her name. I saw it on the No Entry sign at Maria Cardoza's house yesterday." There was an unevenness to her voice as the words rushed out. "I decided Deputy Hawkins might be able to tell me something that would give me an idea where he is so I stopped by her office on the way back from Maria's. She didn't have time to talk then, and we decided to get together last night for dinner."

"Whoa!" Greg lifted a hand. "Slow down. Go back to the Cardoza woman's house. I assume you thought your airman might be there."

"Oh, he was there all right." Joy's voice rang with certainty.

"You sound awfully sure of that."

Reaching into her handbag, she pulled out the insignia she'd found. "After I'd been at Maria's place a few minutes, I realized somebody was watching me through binoculars from the hill across the canyon. It had to be Airman Tuck. By the time I drove over there, he was gone, but I found this."

She got up and handed the silver insignia to Greg.

He took one look at it and his internal alarm system began ringing. Why would the enlisted man go AWOL so he could watch his dead lover's house through binoculars? It didn't make sense.

"You say you found this on the hill opposite Ms. Cardoza's house?" He turned it over in his fingers, noting the clutches fastened to its back and its unscratched, mint condition.

Joy nodded. "By the side of the road where he probably parked his motorcycle. It must have fallen out of his pocket."

"How did you know he was watching you through binoculars?"

"The sun was reflecting off them. It took me a couple of minutes to figure out what was going on."

"And as soon as you did, of course you had to get right over there?" A strange anxiety, like nothing he'd felt before, heightened Greg's alarm. "Didn't it occur to you that somebody else might have been watching the place?" He got up and paced up and down in front of her. "It's isolated as hell out there in the valley. Damn it all, Joy, it's not safe to go running around in the boondocks like that."

Joy glanced at him, surprised. Was he that concerned about her safety?

"Are you suggesting that it might have been Maria's murderer?" she asked. "Even after I found Airman Tuck's insignia?"

"The Cardoza woman's death was an accident," Greg said stubbornly. "So it couldn't have been her murderer. I admit it sounds like Tuck was the one with binoculars. But you didn't know that when you went rushing over there. All I'm saying is that your hidden observer could have been somebody with less than sterling motives."

"But he wasn't," Joy said practically. "It must have been Chris Tuck. It's not logical that anybody else would drop an airman's insignia across the canyon from Maria's house. It had to be him."

In spite of her seeming assurance, Joy shifted uncomfortably on the army-blue sofa. An unseen stranger watching from across the canyon... *It had to be my airman,* she repeated to herself, to quiet her gnawing fear.

"Airman Tuck said he was going to use himself for bait to trap the murderer," she said doggedly. "The logical place to do that is Maria's."

"But why?" Greg asked. "Why would he choose that particular place?"

"I felt it in my bones," she said, shrugging. "So did Santos Mueller. We had different reasons, but we both thought that's where Airman Tuck was."

"Do you still think he's there, watching the house?"

Joy nodded, adding, "If I hadn't found his insignia, I wouldn't be so sure."

"Both you and Santos think he's hanging around there. That *is* curious." Greg slid off his desk. "It might be a good idea to take another look around the place."

As they entered the outer office, Greg spoke to Sergeant Philpott. "If anybody wants me, I'll be in the Carmel Valley for the next couple of hours. Call Colonel Spellman and have him cover for me." He started toward the door and then paused, turning toward his secretary again. "Sometime this morning get in touch with the Salinas Sportsmans' Club and tell them that Mr. Mueller, Captain Donnelly and I will shoot skeet at 0730 Saturday morning. We don't want to get out there and find them shut down."

"Yes, sir." Sergeant Philpott wrote some notes on her calendar.

"And please call Sergeant Blakeman at the 3483rd and tell him that Captain Donnelly is with me and will be back after lunch."

Barbara Philpott jotted a note on her desk pad. She didn't look up when Joy and Greg left.

IN THE THINNING FOG outside, clusters of uniformed students moved toward the academic area for their eight o'clock classes.

Joy's Firebird was parked in a visitor's space. "Shall we take my car?" she asked, fishing around in her bag for her keys. She didn't think he'd take her up on her offer.

"Good idea," he said, surprising her. Greg Weston was an enigma. She never knew what to expect from him.

He opened the door for her. "That way I can keep an eye on you."

She slid behind the wheel and fastened her seat belt. Not until they were under way did she realize what he'd meant. Since his blind eye was on the right side, as driver he couldn't glance at someone in the passenger's seat without a definite movement of his head. The discovery elicited unexpectedly tender feelings for him.

"What do you think we'll find?" she asked, to mask emotions that, if revealed, would embarrass both of them. "I gave the yard a pretty good once-over yesterday afternoon."

"Probably nothing. But you're right about this insignia. Finding it where you did seems to indicate that your man was there. By the way," he went on, remembering that she hadn't said much about her conversation with the deputy sheriff, "did you tell the deputy about it?"

He turned so that he could look directly at her face.

He was surprised to see a pink flush rise from her neck and soar to her freckled cheeks.

"No, it didn't seem like a good idea." The flush intensified, turned a fiery red.

"Why not?" he prodded. "Since you'd told her you were on the trail of a missing airman, it seems logical to let her know why you thought he was still in this vicinity."

"If I'd said anything about the insignia, she would have known I was snooping around at Maria's house because I thought he might be there. As it was, she guessed that he'd had a relationship with Maria. I told her I'd heard some gossip— I guess what Santos said qualifies as gossip."

"Good girl," he said. "Until we've got more to go on, there's no reason to say anything about the man's relationship with Ms. Cardoza or about his drunken ramblings that she was murdered."

He glanced at her again. "I'm surprised the deputy— what's her name? Hawkins?—didn't guess you'd been at the house when you stopped by her office yesterday afternoon. It was directly on your way from there to the Presidio."

Her chin jutted out. "She did guess. She came right out and asked me if I'd been there."

"But you didn't tell her?"

"I flat out lied about it."

There was so much self-condemnation in her tone that Greg kept quiet, careful not to let his amusement show. *Welcome to the real world, Captain Joy Donnelly,* he thought.

"I'm glad you didn't arouse her curiosity," he said.

"I told you I wouldn't say anything to the authorities unless there was a threat to Airman Tuck's life," she reminded him. "So far, what we've seen indicates the opposite. He must have been okay when he dropped that insignia."

"Okay except for a hell of a hangover," Greg agreed. "Did you find out anything interesting about Tuck from the deputy?"

They'd turned off Highway 1 onto the Carmel Valley Road.

Joy replied with the generous smile he hadn't seen much of during the past few days. "More than I really wanted to know," she said. "The one interesting thing he told Amanda—Sheriff Hawkins—was about the crystal. He didn't say anything about giving it to Maria, though."

She spent the next few minutes relating everything Amanda had told her about the piece. How it looked. That Airman Tuck had said Maria wore it all the time. That she wasn't wearing it when she was found. That the police hadn't found it when they searched the house.

"But they weren't looking for it, were they?" Greg asked, when she'd finished.

Joy shook her head. "I suppose not. Airman Tuck didn't mention it to Deputy Hawkins until Tuesday night. Maria's body was found six days earlier."

"Then it's probably somewhere inside. She simply took it off when she went in the water."

"He told me she never took it off. When he found out she wasn't wearing it that night, that's when he knew she'd been murdered."

"My point exactly." There was a triumphant note to his voice. "If she took it off herself, your airman was wrong with his drunken allegations."

"Amanda seemed awfully sure the crystal wasn't there," Joy said. "Maybe she looked for it herself after she talked to Chris Tuck."

"I'd be willing to bet my good-conduct medal it's right there in the house. Too bad we can't get inside to take a look around."

Joy gave him a startled glance. That's exactly what she'd been thinking.

THE RAMSHACKLE gray cottage looked even more desolate in the early morning than it had at noon, because the shadows were longer. To the west the omnipresent fog bank hung over the Pacific, but here the air was clear and cool.

Joy parked the Firebird behind the house in almost the same place she had yesterday, near the attached garage.

Greg helped her out. "Let's have a look around," he said.

Instead of heading for the porch, as she'd done yesterday, he went to the back door, twisting the knob and rattling the door back and forth. Even though it was locked, it appeared pretty insubstantial to Joy.

Next he jerked on the big garage door. It refused to budge. A flimsy door on the far side of the garage was locked with a ridiculously insecure knob lock.

"No problems here if we want to get in," Greg said.

A tiny knot formed in the pit of Joy's stomach. Much as she wanted to see the inside of Maria Cardoza's house, the thought of breaking in sickened her. Military officers didn't do things like that.

But Greg Weston did. Any number of his exploits had involved his unexpected appearance in places where he wasn't supposed to be. Like the time he'd defied official orders to rescue hostages on a hijacked airplane. At least the newspapers said he'd defied official orders—maybe he'd been acting on secret orders nobody knew about. These days, with the cold war over and a dozen third-world countries involved in terrorist and drug operations, actions against them were more hush-hush than ever.

She followed him around the back of the house and went from there to the front door of the porch, also locked. At the far end of the porch, the sliding glass doors were still covered with the heavy drapes she'd noticed yesterday. As far as Joy could determine, nothing had changed.

"Is that where he was watching you through the binoculars?" Greg asked, motioning across the canyon.

She searched for a glint of light or a swirl of dust that would betray Airman Tuck's presence, but saw nothing. "There's a piece of land directly across from here that extends into the canyon. It's the logical place to keep an eye on this house. That's where I found the insignia."

Greg started around the pool, searching the ground just as she'd done yesterday. "We'll go over there as soon as we've seen everything here," he said.

"The pool's empty." She followed him, suddenly anxious, not wanting him out of her sight. "Yesterday I saw the hose somebody used to drain it after the accident. I suppose they put the pool cover on then, too."

"Smart move," he said.

At the far end of the structure she saw him examine the hose used to drain the water into the canyon. A simple garden-variety green piece of tubing, it turned off and on with a spigot, like an ordinary water faucet.

While she watched, Greg twisted the spigot. In a few seconds there was a rush of water 75 feet below from the end of the hose. It gushed into the canyon, following pre-carved channels in the dry earth. He switched the spigot off.

"I thought you said the pool was empty."

"When I saw the hose hooked up to it and the pool cover on top, I thought it was."

"Then you didn't climb up there for a look?"

She shook her head and started toward the small wooden deck at the end of the pool closest to the porch. He caught up to her before she reached it.

"Better let me go first," he said, taking the steps in the four-foot ladder two at a time.

The wooden deck, about fifteen feet long and five feet wide, was curved to fit snugly to the rounded side of the pool. At each end was a wooden bench. The pool cover had been loosened where the vinyl liner joined the wooden deck between the benches. Joy helped him flip the heavy plastic cover backward.

He took one look at the still water and spun around to block her view.

It was too late.

She'd already glimpsed the man's body, dressed in red swimming trunks, floating in the partially drained pool.

She didn't need a second glance to know who it was.

They'd found Airman Tuck.

Chapter Six

Greg hauled the plastic cover forward, hiding the body floating underneath.

Joy's horror couldn't be covered up so easily. Assailed by a terrible sense of grief and guilt, she gulped huge mouthfuls of the clear, cool air.

"If only I'd listened to him," she said, her anguish almost too much to bear. "He knew somebody was after him. If only I'd stayed in the yard and talked to him instead of insisting that he come inside...."

She felt Greg's hands grab her shoulders in a grip that was gentle but firm. "That's B.S., Joy," he growled. "You were doing the man a favor by inviting him inside. Don't get the notion you could have done anything to prevent this."

Tears welled in her eyes, and she turned away so he wouldn't see. Officers didn't cry, at least not in uniform. "He came to me for help, and I refused to listen," she said, her voice choking.

His hand, holding a neatly folded handkerchief, appeared at her side. She brushed it away.

"I'm all right, Greg. Truly I am." Her eyes were filling. She tried to keep from blinking so they wouldn't overflow.

"You'd better take it, Joy."

She heard the compassion in his voice through a mist of pain.

"This has got your name on it."

She grabbed for it as the first hot drops rolled down her cheeks. With her back to him, she dabbed at her eyes and blew her nose. During those first anguished moments, horror and grief yielded to anger. Joy seethed with mounting rage. Maybe there wasn't anything she could do to bring Airman Tuck back, but that didn't mean she was helpless.

"We've got to find out who did this," she said through clenched teeth. "First Maria Cardoza and now Chris Tuck. I'll get the bastard if it's the last thing I do on this earth."

She felt Greg gripping her shoulder again.

"We'll find out what happened," he growled, leading her to the steps from the wooden deck. "I promise you that."

When they'd reached the ground, he turned to her. "I admit it looks suspicious," he said, "but we can't automatically assume he's been murdered."

She gave him a hostile glare. "Are you suggesting we keep quiet about this too, the way you insisted we say nothing about his fears for his life?"

Greg recoiled. Unfair as her words were, they hurt. Joy Donnelly didn't think much of his character or his integrity if she honestly believed he'd walk away from a dead trooper.

She was upset and didn't mean what she was saying, he told himself. This airman was probably the first she'd lost.

"No more keeping quiet, Joy," he said quietly. "When we report this to Deputy Hawkins, you tell her the whole story. It'll be up to the police to determine if it was an accident."

Joy's pent-up fury exploded. "You're going to tell them you think that's what it was, aren't you? An accident? Like Maria's drowning?"

"What I tell them won't make much difference, Joy."

At that moment, she forgot he was her commander, a full colonel with eagles on his shoulders.

"I simply can't fathom how your mind works, Greg Weston," she fumed. "In spite of everything that's happened, you're still so concerned about unfavorable media attention to your precious school that you're willing to pretend you think these murders are accidents. Well, I know better, and I think you do, too." She swung around, intending to get to the Firebird and Deputy Sheriff Hawkins's office as fast as she could.

Greg caught her arm. "I'm not pretending, Joy."

She tried not to see the quiet sincerity in his expression.

"It's not likely Tuck was murdered," he went on. "Drinking is a factor in a lot of drownings, and he was probably intoxicated when he died. The police can tell us that after an autopsy. Plus, we know for a fact he was mourning Maria Cardoza. It's even possible he committed suicide."

"Suicide! How can you even suggest that in the light of what he told me Tuesday night?" She jerked away from him and started around the house.

"Let's call a truce for the moment," he said, following her. "You're upset now and you've got every reason to be. The death of a trooper is the worst thing that can happen to a commander. It's something you never get used to. But instead of arguing about how and why Airman Tuck died, why don't we wait and see what the police have to say about it?"

Joy could taste the bitterness in her throat. "Nobody's going to convince me it wasn't murder, Greg. Not you. Not the police. Not anybody. The sooner I talk to Amanda Hawkins and report this murder along with everything Airman Tuck told me Tuesday night, the better." She opened the car door and got in.

Greg leaned down, resting his arms on the open window. His face was so close Joy could see tiny lines around his mouth and feel the warmth of his breath. She clutched at her anger, struggling to keep hold of it because it was so much easier to bear than grief.

Greg swung her car door open. "If speed is what you're after, the telephone is the quickest way to reach the authorities. Let's see if the one in the house is still hooked up. Even if it isn't, it's a good excuse to look around inside."

Joy didn't get out, but she didn't slam the door closed either. "What you do is your own business, but I'm not about to break into that house."

"Suit yourself." He shrugged and started toward the porch.

Joy stared at Greg's departing back with a jumble of confused thoughts and feelings. Much as she wanted to resist his suggestion, this was a golden opportunity for a glimpse inside.

She got out of the car and went after him.

He didn't seem surprised to find her at his shoulder. "The slider to the bedroom's not locked," he said when they were halfway across the front deck.

"How could you possibly know that?" she gasped.

Reaching it, he pushed it open. "Since the other doors are locked, Airman Tuck must have used this one when he went outside for his swim."

"Or somebody left it open when they carried him outside and dumped him in the pool," she corrected.

"I'm sure the police will have some ideas about that." Greg gathered the heavy draperies to one side and disappeared behind them.

Swallowing the last of her scruples, Joy followed him through the sliding glass door into Maria Cardoza's darkened bedroom.

THE LIGHT SWITCH was beside the open door to the hallway. Greg flicked it on.

"Don't leave any fingerprints you don't want the police to find," he warned. He pulled a couple of tissues from a box on the dresser and wrapped them loosely around the fingers of both hands.

Now that she was inside, Joy found her anxiety fading. With one glance, she took in the lush, gauzy look of Maria Cardoza's bedroom. A plum-colored carpet, rosebud wallpaper with matching draperies and spread on the bed, white French country furniture with gold accents: the cottage's plush interior in no way matched its ramshackle exterior.

On the queen-size bed was a pile of dark clothing. Joy could see a pair of men's pants and a green wool sweater. Tossed on top were boxer shorts and a white T-shirt.

"That's not what Airman Tuck was wearing when I saw him Tuesday night."

Greg was opening drawers in the triple dresser, peering inside, and closing each one. Every so often he would push something aside for a better look.

"Are you sure?" he asked. "That could be important because, if they're not here, it means he stopped somewhere to change."

"The sweater he had on was a turtleneck," she said. "This one has a V-neck. And he was wearing jeans."

He glanced up from a drawer.

"Check the closet," he said, pushing the sliding door on the wall beside him open. "See if you can find what he was wearing when you saw him."

Joy inched along the wall-length closet, examining each piece of clothing. When she reached the midpoint, Greg pulled the doors in the other direction, opening the closet's other side.

Maria's closet was well organized, Joy observed. Skirts, slacks, shirts, work dresses, and dressy dresses were lined up with military precision. At the far end Joy found what she was looking for: a small space where a man's clothes hung—a uniform, several pairs of jeans and trousers, a sweater, and a couple of shirts. Two pairs of shoes were on the rack underneath, but there was no sign of the dark blue turtleneck sweater she was looking for.

"One pair of these jeans has been worn," she said. "It's possible they were the ones he had on Tuesday night, but the sweater isn't here."

Greg came around the bed and felt in the pockets of the jeans and then of the other pants in the closet. There was nothing inside any of them. She watched him go through the pockets of the trousers on the bed.

As he laid everything out so she could see the contents, she noticed his long fingers with their square tips and well-manicured nails. Greg had a pianist's hands. It seemed to Joy that he touched the airman's possessions with great respect.

Don't imagine things, she scolded herself. *He's being careful so nobody will know we went through Airman Tuck's things.*

She surveyed the items on the bed. A billfold and card case. Some change. A key ring. A package of cigarettes. A couple of crumpled tissues.

Greg put everything back where he found it. "If that insignia you found fell out of his pocket, you'd think its mate would still be here."

"Unless when he changed his clothes, he overlooked it. It's probably in the pocket of the jeans he was wearing Tuesday night."

"That means he was wearing those jeans yesterday at noon when he was watching you from across the canyon. It's odd that only one of a pair of insignias would fall out of his pocket."

Joy stood silently near the bed while Greg returned to his search. He'd finished the triple dresser and begun on the bureau. As with Airman Tuck's belongings, it seemed to Joy that he handled Maria's with a respect akin to reverence.

"Sometime between then and now, he changed into these clothes on the bed and put the ones he was wearing somewhere." He nodded toward an inside door. "Maybe there's a hamper in the bathroom."

Joy shoved the door open. Inside, in spite of the wall-to-wall carpeting that matched the bedroom's, the house's shoddy construction was evident. The tile around the tub-shower was a cheap rose-colored plastic and the grout had shrunk leaving gaps between it and the tile.

Thick bath towels embroidered with a large gold *C* hung across from a laminated counter with two white porcelain washbasins. Joy grabbed some toilet paper. Covering her fingers, she gingerly opened the cabinet below the basins. It contained cleaning supplies, neatly arranged from lowest in front to highest in back.

A linen closet beside the tub held toiletries, towels, and sheets.

"Nothing in the bathroom," she said.

Greg was finishing his search of the drawer in the nightstand beside the bed. Joy noticed that he paid no attention to the white telephone on top of the nightstand. Trimmed in gold, like the furniture, the phone was a reproduction of an antique desk model.

"No sign of the crystal so far," he said.

"Is that what we're looking for?" Her anxiety had been replaced with the breathless thrill of doing something forbidden but morally justifiable.

He shrugged. "The crystal or anything else interesting."

"Did you try the phone?"

"When you were in the bathroom. It's still hooked up. We'll call your friend in the Carmel Valley Sheriff's Office when we've finished looking around."

With Joy behind him, he started toward the open door to the hallway.

There was another bathroom at the end of the hall, and a second bedroom, apparently used for guests. While Joy checked the bathroom, Greg made a swift search of the little bedroom.

They met in the hall a few minutes later.

"She used the room to store things she doesn't wear much," Greg said. "A flamenco outfit was all set out in the closet—probably for the carnival next Tuesday."

Joy tried to read his expression. Was that sympathy she saw, or simply curiosity about a well-organized woman who'd taken time to pick out her costume for a party a few weeks ahead of time?

The house's third and smallest bedroom adjoined the second. Maria used it as a den. Joy was surprised to see a computer and printer set up on a table alongside an elegant white country-style French desk. The desk had drawers on each side.

While Greg went through the desk, Joy studied the titles of the books in the painted wooden bookcase beside the computer table. There were many Spanish language titles, a row of teaching textbooks, several recent bestsellers, a stack of newsmagazines, three dictionaries: English, Spanish/English, American slang, and a book of quotations. Joy wondered how Maria used quotations in her language teaching.

Inside a closet next to the bookcase, Joy discovered a two-drawer metal file cabinet. Smoothing the crumpled tissue over her fingers, she examined the manila folders inside.

Alphabetically arranged, the files contained Maria Cardoza's personal records. Joy skipped through folders full of bank statements, rent records, miscellaneous letters, tax forms, and assorted papers involving Maria's house. She'd had the place redecorated when she moved in and folder after folder bulged with estimates, brochures, invoices and samples of everything from carpeting to wallpaper.

The file continued in the second drawer. Under *P* was a folder marked Press. It was chock-full of newspaper clippings.

Joy flipped past it, guessing it contained more decorating information. When she reached the last file folder, she realized that none of the others had included only newspaper items. Curious, she pulled the Press folder out of the cabinet and opened it.

On top was a short article about a navy lieutenant attending the Defense Language Institute who had been hurt last week in an automobile accident. Maria must have clipped the article only days before her death. The lieutenant's name was underlined in red every time it appeared in the article.

Interested, Joy flipped through the next few articles. One featuring Sergeant Barbara Philpott had the title circled. DLI's Iron Lady, the headline read. A red question mark had been penciled in after it.

Beneath the Philpott article was an embarrassing item about Joy herself, written a few days after her arrival. Joy scowled at her picture in front of the Sloat Monument, a large granite eagle overlooking the Army Museum on the Presidio grounds. Before she laid the open folder on the desk in front of Greg, she made sure the article about her was turned over on the left-hand side of the folder so he wouldn't see it.

"Here's something interesting," she said. "Maria Cardoza kept a file of stories about the language school."

Greg bent down and leafed through the rest of the articles in the folder.

Standing beside him, Joy noticed that the items dated back three years—to the time Maria Cardoza first began working at the Presidio. She'd saved every article remotely connected with the Defense Language Institute that appeared in any newspaper or magazine on the Monterey Peninsula since the day she arrived.

As Greg flipped through the articles, he saw one about himself written a few weeks after he became commander. There were several others reporting his "shakedown at the Tower of Babel," a reorganization he'd demanded when he arrived two years ago. Each time his name appeared, it was underlined in red ink.

When he came to the end of the file, Joy reached for it.

"If you're through, I'll put it back," she said.

Greg sensed an anxiety in her eagerness, as though there was something inside she didn't want him to see. Closing the folder, he picked it up from the desk.

"I want to glance through the articles on top," he said. "Don't want to miss anything." From the way she sighed and stepped back, he could tell he'd been right. She didn't want him to see one of the items. It had to be about her.

Starting at the beginning he leafed through them until he came across a long piece, with a picture, about Joy. Her photo in front of the Sloat Monument smiled at him from the printed page. Too bad he wouldn't have time to do more than glance at it. He'd have another copy brought to him when he got back to his office.

She brushed closer to him, staring down at the picture of herself. He could see a small vein throbbing in her temple. A rosy blush turned her face crimson.

"It's a pretty good picture," he observed, amused at her obvious embarrassment.

"My usual toothy grin." She laughed nervously. "But at least I don't look slaphappy."

Toothy grin? Slaphappy? He thought she must be kidding, but one look at her face told him she wasn't.

"Were you satisfied with the article this reporter—" he checked the byline "—Nadine Robinson wrote about you in the *Monterey Tribune*?"

"Then you haven't read it?"

He heard the relief in her voice.

"I'm sure I read it when it was printed," he said. "Major Easely makes certain I see everything in the local press that concerns the school." He noticed that she hadn't answered his question. "Sounds like Ms. Robinson said some things you didn't like."

"She misquoted me," Joy said. "Or rather, she emphasized my personal life when the interview was supposed to be about the role of women in the military service. I considered asking for a retraction, but Donna—Major Easely— said that would only give her an excuse to write another article about me. I decided to drop it."

"Smart move," Greg said. "You've already heard my opinion of the fourth estate, so you have my sympathy."

Resisting his urge to scan the item, he closed the folder and handed it to her.

Damn that reporter, Joy thought. *If Greg reads that article, he'll think I'm a snooty snob.*

Almost as annoyed with Greg for commenting on the article as with the fool reporter who wrote it, Joy shoved the file of clippings in the metal cabinet and slammed the drawer shut. The cabinet responded with a jerk, followed by the hollow clack of something falling to the uncarpeted closet floor. She peered into the small space beside the cabinet. A pair of glasses lay there. They'd been wedged between the cabinet and the wall and had fallen when she jarred the cabinet.

Careful to keep her fingers covered, Joy picked them up. They were reading glasses. Maria must have been wearing them while she used her file, had placed them on top of the cabinet and had somehow knocked them off.

Joy was about to put them back where she found them when something struck her as not quite right. The horn rims didn't suit Maria Cardoza's delicate features. Curious, Joy held them up to her own face. The bridge was too wide to sit comfortably on her nose.

These are a man's reading glasses. The revelation sent her blood pressure skyrocketing. She straightened and turned to Greg, who was still going through the desk.

"Know anybody who wears glasses like these?" she asked. "It couldn't have been Airman Tuck. He was too young for reading glasses."

Greg took them from her and shook his head. "Where did you get them?"

"In the closet beside Maria's file cabinet." Her words tumbled out in a rush. "As though somebody was going through the cabinet hunting for something and was interrupted. Or took them off when he was finished and just plain didn't notice he'd knocked them off the cabinet."

Greg's expression was solemn. "These glasses could mean somebody's been out here snooping around—or maybe they were left here months ago."

He handed them back to her. "We have to be careful not to jump to conclusions, Joy."

"C'mon, Greg. Somebody besides me has been in this file since she died, and you know it." Wrapping the glasses in a tissue, she put them in her shoulder bag.

Joy saw Greg's reproving look.

"If you want to remove them from the house, let me take them."

With a determined snap, she closed her shoulder bag, the glasses inside. "Finding out who owns these is something I'm going to do for Chris Tuck."

"It's something we're both going to do. They're men's glasses, Joy. I can pretend they're mine. It might give us an edge."

Reluctantly, she gave them to him.

IN THE COMBINED living and dining room across the hall, elegant white French provincial furniture and Oriental rugs transformed an ordinary interior into a showplace.

When Joy opened the ceiling-to-floor draperies on the outside wall, the magnificent view of the canyon and surrounding hills added to the elegance. Since the ground sloped down from the house, the pool lay below, almost out of sight of the wide-screen panorama from the windows.

"Maria Cardoza had expensive tastes," Greg observed, examining the material of the draperies. "These drapes alone are worth thousands. Add in the furniture and carpeting and items like that marble fireplace—" he nodded toward it "—and we're looking at expenses in the neighborhood of forty to fifty thousand dollars."

"Some of the folders in her cabinet had information about the remodeling she did when she moved in," Joy said. "You think she had the fireplace done especially?"

"No doubt about it. Contractors of cheap houses like this don't install items like that real marble fireplace." His brow furrowed. "I wonder where she got the money."

Joy thought for a minute. "You don't suppose she was using the information in those articles to blackmail people?" The notion popped into Joy's head, and she voiced it before realizing how ludicrous it sounded. Information in newspaper articles couldn't be used to blackmail anybody.

Ludicrous or not, Greg took her seriously. "The same thought occurred to me," he said. "But it just doesn't make sense, no matter how I twist it around. Even if she combined information from the various articles and made deductions about people, she'd still be working from published articles everybody's read."

"Maybe she combined it with private knowledge she picked up somewhere." Joy pulled the drapes shut.

"Possible," he said. "But in that case, why would she collect every article about every person remotely connected with DLI? Why not just about the person or people she was blackmailing?"

Joy studied his face. "If not blackmail, where did the money come from to pay for all this remodeling? You know, Greg, it might be worth a check of the personnel files to see if she had wealthy relatives in Spain or some other source of income. With an okay from you, I'm sure Personnel would let me have a look at her file."

"It'll be easier if I do it," Greg said. "I've told Personnel to restrict access to those files. We can compare notes tonight before the Spanish Department party."

"The Spanish Department party! I'd forgotten all about it." Suddenly Joy's anguished feelings at the pool flooded back and a vast emptiness swept over her. Dark images of the floating body filled her mind, changing her mood. "Do you think they'll still have the party?"

He nodded. "There won't be an announcement about Airman Tuck's death until his family's notified. Tomorrow at the earliest."

"Where do you want me to meet you?" she asked, her voice breaking. No matter how miserable she felt, she had to go to that party. Somebody there might be able to tell her something, anything, that might help.

He looked at her strangely. "I'll come by for you, of course." He sounded surprised at her offer to meet him. "The party's not until eight. Would you like to go somewhere first for an early dinner?"

Much as Joy wanted to accept Greg's invitation, she couldn't escape her anguished feelings.

Wearily, she shook her head. "I'm sorry, Greg. The party's all I can manage tonight. I'll fix myself something at home."

To her relief, he didn't argue with her about it.

"Quarter to eight tonight, then, at your house." He went through the dining room into the kitchen.

Struggling to free herself from the raw grief that overwhelmed her again, she followed him to the kitchen.

Like the rest of the house, it was an odd mix of elegance and trashiness. The appliances were top-of-the-line, their shiny black fronts accented with gleaming chrome; but the laminated countertops and cabinets matched the house's cheap exterior.

A door led outside. It was one Greg had already tried, and he didn't bother opening it.

"Time to make that phone call." He headed back down the hall toward the master bedroom.

He unwrapped the handkerchief from his fingers before he picked up the phone and dialed the emergency numbers. Joy knew he wanted the authorities to find his prints on the phone. Otherwise they'd know he kept his hands covered while he was inside. After he'd reported finding the body in the pool, he agreed to wait on the premises until an official arrived.

When he'd finished, he turned to Joy. "Let's take a look at the garage before they get here."

Access to the garage from the house was through the guest bedroom. Inside were two vehicles. One was a car, an American-made compact that must have belonged to Maria. The other was a motorcycle with a shiny red helmet propped up on the luggage rack behind the rear seat.

"Looks like he came out here under his own steam," Greg said.

"More proof to you his death was accidental?" Joy asked.

But Greg shook his head. "I don't know, Joy. I don't know."

Chapter Seven

A sensation of sickness and desolation swept over Joy as she watched the scene below the deck where she and Greg were sitting. She pulled her faded patio chair closer to his, so close they were almost touching.

Beside the aboveground pool, a cluster of officials was gathered around the body of Airman Christopher L. Tuck, which had been pulled from the pool and placed on a stretcher. Greg had gone for a close look a few minutes ago and had just returned to the deck.

Unable to continue watching, Joy turned her chair around so that her back was to the railing. She was starting to perspire, but didn't consider removing her uniform blouse. Not only would that be militarily incorrect, since they were outside, but it would also remove her captain's bars, worn on the shoulders of the blouse. At that moment the authority and responsibility the bars represented were slender threads holding her nausea and grief in check.

She felt Greg's hand on her arm and saw his knowing glance at her face. He stood up.

"Deputy Hawkins." He didn't yell, but there was an intense timbre to his voice that made everybody below look at him. "We need to get back to the Presidio. Call me for an appointment when you're free to talk."

The policewoman immediately detached herself from the small group around the body. "I'm free now, Colonel."

In a moment she'd joined them on the deck. To Joy, her bulky frame, clad in a tan sheriff's uniform, looked even firmer than it had last night. There was no sign of distress on her face at the unfortunate events taking place only yards away.

"I've got a few questions for you people now," she said. "Later on, maybe there'll be more."

Greg sat down again, facing the pool. Amanda took a chair next to him.

"After talking to Joy yesterday, I knew you were looking for Chris—Airman Tuck," she said. "Too bad you had to find him like this. If I might ask, what made you think to come out here?"

Joy responded quickly, before Greg could answer. "Because of something you said last night. You told me you thought he was having an affair with Ms. Cardoza. That gave me the idea he might be hanging around her house."

Amanda turned to Greg. "I'm sure Joy's told you about the rest of our conversation over steaks at the Foghorn Inn."

Greg nodded. "When she said she was coming out here, I decided to tag along."

Although still fighting her nausea, Joy noticed that Amanda's aggressiveness at the Foghorn Inn had disappeared for the moment. She wondered what was behind the woman's sudden congeniality.

Grinning at Joy, the policewoman turned her gaze back to Greg. "As I told Joy, I suspected Chris was... um... intimate with Maria Cardoza as soon as he starting asking questions about her accident and about the crystal he said she always wore." Amanda's expression didn't change when she mentioned the crystal. "I don't suppose you had a chance to look for it while you were inside using the phone."

Greg leaned back in his chair. To Joy he seemed as relaxed as in his office.

"We walked through the house while we were waiting," he said, "but didn't want to get fingerprints on anything, so we were careful about opening drawers."

It wasn't a lie, but not the complete truth, either.

Amanda stood up. "That's it then. We'll be in touch."

Joy couldn't believe her ears. "You mean that's all the questions you have for us in a suspicious death like this?" Her stunned astonishment swept away the icy lump in her stomach.

"Who says it's a suspicious death?" Amanda said.

For all Greg's arguments about the drowning being accidental, he looked as startled as Joy felt.

"Nobody goes swimming under a pool cover," he said.

"Plus," Joy added, "Airman Tuck seemed scared to death when I talked to him Tuesday night. He was convinced somebody was after him. If that's not reason enough to consider his death suspicious, I don't know what is."

The deputy sat down again. "You didn't say anything about that last night, Joy," she said softly. "If there's anything else you're holding out on me, let's have it."

Joy felt the blood pounding in her temples as she stared at Amanda's alert eyes in her smiling face.

"I didn't say anything about it because I didn't want to make him sound paranoid or get him into trouble with the police. Now that he's dead, it's a different matter."

Amanda took a deep breath. "He didn't sound scared to death when I talked to him at the bar. That must have been only minutes before he arrived at your house. Maybe you misunderstood him. He was pretty drunk, and you only said a few words to him."

Amanda's catlike eyes peered into Joy's green ones.

"I didn't misunderstand him," Joy said stubbornly. "The man was scared to death."

Greg, who had been watching Joy, turned to Amanda beside him. "There *is* going to be an autopsy, isn't there, Deputy?" Joy detected a subtle hardening of his expression as he eyed the policewoman.

"Affirmative, Colonel, although I've got to tell you that it looks like an accidental drowning to me—or maybe even a suicide."

Even though Greg had voiced the same thought only a short time ago, the disbelief on his face matched Joy's.

Amanda hurried on, as if eager to convince them. "The man was drunk, he came out here to his lover's cottage in the middle of the night, ended up drowning in the same pool where she died just a week before. What does that sound like to you people? So what if there was a cover over the pool? There was plenty of room underneath."

Joy caught Greg's eye and saw a reflection of the same startled shock she was feeling.

"Are you telling us that Airman Tuck's been in that pool since Tuesday night?" she asked, her heart in her throat.

"That's my guess," Amanda said. "From the way the body looks, it's been in the water at least twenty-four hours, probably closer to thirty-six."

Joy winced. The deputy must be wrong. If the body had been in the water for twenty-four hours, that meant it had been in the pool yesterday, at noon, when Joy was prowling around on the property.

The icy lump returned to her stomach, twice as big as before. "When will we get the official report of the autopsy so we'll know for certain when he died?"

Amanda had a way of smiling with her lips closed and her eyes round as saucers. She beamed first at Joy and then Greg before she answered Joy's question.

"Here on the Peninsula autopsies take a while," she said. "We're looking at a few days to a week for a preliminary report, but it may take a month or longer for the final."

"A month! I knew civilians were inefficient, but that's absolutely ridiculous." Greg's low growl brimmed with disgust.

Amanda wasn't smiling now. "An autopsy isn't a simple procedure, Colonel. Lab tests have to be made, tissue samples taken and analyzed."

A muscle twitched in Greg's jaw. "That means there's no final report yet on Maria Cardoza, either."

"That's right. But since the preliminary report gave us no reason to think her death wasn't accidental, she's not a high-priority case."

"After this second death you'd be well advised to reexamine your priorities, Deputy."

Joy heard the command of authority in Greg's voice. Amanda Hawkins did, too. Her round eyes narrowed.

"Before you go, I'd like to give you a little friendly advice, Colonel Weston, Captain Donnelly."

Joy noticed they were no longer on a first-name basis.

"We police officers are quite capable of establishing our own priorities," she went on. "We don't need any help from you people. If you've got any ideas about meddling in matters that don't concern you, I'd strongly advise against it. This is not your line of work."

Joy had been holding her breath without realizing it. She exhaled in one long, slow motion.

"I'll certainly take your advice under consideration, Deputy," Greg said, standing up. "Now, we've got to get back to the Presidio. You've got our numbers if you have questions."

When Joy turned, she noted that Airman Tuck's body was gone.

"I doubt we'll have to bother you again, Colonel," Amanda said, also standing. "This looks pretty cut-and-dried to me." She waited until they'd reached the edge of the deck before delivering her ultimatum. "You seem like sensible people. I realize that you're shocked and upset by what's happened here, but don't let that confuse you into making a simple accident into murder. If you want to stay out of trouble, let us handle it. That's what your civilian security forces are getting paid for."

In back of the house, three police cars were parked near the Firebird. The ambulance was gone.

Joy didn't argue when Greg took the keys from her. Gratefully she climbed into the passenger seat. After he started the engine and the radio came on, she felt better.

With the windows closed, they were out of earshot of Amanda Hawkins and her minions.

"Still think Maria Cardoza's drowning was an accident?" Joy asked. "And Airman Tuck's, too?"

Greg drove down the gravel road leading away from the ramshackle house. "The deputy was trying too hard to convince us, Joy. Makes me suspicious when somebody does that."

Joy swallowed her gasp of surprise. "Then you think the police are covering up something?"

He shifted in the driver's seat as though her question made him uncomfortable. "I wouldn't go quite that far, Joy. Let's just say my mind's a lot more open than it was."

Joy made sure Greg didn't see her satisfied smile.

Suddenly a frightening new thought intruded. "Amanda couldn't possibly have been right about the thirty-six hours, could she, Greg? About Tuck's body being in the pool since Tuesday night?"

There was an odd silence, as if Greg were reluctant to respond. "I took a close look at the body, Joy, and it was somewhat bloated, a sign it could have been submerged that long. It's been warmer than usual in the Valley the past few days, and that had a noticeable effect."

"If Airman Tuck came straight to Maria's after talking to me, why weren't his clothes at her house?"

Suddenly dark shadows filled the car. And Joy's eyes glittered with a sudden new fear. "If he was already dead yesterday, then who was watching me through binoculars from across the canyon?" She glanced wildly at Greg, knowing he had no ready answers. "Who dropped his insignia in the dirt over there if it wasn't Chris Tuck?"

IN AMANDA HAWKINS'S small office in Carmel Village, the phone was ringing as she walked in. She didn't run to answer it. That's what answering machines were for.

In a one-person office like this, nobody expected her to be sitting by the phone twenty-four hours a day. It was one of the things she liked about her job, established only months earlier to serve the burgeoning, conspicuously prosperous population of the pristine Carmel Valley. The freedom appealed to her even though it meant she was on duty all the time. When she wasn't in the office, she worked out of her house, high on a hilltop just above the village, and from a beeper system tied into the Monterey Sheriff's Office.

If being the lone peace officer in the Carmel Valley meant she was sometimes called out of bed at 3:00 a.m. to handle emergencies, it also meant that she was relatively independent and that she'd become something of a personality in the small community during the short time she'd been Deputy Sheriff. Everybody knew her. For Amanda Hawkins, that was compensation enough for the long hours.

Now, tossing her broad-brimmed hat on top of a four-drawer safe behind her desk, she listened to the hoarse voice of her superior speaking over the telephone line into the answering machine. Captain Frank Peterson, sheriff of Monterey County, was another reason Amanda liked being where she didn't have to rub elbows with him every day.

"Absolutely urgent that you call me before you do anything else," he said to the machine. "*Anything*, Deputy. Don't even take your hat off first."

Frowning at the telephone, she got a Pepsi out of the fridge next to the filing cabinet, and took a long swallow. Then, settled behind her desk with her feet up, she dialed his number.

"I just walked into the office from the Cardoza place, Captain," she said. "Don't tell me what this is all about. Let me guess. You've talked to the Feds again. They want us to put the wraps on this kid that drowned, just like on the Cardoza woman."

Amanda tried to keep the sarcasm out of her voice, but some of her bitterness must have seeped through.

"That better not be a problem, Deputy Hawkins," the sheriff said in his most threatening manner. Amanda had noticed that whenever Frank Peterson wanted to sound menacing, he affected a southern drawl—probably to give the impression he was a tough lawman from Texas or Georgia. She'd heard he was a native of Oregon but had never bothered to check.

"Those military people who found the airman's body aren't dummies," she said. "They're already asking questions about the Cardoza autopsy."

"Of course you didn't tell them anything."

Amanda detected a trace of anxiety in his voice.

"We can put them off for another month, if we have to," she said, deliberately avoiding a yes or no answer. "Final reports on autopsies have been known to take that long."

She paused, wondering how blunt she dared to be about the possible consequences of covering up two murders. Pretty blunt, she decided. If it got her in bad with her stupid boss, at least she'd have given him fair warning.

"No matter what Washington says, we'd better not have to stall for anywhere near that long, Captain. We've got a killer on our hands. The press finds out we've covered it up, and there'll be big trouble. That's big with a capital *B*."

"The Feds know who's behind these killings." His voice was stubborn, the way Frank Peterson's voice always was when he was unsure of himself. "All they need's a few days to grab him."

Amanda snorted. "That's what they're telling you. If they know who the killer is, what are they waiting for? What if he, or she, hits again and the press finds out you've been sitting on this? You really think those government people will back you up? Not a chance, Sheriff. They'll disappear into the woodwork like the man who never was. Guess who'll be left holding the bag? Tonight I'm going to get down on my knees and pray that nobody else around here has a suspicious fatal accident because if they do, I'm going to feel damned guilty for not warning people about what's going on."

"You do that, Deputy Hawkins." His southern drawl was back, stronger than ever. "While you're at it, you might pray a few words for yourself to remind you to be very careful about what you say and whom you say it to until the Feds clear this mess up."

There was a moment of silence. Then, as an afterthought, he added, "You *do* know that the Carmel Valley Sheriff's Office was set up on a trial basis for the first year? Foul up and you're out."

This was at least the third time in the past month that Peterson had reminded Amanda of that fact.

"I seem to recall your telling me about it, Sheriff," she said.

He grunted. "Good. This is your first big case. It'd be a shame to screw it up by talking when you should have been listening."

Amanda was still frowning when she hung up the receiver.

Thursday Afternoon

THOUGH IT WASN'T yet four, the fog wrapped itself around Pacific Grove like a dank, spongy blanket. Joy turned on her car's lights and heater as she threaded her way through the late-afternoon traffic toward the house she shared with Donna Easely.

Joy had spent the afternoon taking care of the innumerable reports, inventories, forms and personal details connected with Airman Tuck's death. Now, exhausted, she couldn't wait to get to the place she'd called home for the past three months.

Located on a secluded street about a mile from the Presidio's Taylor Street Gate, the house was a boxy, stucco building that looked singularly unloved thanks to its untended, weedy lawn and scraggly bushes. With its inverted-V composition roof and unshuttered windows, it reminded Joy of a giant birdhouse, an impression that was reinforced by the porch's miniature roof, a replica of the parent structure.

At least the house itself was well maintained. With property values soaring on the Monterey Peninsula, Donna—who owned it—was highly motivated to keep the place up. The first thing she'd told Joy was that she needed help paying the mortgage and other expenses, and that was the sole reason she'd consider letting a female live with her.

"If you don't like having a woman around, why not share with a man?" Joy had asked.

"Too messy," Donna had answered.

Joy thought she knew what Donna meant. Although her roommate's reputation around the Presidio was spotless, she appeared to be involved with several men who occupied most of her off-duty time. Not that any of them ever stopped by the house in Pacific Grove. Joy knew them only by their voices on the telephone.

Joy's tentative questions led Donna to tell her to mind her own business or find other quarters. Since Joy liked the house and the convenience of living only ten minutes from work, she curbed her curiosity. After a month or so, she developed a certain fondness for Donna's sharp tongue. It masked, Joy discovered, a deep-seated sense of duty that seemed to embarrass her roommate.

Since Donna was gone so much, Joy had the house to herself most of the time. Not today, though, she thought, parking her car at the curb in front. Through the thickening fog, she could see a light in the living room, a sure sign that Donna was home.

Joy looked for her car. It wasn't parked in the driveway where she usually left it. The front door wasn't locked, Joy noticed, trying the knob. This wasn't like Donna, she told herself uneasily. It was early for her to be home, too. Although the hours at the Defense Language Institute were flexible, Donna, like most of the headquarters staff, considered 0800 to 1700 to be the normal duty day. Joy had left early this afternoon to gather strength for tonight's ordeal.

She felt a quick stab of fear that quickened her heartbeat.

Slowly she pushed the door open.

Be careful, she warned herself, pausing in the doorway. *Just because a light's turned on doesn't necessarily mean she's here. Maybe it's somebody else.* The shot of adrena-

line she'd felt last night when she saw the panel truck behind her jolted through her again.

"Donna?" Joy called, poised for flight if she got no answer. "Donna, are you here?"

Her roommate appeared from the kitchen. Tall, blond,
and slimmer than Joy, she was wearing her favorite around-
the-house outfit: blue jeans and a sweatshirt decorated with
sequins. As usual, her perfectly proportioned face was
beautifully made up.

She took one look at Joy and frowned. "Don't stand
there yelling, Air Force," she said in her clipped New Eng-
land accent. "Since you live here, you don't need my per-
mission to come inside. What's the matter with you,
anyhow?"

At seeing her, Joy's surge of relief was so great that she
practically collapsed on the sofa.

"The door was open," she said. "Since I didn't see your
car out front, I was afraid it might be a burglar."

Folding her arms in front of her, Donna walked around
the couch and faced Joy. "The car's in the garage," she
said. "Lucky you. Tonight I'm staying home for a change."

Usually Joy looked forward to the few evenings Donna
spent at home. She found their verbal exchanges stimulat-
ing. But this wasn't a usual evening.

"I've had a bad day, Donna," she said. "And I've got a
command performance to get ready for tonight. I'm afraid
I'm not going to be very good company."

"What's the matter, Air Force, no guts?" There was a
subtle taunting tone underlying Donna's Boston accent. "If
you think you're the first military officer who ever lost one
of his people, think again, ma'am."

Damn her, Joy thought. *If she makes one smart remark,
I'll flush her precious skin rejuvenator down the john.*

"Who told you about it?" she asked.

Donna's eyebrows lifted. "I can't imagine why you should
care," she said, "but the first person who called was your
very own first sergeant. I am the Public Affairs Officer, you

know. Not long afterward your airman's instructor stopped
by the office with the news.''

"Santos Mueller?" Much as Joy didn't want to give
Donna the satisfaction, she couldn't contain her surprise.
"How in heaven's name did he find out about it?"

"Colonel Weston told him, since he was the airman's new
instructor. Santos said he was the only one in the Spanish
Department who knew."

Joy frowned, wondering why Greg had told Santos.

"Why did Santos want to talk to you about Airman
Tuck?" she asked.

Donna smiled with that knowing, sexy way of hers. "I
could be wrong, of course, but I got the impression that he
wanted an excuse to meet me." Her self-assured tone said
she was only being modest by suggesting she might be
wrong. "He said he wanted a briefing so he'd know what he
should and shouldn't say if reporters asked him about it."

Joy had no desire to hear about Santos Mueller's romantic machinations. If Donna wanted to add the burly instructor to her stable of admirers, that was her business.

"And just after Santos left, I got a call about the drowning from the commandant himself," Donna said.

"From Colonel Weston?" Joy took a quick gasp of air.
"What did he tell you?"

When Joy saw the interested expression on her roommate's face, she warned herself to be careful. *Remember she
deals with the press. Don't make her curious about Airman
Tuck's relationship with Maria Cardoza or about the way
they died.*

Donna leaned toward her. "The commandant told me
that you and he were looking for an AWOL airman and
found him in the pool of that Spanish instructor who died
last week. An odd coincidence, isn't it? That they should
both drown in the same pool, I mean. Colonel Weston was
rather mysterious about it. Said that was all I needed to
know and that I shouldn't pester you with questions about
it."

She smiled smugly. "Sounds like you and the colonel had a—" she paused and lifted an eyebrow "—meeting of the minds concerning what to tell the rest of us about what went on out at Ms. Cardoza's place this morning."

Detecting a subtle insinuation, Joy forgot her unspoken resolution never to let Donna get to her. She shot off the couch like one possessed. "If finding a body in a damned pool is your idea of a fun morning then you're right, Donna. We did have a meeting of the minds. But for your information the only thing we agreed on was how awful it was."

"Don't get excited, Air Force." Donna examined her warily, the way a hospital attendant eyes a potentially dangerous mental patient.

Trembling, Joy returned to the sofa. The living room, with its eclectic mix of modern and traditional furniture, spun around her.

"If the commandant hadn't had some kind of a meeting of the minds with you, I wouldn't be here tonight," Donna said smugly. "Instead, I'd be having dinner overlooking the ocean at Big Sur."

From the kitchen came the delicious smell of a curry simmering on the stove. In spite of herself, Joy felt her mouth watering. Donna cooked almost every evening she was home, and the results were outstanding.

Sniffing the air, Donna stood up and started toward the kitchen.

Joy hurried after her. "Tell me what you're talking about, Donna," she demanded. "Either that, or stop making vague insinuations."

Her roommate lifted the lid of a large frying pan and stirred a mixture of curried vegetables and seafood with a long wooden spoon. A salad bowl full of greens and cherry tomatoes had been set on the round kitchen table between two place settings. A folded newspaper was neatly positioned beside one of them.

"I'm here because Colonel Weston didn't want you to come home to an empty house tonight," she said, in a smug, superior way that made Joy burn in spite of herself. "He told me you were going to a party with him later, but he didn't want you to be alone when you got here. He sounded very concerned. Looks to me like our supreme leader's got the hots for you, Air Force."

"Looks to me like you ought to mind your own business," Joy said, ignoring the envy in her roommate's voice. "Anything the commandant and I do together is strictly in the line of duty."

So Greg thought she couldn't handle herself in a crisis and had said as much to her roommate. He was underrating her again, the way he always did.

"I'm sorry you've gone to all this work on the dinner, Donna," she said, too disappointed in Greg to do justice to Donna's cooking. "I think I'll just fix some soup for myself."

Her roommate shrugged her shoulders. "Your loss, Air Force. For your information, I made this shrimp curry for myself, not you. It's one of my favorite dishes." Leaning over, she pulled a pan of hot rolls from the oven and arranged them in a wicker basket with a checkered napkin around them. Then she piled rice in the middle of a plate and ladled sauce over it. "Looks good, doesn't it?"

Joy had to admit that it did. She'd missed lunch again and hadn't realized how hungry she was. "If you'll give me a minute to change out of this uniform, Donna, I believe I'll take you up on your offer after all."

Her roommate headed for the kitchen table with her heaping plate. "Make it snappy," she said. "There's something in today's paper you'd better take a look at before you go to that party with the commandant."

Chapter Eight

In her room, Joy changed into an aqua sweat suit. When she reappeared in the kitchen, Donna was halfway through her first plate of shrimp curry. She didn't apologize for not waiting.

"Help yourself," she said, nodding toward the two covered pots on the gas stove. Like the rest of the kitchen, the stove was old, but clean and in good condition.

After filling her plate, Joy sat down at the table. Next to her napkin was a folded newspaper. She reached for it.

"You'd better eat before you look at it," Donna warned. Her taunting smile was close to a smirk. It was obvious that she couldn't wait to see Joy's reaction to something inside.

Deliberately, Joy put the newspaper down and took a bite of curry.

"Thanks for warning me, Donna," she said, helping herself to salad and a roll. "I'll look at it later, after my shower."

She took another bite of curry. It was delicious.

Across from her, Donna backed away from the table and started toward the stove with her plate. She could eat three times what Joy did and never seemed to gain an ounce.

"At least, your picture turned out pretty good," she said. "They used the same one they took a couple of months ago when you first got here, only it's even bigger this time."

Joy paused with her fork halfway to her mouth. "My picture's in this paper?"

At the stove, Donna piled her plate higher than before. "Don't act so surprised. You must have known they were going to run it."

Joy jerked the paper open and spread it out on the table beside her plate. Donna had put the *B* section containing local news on top. The first thing Joy saw was a huge picture of herself, smiling, in front of the Sloat Monument. It was the same picture published in the *Tribune* three months ago.

A wave of apprehension swept over her. There was something frightening in the picture's unexpected appearance so soon after she'd seen it—and the embarrassing story that went with it—in Maria Cardoza's file of newspaper clippings.

MORE BABBLE FROM THE TOWER OF BABEL was written in big letters across the top of the picture. Below it were two lines identifying her as Joy Donnelly, the commander of the 3483rd Air Force Student Squadron at the Defense Language Institute.

An anxious tremor rippled down her spine. In addition to every horrid thing that had happened today, why had the *Monterey Tribune* chosen this particular date to run that disastrous picture again?

Her eye skipped to the article's headline. SCHOOL FOR SPIES? it read, in capital letters at least half an inch high. *Funny,* she thought. *What does a story about spies have to do with me?* She took another bite of curry and scanned the first couple of paragraphs.

SCHOOL FOR SPIES?
By Eye of the Peninsula

Describing the Defense Language Institute as a "School for Spies," Air Force Captain Joy Donnelly claims that most DLI graduates end up in intelligence career fields.

"Many are sent directly to the top secret National Security Agency at Fort Meade, Maryland," said Captain Joy the other day over lunch and a glass of white wine at the Highlands Inn. "Others fill slots in the country's military attaché program where their training at the school permits them to eavesdrop on the conversation of their hosts."

She told friends—who later passed the exciting news to Eye—that if DLI went out of business, the nation's intelligence capabilities would be irreparably damaged. . . .

Shaken, Joy looked up. "This is absolutely ridiculous," she said, her voice trembling. In her dismay she barely noticed the offensive reference to herself as Captain Joy. "Whoever this Eye person is has implied that we teach cloak-and-dagger techniques at DLI when everybody knows this a military language school pure and simple. The Presidio is so open, we don't even have guards at the gates."

Her roommate put her plate on the table and, sitting down, helped herself to more salad and another roll. "My, my, my! For somebody who claims to be reasonably well informed as to the DLI mission, you certainly rattled on to your friends at the Highlands Inn about the school's alleged relationship to the U.S. espionage program. As I read the article, I was half expecting you to make some kind of outlandish statement about the language school being funded by the Central Intelligence Agency."

Joy stared at her. Coming on top of everything else, Donna's sarcastic comment about the CIA was too much. The Defense Language Institute had no connection whatsoever to the Central Intelligence Agency.

"Get off my case, Donna," she snapped. "You ought to know I'd never say something like this. The only time I've ever been to the Highlands Inn I was with a lieutenant from the Navy Line School, and all he could talk about was his engineering exams. We never once mentioned DLI."

Donna took a huge bite of curry and studied Joy skeptically until she'd swallowed it. "You mean you never said anything about the Defense Language Institute being a school for spies?"

"Never."

"Not to anyone?"

"Not to anyone." Joy was emphatic. The idea that somebody would fabricate a story like this made her mad as hell. Mad and scared. Why would anybody pull a stunt like this except to hurt her?

"Whoever wrote this isn't going to get away with it," she fumed. "That paper's going to print a retraction, or it's going to get hit with a libel suit that'll make publishing history."

"If you didn't say these things, they'll print a retraction," Donna predicted confidently. "I'll call them first thing tomorrow."

"I'll call them myself," Joy said. "I want to find out who this Eye person is and why they think they've got a right to print lies like this." She stared across the table, her eyes narrowed. Donna had been awfully quick to show her the newspaper. Maybe she knew more about the article than she was letting on.

"You don't know who Eye is, by any chance, do you, Donna? You're the one with all the press connections." *And the mysterious phone calls at all hours,* Joy added to herself.

Donna shook her head. "Nobody knows who Eye is, Air Force. The paper keeps that information confidential. I'm just guessing, but probably it's one of the people on the staff who compiles a column of gossipy little items about personnel assigned to the military bases in the area."

"I'd hardly call this a gossipy little item."

"Read on," Donna said. "It gets gossipy when Eye starts telling your life story."

The sick, frightened feeling in the general vicinity of Joy's solar plexus had nothing to do with the food she'd just eaten. If the columnist had printed outrageous lies that could hurt her professionally, what in the name of heaven had Eye made up about her personally?

With a trembling hand, she picked up the newspaper and read the article from start to finish.

When she put the paper down she didn't know whether to cry or scream. There was something horribly threatening about lies published for only one purpose: to hurt her.

In chatty terms, sprinkled liberally with supposed quotes from Joy herself, Eye had dredged up most of the personal information in the previous article.

But this column was much worse because of the way it was written.

In this piece, the quotations attributed to Joy sounded idiotic because of the gossipy little comments that went with them. Her stomach churned as the words repeated themselves over and over again in her head.

"I fully intend to make general before I retire," said Captain Joy in describing her goals. "I've always known I had the leadership potential to be a top officer." She spoke with the supreme confidence of a woman totally aware of her many assets.

Or this one: "Any man I marry will have to put my career first." Captain Joy's face flamed with righteous conviction. "If a man's unwilling to do that, he's not for me."

Even though Joy hadn't made the statements exactly as quoted, they were close enough to what she'd said in the original interview to bring fire to her cheeks. Was it possible that Nadine Robinson, the reporter who'd written the earlier story, was Eye? And if she was, why would she risk exposure and a libel suit by rewriting the piece in such lurid terminology?

More important, could this outrageous article somehow be connected to Joy's investigation into the death of Maria Cardoza and, now, Airman Chris Tuck?

Joy pushed her half-eaten plate of shrimp curry aside, unable to finish it. She'd been avoiding the most disturbing question of all.

What would Greg Weston think after he'd read it?

WHAT THE HELL was going on in Joy Donnelly's pretty little head?

Irritably, Greg asked himself the same question for the hundredth time since reading that fool article this afternoon. Sergeant Philpott had made sure he saw it. He'd no sooner settled himself in his office when she marched in and handed him a copy of the *Monterey Tribune* open to the local section. Joy's picture, half a page high, smiled back at him.

Was Joy deliberately trying to antagonize him, he wondered, or did she have some other reason for making such revealing statements about the language school's relationship to Intelligence? Just when he thought he'd halfway figured her out, she had to throw something like this in his face.

Even though he'd long since finished his early dinner in the Soviet area's enlisted mess hall, Greg made no move to leave. School for spies, indeed! Even though there was nothing remotely connected with cloak-and-dagger work at the Defense Language Institute, everything Joy Donnelly said about its graduates' ultimate assignments to the top secret National Security Agency was true.

More ammunition for the do-gooders in Congress who think there's something nasty about eavesdropping and are trying to shut us down, he grumbled to himself.

And the revelations in the article about Joy's personal life! As if the first article about her hadn't been bad enough, here was another that was infinitely worse.

After reading the two articles, he was convinced that her goals could never include him. Annoyed with her for having them, he was absolutely infuriated with himself for being so upset about it.

A man in a white cook's outfit appeared across the table with a steaming cup of coffee in his hand.

"Thought you might like a second cup, sir," he said.

Greg nodded his thanks. Several times a week he ate a meal in one of the school's enlisted messes so that he could check the food being served the students. This evening he'd tried the roast pork at the big McDonald's-style mess hall in the Soviet academic area. An array of tropical-looking artificial plants—one result of Joy's mess-hall beautification project—lined the big windows on two sides of the room.

Greg frowned at the coffee cup on the table in front of him. Thanks to Joy's latest indiscretion, he couldn't think about anything but what she'd said in that damn fool article. What was the matter with him, anyhow?

Checking his watch, he saw that it was nearly 1830—time to get to his quarters and change for tonight's party. The thought of seeing her again left him feeling trapped and empty. She should probably be transferred. Then he'd be rid of her once and for all. He could chew her out about her "school for spies" comment in the article and then send her lovely little backside packing all the way to Texas. If the assignment people at Randolph Air Force Base liked her so much, let *them* have her.

Even better, wasn't it about time for him to find out if he'd been selected to command the new special forces school in Florida? The informal notification could come any time now, followed shortly by official orders. After missing out on Operation Desert Storm, Greg was itching to get back with combat troops again.

Frowning, he put the thought aside. Somehow it was just as upsetting as the idea of transferring Joy from the Presidio.

Usually Greg ended his mess-hall visits with a brief walk through the kitchen. It was amazing how much information about the basic soundness of a food operation a commander could pick up with a quick glance into sinks, refrigerators and garbage cans.

Tonight, to the relief of the civilian staff, he forgot about the kitchen. Placing his service hat carefully on his head so that it wouldn't disturb the cord holding his eye patch, he

started toward his Cherokee, parked in the commander's
slot in a nearby lot.

As soon as Joy opened the front door, she knew Greg had
read Eye's column in the *Tribune*.

And believed every word, of course. Why had she hoped
he might not?

From the firm line of his mouth to the determined set of
his shoulders, his whole demeanor suggested anger and dis-
appointment. Even though he was in civilian clothes, he
looked every inch the commander, about to take one of his
subordinates to the woodpile.

Folding her arms, she stood in the doorway waiting for
him to chew her out right there—without giving her a chance
to defend herself and with Donna listening in the living
room.

The moment passed. She watched his tautness melt into
grudging admiration.

"Nice dress," he said. "I never thought I'd see you in
anything I liked better than your uniform."

"Thank you," she said. "It's my favorite."

To get her in the mood for tonight's party, Joy had put on
her brightest outfit—an orange-red silk dress with green accents.

"You're looking pretty good yourself, sir," she said, using the "sir" for Donna's benefit.

Unfolding her arms, she stepped back and eyed him up
and down. He was wearing a smoky-blue flannel blazer over
gray slacks. It was the first time she'd seen him in civilian
clothes and the difference was remarkable. Unlike the bulky
uniform blouse the blazer emphasized his broad shoulders
and narrow hips. He was clean shaven, his straight brown
hair combed back.

An unwelcome flicker of excitement pulsed through Joy.
She backed into the room to let him enter.

As soon as Greg came into the living room, Donna stood
up.

Always the good soldier, Joy thought. She listened to the brief exchange between them while she slipped into the coat she'd hung in the front closet.

Greg: "Thanks for staying home tonight, Major Easely. I owe you one."

Donna: "No problem, Colonel. I'm glad to do it."

Greg: "You're going to be home the rest of the night?"

Donna: "Yes. I've rearranged my schedule."

Aggravated, Joy broke in. "You don't have to rearrange anything because of me, Donna."

"I'm not doing it for you, Air Force. I'm doing it because the commandant asked me to."

Joy faced Greg. "Did you really?" she asked. "Whatever for?" She struggled to keep the irritation out of her voice.

"Sometimes it's better not to be alone," he said matter-of-factly, as though surprised she would question him about it.

Joy didn't argue. Not there in front of Donna. She'd straighten him out later, when they were alone.

HEADING NORTH on Del Monte Avenue, they went several blocks without speaking.

When they passed the Naval Postgraduate School and Greg still hadn't brought up the Eye column, Joy decided to take the offensive.

"I've got a bone to pick with you, Greg Weston," she said.

He twisted his head so quickly that she was sure she'd caught him unawares. He probably thought she was going to make excuses for that stupid column, she thought. No way she'd do that. If he wanted to chew her out about it, he'd have to bring it up himself.

"It's about ordering Donna to baby-sit me tonight. I'm a big girl, Greg. I know when I need company. Please don't do that again."

He grunted. "As long as you're one of my people, I'll do what I think best for you—just as I would for any of the others."

Joy could see she hadn't gotten through to him. "You're meddling in my private life, Greg," she said softly. "Please stop it."

That got his attention. "Sometimes a commander's got to do a little meddling to keep his people in line and protect the mission of his organization. That's why he's the boss." He cleared his throat. "Speaking of protecting our mission, I'm sure you saw that article about yourself in this morning's paper. You managed to drive a few more nails in DLI's coffin with the interview you gave that reporter."

Here it comes at last. Relieved but wary, Joy waited for the expected reprimand.

"Yes, I saw it." She didn't offer any excuses. If he jumped to the wrong conclusion, so be it. She already knew what he thought of her judgment.

Even though Greg's face was impassive, Joy noticed that he was clutching the steering wheel in a viselike grip.

"Damn it all, Joy, how could you say we're a school for spies? You know how offensive our connection to the National Security Agency is to those people in Congress who want to close us down."

Joy stiffened. "I can't imagine how you can think I'd say a thing like that, Greg. Don't you know me better by now?" Determined as she was to stay cold and aloof, she felt the heat rise to her cheeks.

"You mean you didn't make those statements?"

She could hear the puzzlement in his voice. It meant he didn't believe her.

"From the first day we met, you've never given me credit for being able to do anything right." Joy tried to keep her voice steady. "Now here you are taking an article in the paper as gospel when I've just told you it's not true."

He twisted his head again to look at her. "You mean you were misquoted?"

He sounded incredulous, his voice filled with disbelief. She felt pressure in her sinuses and swallowed hard. It wouldn't do to let him see how hurt she was that he didn't believe her.

"You said you were misquoted in the first article," he prompted. "Did they do it again in this one?"

"No, they didn't." Her chin rose defiantly. "No matter what you think of me personally, you can't believe one of your officers is stupid enough to call this a school for spies." She paused to let what she'd said sink in. "They didn't just misquote me, Greg. They made the whole thing up."

"Made the whole thing up?" It was plain he still didn't accept what she'd said. If she needed proof that the man didn't have any faith in her abilities, this was it.

She leaned forward, turning toward him so he could see the determination on her face. "You heard me, Greg Weston." The grit in her voice was unmistakable. "They made the whole thing up. Every word."

His usual impassive expression was replaced by stunned amazement. "Explain, please."

"The first part—about the school for spies—was a complete fabrication. The second part, about me personally, was taken from that article printed when I first got here. Except that this column was written to make me sound like an empty-headed fool. Nothing came out the way I really said it."

The Cherokee's tires squealed as Greg pulled into an open spot at the curb near a row of stucco houses. After he'd switched the engine off, he turned to face her.

"Are you sure you never said anything like this to anybody who could have passed it on to that columnist?"

"Absolutely positive."

At her response, his nostrils flared. His one eye narrowed. His mouth turned to a thin, hard line. Joy had never seen him look so angry. Or so magnificent.

"Then we've got business with the editor of the *Tribune* first thing tomorrow morning," he said. "Nobody prints lies about my people and my school and gets away with it. *Nobody*." As he drove on, he couldn't help but feel half-sick that the article was tied into the Maria Cardoza affair.

ALL CONVERSATION STOPPED when they walked in on the Spanish Department party a few minutes later. From the way everybody gawked, Joy in her flame-red silk dress felt she must look like a contemporary Scarlett O'Hara, cloaked in shame. It was plain the guests had been reading the Eye column when Señora Ramon, the wife of the department chairman, ushered Greg and Joy into the living room.

Several men holding newspapers were wearing reading glasses. Joy cast a quick look around the room, but saw none like the pair she'd picked up at Maria's.

A soft-spoken, plump little woman in her late fifties, Señora Ramon handed a copy of the newspaper to Joy. A group of instructors and spouses clustered around them with the alert expressions of people who expected something interesting to happen momentarily.

"It's a beautiful picture, Captain Donnelly," she said. "We were admiring it when you walked in."

On the spot, Joy decided to deny the whole thing. The sooner she put these detestable lies to rest, the better.

To her surprise, Greg spoke before she could say anything.

"Captain Donnelly didn't make these statements."

His voice rang with conviction. He seemed to be trying to make up for his earlier doubts. Of course it took sworn testimony on a stack of Bibles to make him change his mind, Joy thought grimly.

"The entire column's a fabrication," he continued. "I don't know who wrote it or what's behind it, but I certainly intend to find out."

The small group around them had now swelled to include everybody in the room.

"If any of you has an idea who's behind these lies, I'd like to hear it," Greg went on. "And so would Captain Donnelly."

Joy glanced around the group, looking for some reaction to Greg's request. Several instructors shook their heads as her eyes met theirs. In her quick scan, she missed Santos Mueller's bulky frame. She nudged Greg. "I wonder where Santos is."

Their host, Julio Ramon, chairman of the Spanish Department, overheard her question. A craggy man in his sixties with a Dutch-boy haircut and a graying mustache, Ramon was Don Quixote with a glass of bourbon in his hand. Joy noticed that he wasn't wearing glasses.

The department chairman chuckled. "We all miss Santos. Especially the ladies." His expression sobered. "He had work tonight at the warehouse unloading a big shipment of olive oil."

"Warehouse?" Joy said. "Does Santos have an outside job, Señor Ramon?"

The department head smiled nervously as he shot a quick glance at Greg. "It's no secret, Captain. I'm sure the *Comandante* knows about it."

Joy caught the subtle shake of Greg's head.

"As a matter of fact, I didn't, Julio. But there's nothing wrong with an instructor having an outside job as long as it doesn't interfere with his duties at the school."

Señor Ramon cleared his throat. "It doesn't amount to much, *Comandante*. More of a favor to friends than a job. They own a Spanish market near Seaside and are on a...how do you say? shoestring. He manages their warehouse for a small salary."

So Santos Mueller was doing a favor for friends by managing their warehouse? No matter what Julio Ramon called it, to Joy it sounded like a second job, a second job he'd never mentioned to Greg. It might be interesting to stop by the market, and, in the process, to get a firsthand look at the warehouse.

"What's the name of the place?" she asked.

"The Iberian Market," he said quietly. "They sell the best olive oil this side of Madrid."

As the group around them dispersed, they followed Julio and his wife to a spot near the improvised bar on the dining room buffet. Señora Ramon scurried toward the kitchen a few minutes later.

When Señor Ramon had fixed drinks for them, Joy thrust the newspaper she was holding toward him.

"Did you notice this paragraph about our military attachés in Eye's column?" she asked, watching him closely.

He didn't look down at the paper. "Nothing but lies, Captain."

Beside her, Greg turned toward the department head. "I must have missed that part, Julio. Would you mind reading it?"

Señor Ramon handed the paper to Greg. "I'm sorry *Comandante.* I misplaced my second pair of reading glasses and left the others at the office."

When Greg adjusted his eye patch and put on the glasses Joy had found at Maria's she caught a flicker of surprise in the department head's expression.

"Those look just like the glasses I lost, *Comandante,*" he said. "Where did you get them?"

Joy felt as if she'd just received another medal. If the glasses were Julio's, that meant he'd been snooping in Maria Cardoza's file cabinet. But why?

"They're from a place downtown," Greg returned. "I've been leary of military eye doctors and glasses ever since I lost my eye."

Señor Ramon smiled, warming to the subject. "Since my cataract surgery, I've needed glasses only for reading and working with my computer."

Joy sensed that they'd found out all they were going to. Elated, she touched Greg's arm. "If you and Julio will excuse me, I think I'll see if I can lend our hostess a hand in the kitchen."

"Good idea," he said, smiling.

Señora Ramon was lifting two trays of puffy canapes out of the oven. Joy grabbed a potholder and took one tray from her.

"Gracias," the woman said, beaming. In her own kitchen there was no hint of the submissiveness Señora Ramon had shown when her husband was within earshot.

For the next few minutes Joy engaged the department head's wife in small talk ranging from the price of real estate to the big earthquake of 1989. Without too much difficulty, she managed to work the conversation around to another horrendous event: the death of Maria Cardoza. Señora Ramon seemed eager to talk.

"You know, Captain," she said, after she'd popped another tray of canapés into the oven. "When my husband found her body in the pool last week, my first thought was that maybe now the embarrassing articles would stop. Yet, here comes one about you a week later. It's as though she came back from the dead to write it."

Chapter Nine

Thursday Night

Joy's body stiffened with shock. She forced herself to keep stuffing cheese and sausage into the pastry dough on the counter in front of her.

Had Maria Cardoza been Eye? If she'd been writing gossip for the newspaper, that explained the clipping file: she'd kept it for background. It also explained the dictionaries, the book of quotations, the computer and printer. Might it be the reason she was killed?

Joy tried not to let her excitement show. "Did she write that gossip column, Señora Ramon?"

The older woman shrugged. "Who knows? Like I told you, she couldn't have written the one about you unless she came back from the dead. I shouldn't have said anything."

"Why do you think she had something to do with the Eye column?" Joy asked, hoping to overcome the woman's obvious reluctance.

Señora Ramon glanced toward the door. There was nobody else in the kitchen. Another instructor's wife had just left with a canape tray. She'd be back in minutes.

"My husband warned me not to say anything about this," Señora Ramon said, her timidity returning. "If it hadn't been for the *Comandante's* request for information about your article..."

"Then nobody else in the Spanish Department knows anything about the column Maria wrote?"

"The Ramons know nothing either." The words came out in a rush.

"You know something," Joy persisted, "or you wouldn't suspect she was connected with Eye."

"We know nothing," the woman repeated. Her chin jutted out. "Absolutely nothing."

"But you're suspicious," Joy said. "Believe me, Señora Ramon, this will go no further than the commandant and me. We've got to find out who wrote that article about me and why. It's terribly important—especially if it's connected in some way to Maria Cardoza."

"If you're sure it will go no further..."

"On my honor as an air force officer..."

Señora Ramon appeared to relent. "It was because she was so curious. That is why we thought she had a connection to the column. She wanted to know personal things about everybody."

Joy was sure Señora Ramon wasn't telling her the whole story. She and her husband must have had a more definite reason than Maria's "curiosity" for believing she wrote a gossip column. Was it possible that the Ramons themselves had been among those Maria was curious about? Probably they were at the top of her list, Joy thought grimly. After all, he was the chairman of her department and in a position to affect her career. I'll bet she had something on him, and that's why he was snooping in her file.

"What kind of personal things did she ask about?" Joy asked.

Señora Ramon looked down, avoiding Joy's direct gaze. "Oh, she asked questions about relatives in the home country, about friends here, about the social life, things like that."

A moment later the other instructor's wife returned to the kitchen, effectively ending the conversation.

Later, on the way home, Joy repeated to Greg what she'd been told. "Señora Ramon wasn't telling me the whole story, but it was pretty clear she thought Maria wrote, or contributed to, Eye's gossip column. Did Julio say anything after I left?"

"Not much. He's a computer nut. We spent the time you were in the kitchen talking about his setup." They'd left Seaside and were heading for Joy's place in Pacific Grove. "It sure looks like he was the one who left the glasses at Maria's place."

Joy nodded. "He was the one who found her body, too. After Señora Ramon mentioned it, I remembered reading in one of the news stories that he called the police from her house. That's probably when he went through her file cabinet. What do you suppose he was looking for?"

"He's been a model department head," Greg said thoughtfully. "But I wouldn't be surprised if there were a skeleton or two in his family closet."

"It fits, Greg. Señora Ramon mentioned family as one of the subjects Maria Cardoza was quote curious unquote about." Joy didn't try to hide her excitement. "You don't suppose whatever Maria found out about the Ramons was serious enough for them to murder her?"

"Whoa," he cautioned. "We still haven't agreed there's been a murder."

In the glare of the oncoming headlights, she studied his profile and caught a trace of a smile. Maybe he wasn't totally convinced the deaths weren't accidental, but he at least seemed willing to accept her conviction with good humor.

"Murder or not," he said, "Ms. Cardoza might have been putting some sort of pressure on him to raise her ratings. It might be a good idea to take a closer look at her file."

"I wonder what Santos Mueller thought of her," Joy said thoughtfully. "By the way, Greg, why did you tell him about Airman Tuck's death? Donna said he stopped by her office, and that you'd told him."

"To get his confidence. I warned him to keep it quiet."

Joy sat silently for a moment. "Do you think he suspected Maria might be writing Eye's gossip column? Señora Ramon said nobody in the department knew about it, but maybe she was wrong."

"That's something else we'll find out on Saturday," Greg said. "And maybe we can get him to tell us about that damned warehouse job that he's never bothered to mention."

"Let's not, Greg," Joy said quickly.

He shot her a surprised glance. "That's the whole point to Saturday morning. Getting him to open up."

"No, no." Joy's words tumbled out in her hurry to explain. "I meant let's not ask him anything about the warehouse job. That'll give us a chance to look around the place ourselves first. No sense letting him know we're interested."

Greg turned toward her. His smile broadened. "Have any special schedule for this little snooping expedition of yours?"

Joy could tell from the way he asked the question that he thought a visit to the Iberian Market would be a waste of time. She didn't let his opinion deter her. "I thought I'd stop over there Saturday afternoon."

"After our morning at the skeet range? It'll work out fine for us to go then."

Waste of time or not, it was plain Greg intended to go with her to the market. Joy was helpless to explain the sense of pleasurable anticipation that coursed through her at the thought of spending all day Saturday with him.

Greg pulled up to the curb in front of Donna's house. The living-room lights were on.

"Looks like your roommate's still up," he observed.

"Did you order her to burn the midnight oil until I got home safe and sound?"

Imagine! she thought. *An army major ordered by her commander to baby-sit an air force captain.* What was going on in Greg Weston's head to do something like that?

Instead of being annoyed, Joy now saw the humor in the situation. The fact that this tough jungle fighter thought she, of all people, needed a baby-sitter and had selected Donna for the job, tickled her funny bone.

She wasn't sure whether it was the Scotch and soda she'd had at the party or her delight in what they'd found out. But Greg's order that Donna stay home tonight suddenly seemed hilarious. Unexpectedly, she felt the urge to laugh and covered her mouth with her hand. The harder she tried to hold in her laughter, the more she wanted to let it out. Her eyes began watering.

Greg glanced quickly in her direction.

"No," he said thoughtfully, "I didn't say anything to Major Easely about when to hit the sack. Just to stick around the house tonight."

Joy was certain he was dead serious. Peals of merriment spilled from her lips, filling the Cherokee with sound.

"'Fess up, Greg," she said, her voice quivering with laughter. "You told her to wait up for me so she could make sure I got safely into bed."

Unfastening his seat belt, Greg swung around to face her. A surge of relief coursed through him, relief that Joy was smiling and happy again, almost her old self. The fact that she was laughing at him didn't bother him in the slightest.

"Actually, the only reason I didn't give her a specific bedtime is that I wasn't sure when we'd be home," he teased back.

She pulled a handkerchief out of her bag and dabbed at her eyes. "You sound like a proud papa keeping an eye on two teenage daughters."

He smoothed the hair on the back of his head where it had been disturbed by the cord holding his eye patch. "My one good eye would be mighty busy if it tried to keep track of you two. Actually, I was following Rule Number 1 in the Commander's Standing Operating Procedure."

Joy swallowed another peal of laughter. "What's that? I'm a commander, and I've never heard of it."

"Thou shalt make sure thy loyal troops are well protected." His voice was even gruffer than usual. There was something so sincere in it that the laughter died in her throat. She leaned toward him so that she could see his features more clearly in the darkness.

Watching her, Greg marveled at the whiteness of her complexion, the curving line of her throat. He reached out and took her hands in his, expecting her to pull them back. Her breathing quickened in response to his touch, but she didn't move away.

He drew closer to her, reveling in the electric current connecting them. Whether she knew it or not, she wanted him to hold her. He could feel it in her quickened pulse, could smell it in her warm, fresh fragrance.

For an instant he hesitated, giving her a last chance to back away. *This isn't right,* he told himself. *She wants to be a general, and I refuse to be tied to some woman's apron strings—especially if they've got stars on them.*

She inched closer to him. It was the slightest of movements, but he was intensely aware of it. Gazing down at her closed eyes, he saw her long dark lashes curl against her porcelain skin and heard his blood pounding in his ears. Finally, unable to help himself, he pulled her close, pressing his mouth on hers with the urgency he'd carefully held in check since the minute he'd first seen her.

Joy tried to push herself away and found she couldn't. His lips drew her like a magnet. Once she'd felt them, she was powerless to do anything but press more closely to him. Putting her arms around his neck, she drank in the heady excitement of his closeness. His chest felt hard and warm against her breasts, and her insides responded with an aching approval that demanded more.

When his mouth left hers and traced a slow line from her mouth to her neck, she gasped with pleasure. Greg Weston was more than the most attractive man she'd ever known; he was also the strongest leader. Images of him standing in front of a mirror, his face lathered with shaving cream, passed through her mind. So did a picture of him at the head of a division of troops. The strident sounds of a John Philip Sousa march played loudly in her head.

What would it be like to live with a man like this?

Her eyes flew open. Exciting or not, Greg Weston was off-limits for her. Hadn't he made it clear only a few hours ago that he considered her judgment incredibly poor?

Besides, this evening was part of an investigation they were conducting in the line of duty. She took her arms from around his neck and pushed herself backward. Even in the darkness, she could see the surprise on his face.

"It isn't right, Greg," she said. "Tonight's for Airman Tuck."

His face showed no expression. "I can't argue with that."

For some reason, his acquiescence aggravated her. Without waiting for him to come around and help her, she opened the door and got out.

"I can get to the house by myself." She started up the walk.

"I'm sure you can." He reached for her arm. "But as long as I'm here, I might as well go to the porch with you."

"That's not necessary." Joy struggled to keep her voice calm. It was difficult because every cell in her body seemed to pulsate with an awareness that he was at her side, that his hand was touching her arm.

"I want to be sure Major Easely's home before I leave."

"You sound like you think I'm in some sort of danger." For the first time it occurred to Joy that Greg's order for Donna to stay home might have been motivated by something other than concern for her grief.

His grip on her arm tightened as they walked up the steps.

"When two of my people have died under unusual circumstances, it makes sense to protect the person who knows most about what happened. That's you. Any commander would do the same."

When Joy closed the door behind him, she felt light-headed. Whether it was from relief or regret, she wasn't quite sure.

Friday Morning

A THIN, BIRDLIKE MAN with bushy blond hair bustled to the front counter only moments after Joy and Greg arrived at the *Monterey Tribune*. He was wearing round, horn-rimmed glasses.

"I'm Bill Tarnow, city editor of the *Tribune*," he said, shaking Greg's hand first and then Joy's. "Your public affairs officer just called. I want to assure you that we'll print a retraction of Eye's column yesterday." His voice was squeaky, like a boy's, even though he appeared to be in his forties.

Joy had been prepared for a fight. Having her enemy run up the white flag before she'd said so much as a word left her with all guns loaded and nobody to fire at.

On her left Greg tensed. She could see he was as astonished as she was at the man's total capitulation. If one phone call from Donna could inspire such a prompt apology, then the *Monterey Tribune* was a lot more impressed by the military presence on the Peninsula than seemed logical.

"I want more than a retraction," she said, wondering how far the editor would go to appease her. "I'd like an explanation. What makes you think you can make up lies like the ones in that column and get away with it?"

"My dear lady, you shall certainly have an explanation," Tarnow squeaked. "Come with me, please." He opened a waist-high door at one end of the counter.

Joy noticed curious looks in their direction as they followed the editor through a maze of cluttered work stations topped with video monitors and telephones. His desk was in one corner.

"First, let me apologize for the column," he said when they were seated. "We do the best we can to prevent mistakes like this, but once in a while something slips through. When it does, we do what we can to make amends."

Greg swung his loaded artillery into position. "Not good enough, Tarnow," he said. "We want to know exactly how this happened and who this Eye character is."

Tarnow leaned toward them with a nervous smile. "Eye's identity is a secret," he said. "A gossip column loses its effectiveness if everybody knows who writes it. As to how this happened, I can only say that we shouldn't have printed this column. Although it was written a week or so ago, it hadn't been properly coordinated."

It was written before Maria Cardoza died, Joy thought, elated. The editor's admission made it possible—indeed, likely—that Maria had written the article. Her eyes met Greg's in silent triumph. This morning he was acting as though last night's kiss had never happened. *Good!* Joy thought—and wondered why she didn't feel more relieved.

"Exactly how did it get into print?" Greg asked.

Nervously, Bill Tarnow answered. "Eye wrote the item at home and sent it to us by phone wire with the notation 'Hold for Thursday next,' and yesterday's date across the top. When our editor found it logged on her computer, she thought it was finished copy. Apparently, it wasn't. She's new and wasn't aware that some of Captain Donnelly's comments came from an article written three months ago—until Major Easely complained about it this morning."

Joy tried to make one and one add up to two and couldn't. "If it wasn't finished copy, I don't understand how your editor got hold of it."

Tarnow shrugged. "Your guess is as good as mine, Captain. Maybe Eye intended to rewrite the item and wanted the editor to take a look at the draft first. Whatever Eye's reason for sending it, I doubt she wanted the column to be published as is."

Joy noticed Tarnow's use of the feminine pronoun and smiled to herself. "Why didn't your editor take a minute to discuss it with Eye after she found the article? Surely that's part of your procedure?"

Tarnow took a deep breath. "Ordinarily, yes. But not possible in this case because Eye's no longer with us. As a matter of fact, this is the last column Eye wrote. Our editor published it partly as a sentimental tribute."

So it was a "sentimental tribute," Joy thought. Sentimental tributes are made to dead people. That cinched it. Maria Cardoza was Eye.

"You'd better tell us who this Eye person is," Greg demanded. "Or you'll get hit with a libel suit that'll make publishing history."

"As a matter of fact, Colonel, the *Tribune*'s been asked by the police not to reveal Eye's identity and our editorial board decided to comply. So it's not up to me. If it were, I'd certainly tell you."

"The police! What the Sam Hill have they got to do with this?"

The birdlike little man sat back and stuck his hands out, palms up. "No can say, Colonel."

"About the retraction, Mr. Tarnow," Joy said. "I'd like to see it in the same place where the column was printed, under the same picture, with a headline reading RETRACTION that's just as high as the headline on that story. The accompanying apology should include a statement to the effect that I made none of the remarks attributed to me."

The city editor looked so perturbed that Greg came close to smiling. "You heard the lady," he said. "If we see that picture and retraction in tomorrow's edition, we'll forget how embarrassing it's been to Captain Donnelly and the Institute. Otherwise..."

Tarnow jumped to his feet. "The first of next week is the earliest I can find that much space. But if you'll be happy with a few sentences, we can print it tomorrow."

Greg glanced at Joy. "Which is it? Sentences tomorrow or the picture, headline and story in a couple of days?"

"I'll wait for the full story," Joy said.

OUTSIDE THE *TRIBUNE* building the fog was beginning to lift. Perhaps there would be hazy sunshine in Monterey later this February morning.

Greg helped Joy inside the Jeep and then got in himself.

"Judas Priest!" he exclaimed, as soon as the doors were shut. "Now we find out the police are interested in Eye—

whom we strongly suspect to be Maria Cardoza—and are keeping their interest under wraps. What's going on?''

"A murder investigation, probably," Joy said. "I wonder why Maria made up those lies about me in the first place. If she wanted to say something about the school's connection to Intelligence, why not use you or somebody like Erick Spellman or the chief of staff? Your words carry a lot more weight than mine.''

He slowed down. She guessed that he was deliberately lengthening the time required to get back to the post so they could talk.

"Maria Cardoza was an orderly woman, Joy. I'm betting she had a good reason for connecting you with this story.''

Joy's face reflected her bewilderment. "But why should Maria involve me?" she asked again. "I've got no background in Intelligence. I know absolutely nothing about the nuts-and-bolts aspects of those career fields.''

He turned his head from the road, and Joy caught an aha look in his eye. "You've suggested an intriguing possibility: that Maria wrote that column to focus attention on the school's relationship to the Intelligence field.''

"Why in heaven's name would she do that?''

When Greg shook his head in response, Joy remembered that he'd said something about checking on Maria's relatives. "Did you get a chance to go through Maria's file?" she asked.

Greg nodded. "I found nothing so far but I've got the personnel people looking into her finances. They should have a preliminary report for me this afternoon.''

"Would it be possible for me to take a look at her file, Greg?" Joy asked. "Maybe I can spot something you missed. Maria seems to be the key player in whatever's going on." She paused. "While I'm at it, maybe I should take a look at Julio Ramon's file, too.''

For a long minute he didn't answer. Joy sensed an inner struggle between his ego and his common sense.

Common sense won. He turned to her and nodded. "I'll arrange it with Personnel when we get back."

He was making progress, Joy thought, careful not to let her amusement show. If he could admit she might be able to improve on his research, maybe his opinion of her ability wasn't as low as he tried to make her think.

They'd reached the Presidio's Franklin Street entrance. He turned right, away from Joy's office, heading downhill again on the winding maze of post roads.

"Eye wouldn't be paid much for her columns, would she, Greg?"

"Probably not. But snooping can carry its own reward."

Joy saw what he was getting at. "I thought we decided blackmail wasn't logical because everything in Maria's file was in the public domain."

"No, it wouldn't be logical," Greg said. "But what if she uncovered sensitive information in the course of her snooping and threatened to write about it in Eye's column unless someone paid her to keep quiet? That could account for her extra income."

Joy's voice rose with excitement. "It could also account for her murder."

"The only thing that doesn't fit is this story about you," he said.

Joy noticed that he didn't deny Maria had been murdered.

"Since it's a pure fabrication," he continued, "there's no way she could have used it to blackmail you. It's possible she was working with somebody else. Nobody's threatened you with anything like this in the past couple of weeks, have they?"

"Nobody," she said. "But something sort of unusual happened the other night."

He swung into the parking area near the statue of Junípero Serra at the Presidio's eastern and lowermost tip. As soon as he turned off the engine, Joy could hear the hoarse barking of the sea lions in the harbor below. A thousand animal voices from the bay bellowed over the distant traffic noises coming from the streets along the waterfront.

Greg turned in his seat so that he was facing her. "What happened?" he asked. "We're going to have to start comparing notes about everything, I can see that."

She hesitated. He hadn't believed her before. Why should she think he'd believe her now when she had a lot less to go on?

"After the way I took the stupid article at face value, I don't blame you for not trusting me," he said, apparently understanding her reluctance. "It won't happen again, I promise you that."

He leaned toward her and took her hands. Remembering last night, Joy wanted to draw them away, but she couldn't. There was such magnetism and strength in his touch that she felt locked to him, the same way she had then.

"Tell me about it, Joy," he said.

His sincerity burned from his fingertips onto hers.

"I'm sure I was followed Wednesday night after I left the Foghorn Inn where I had dinner with Amanda Hawkins," she said.

His grip on her hands tightened. It was the only outward sign of the stab of fear that shot through him at the thought she might be in danger. He didn't understand the feeling or the helplessness that went with it.

"Go on," he said, releasing her fingers as though that would put him back in control.

She clasped her hands in front of her. "It was a van with something printed on the side. You know that curving hill going to the Foghorn Inn? The way the van stayed just out of sight coming down it and then turned off as soon as its driver saw I was watching— I'm pretty sure I was followed, Greg. It shook me up because Airman Tuck said he was being followed—and now he's dead."

Greg rolled down his window. The sea lions' coarse yelps echoed clearly through the salty damp air.

"Have you noticed anybody following you since?"

She shook her head. "I'm sure I'd recognize that van if I saw it again."

"Whoever it was knows that," he said. "They've probably switched vehicles." He leaned toward her. "Maybe whoever was across the canyon wasn't watching Maria's house, Joy. Maybe he or she was watching you."

Joy felt as though the breath had suddenly been choked out of her. She fought to block the fearsome image of someone waiting and watching for her until she'd arrived at Maria's isolated cottage.

"That's ridiculous, Greg," she said, fighting her fear. "Nobody knew I was going to Maria's house."

"Maybe you were followed. When you turned off to her place, it was obvious where you were going. Someone familiar with the area would know about the observation point across the canyon."

His expression darkened. "It's not safe for you to be in Major Easely's house alone."

"So that's what this is all about!" Masking her fear with anger, she flung the car door open and got out. The ground was spongy, and her heels sank into the grassy turf as she started toward the statue of Junípero Serra.

Greg caught up to her when she reached it.

She pulled away from him when he reached for her arm. "We've already had this talk, Greg. Maybe it seemed funny to me last night, but it sure doesn't now. Don't you dare order Donna to stay home and baby-sit me."

She didn't look at him but at the harbor below. "You're meddling in the personal lives of your officers, Greg. Maybe that's the way you do things on the battlefield where nobody has a personal life, but it's not right in a situation like this. Anybody knows that."

He scowled. "Any officer knows enough not to meddle? Even a mustang colonel?" *A mustang colonel who will never go any higher.*

"Especially a mustang colonel," she said, so intent on convincing him that she missed the anguish in his question. "Of all people, a man who came up through the ranks should appreciate how important it is not to interfere in his subordinates' private lives."

He stepped beside her, also facing the bay. "Since you're the one who's going to make general someday, how would you suggest we handle this situation?"

She glanced at him but couldn't read his expression. "Don't kid me about that stupid article, Greg. I'll be lucky to make 0-6 before I retire."

"I wasn't kidding. I want to know how you'd protect one of your people who might be in serious danger—and who refuses to take logical precautions.

"I'm no expert at protecting anybody," she said, turning so that she could see his face. Impossible though it seemed, he looked vulnerable somehow, as though she'd said something to hurt him. For a crazy minute she wondered if his blind eye caused him pain, pain that might be making him look so tired and drawn. Surely she couldn't be responsible.

"After what happened to Airman Tuck, that's pretty obvious. The one thing I don't want is for you to order Donna to stay home nights with me."

"Okay," he said. "No order for Major Easely that might humiliate you and interfere with her regular off-duty schedule. But I'm going to insist that the security be tightened around the place. I'll get a locksmith out there this afternoon."

Joy started to protest and discovered she didn't want to. She would sleep better with bolt locks on the doors and windows. That Greg Weston was concerned enough about her to take care of it sent warmth surging through her.

Of course, he was doing it only because she was one of "his troops," as he himself said only last night.

Unable to understand her jumbled feelings, she stared at his angular face in the lifting fog. His beard was showing darkly against his tanned skin. His wide mouth, set above the curve of his chin, was almost smiling. The tension across his forehead that she'd noticed only moments ago, where the black cord crossed it, had disappeared. His service hat was set at a jaunty angle toward the back of his head, not squarely on top the way he usually wore it. Somehow it made him seem even more adventurous.

In the distance the discordant barking of the sea lions swelled, faded, swelled again. Joy hardly heard them.

Incredible as it seemed, during the past few days something had been happening that she hadn't been aware of.

She'd been falling in love with Greg Weston, an officer married to the Army who put mission above everything. Even worse, as her commander his opinion of her abilities hovered somewhere around minus zero.

What in God's name was she going to do?

Chapter Ten

Joy's knees were shaking when she started for the car. Of all the officers in the military service, why did she have to fall for Greg Weston? To get herself in hand, she hurried ahead of him, struggling to maintain her stride when her heels sank into the spongy grass.

After they were inside the Jeep, Greg suggested another visit to the Carmel Valley Sheriff's Office. Joy wanted to say no, but the image of Chris Tuck's body stilled her tongue. She had to continue with her investigation no matter how mixed up she felt about Greg. It was the only way to assuage her guilt and grief over the young airman's death.

"I want to see Deputy Hawkin's face when she realizes we're asking a few questions of our own," he said, starting the car. Joy clasped her hands in her lap and forced herself to concentrate on what he was saying. "Should we tell her about talking to Mr. Tarnow? Or that we know the official investigation into Maria's death is being hushed up?"

"Probably not," Greg said, after a moment's thought. Incredibly, he seemed unaware that she was waging an emotional dogfight with herself.

"Let's let her do the talking, Joy. If she keeps denying there's reason for an official investigation, that'll be an indication she's in on the cover-up. Meantime we can pump her about who owns the Cardoza woman's house. The owner will know who paid for all that expensive remodeling."

"Do you think she'll tell us who owns it?" Joy asked.

"She won't like it, but my guess is that she will. There are other ways to find out if she won't cooperate."

"She'll be sure to ask why we're interested. You know, Greg, it might not be a good idea to tell her we're curious about who paid for the remodeling. If we do, she'll know we were snooping around inside the house." Joy studied his profile. "Maybe we ought to come up with some other reason for wanting to know who the owner is."

Greg smiled, letting himself forget, for the moment, his real reason for wanting to talk to Deputy Hawkins.

"As I live and breathe," he said, shaking his head and swatting at his ear with his hand. "Can I be hearing correctly? From where I'm sitting, it sounds as though the veracious Captain Donnelly is suggesting that we fib to the good deputy about our intentions."

When he glanced at Joy, he noted that her smile had been complemented by a luscious rosy glow. Damn, but she was wholesome-looking! And he'd never known a more loyal officer.

"I wasn't thinking of it as an out-and-out lie," she said, her cheeks turning an even brighter shade of red. "Just giving Amanda a good *other* reason, the way you do when you'd rather not tell somebody something point blank."

Greg faced front again and increased the Jeep's speed. The road had narrowed to two lanes, and three cars were already backed up behind him. When he concentrated on Joy instead of on his driving, the car had an annoying tendency to slow down.

Greg finally admitted it to himself: he liked being with Joy Donnelly. Why the hell should he care if she had stars in her eyes? Actually, he told himself, he should consider himself fortunate that she had no designs on him. He wasn't the settling-down type.

He glanced at Joy again and caught a questioning look. It reminded him that he hadn't answered her. "Of course, we don't have to mention that we searched the house. Only that while we were inside telephoning, we noticed some remodeling that looked expensive and wondered who paid for it.''

He frowned, recalling why he'd insisted on returning to the Carmel Valley this morning. Their talk with the *Tribune* editor had convinced him that something evil was abroad, something that threatened the woman sitting beside him. She was being watched and followed and libeled. Even now, her life might be in danger.

Add to that the fact that the local police were covering up two probable murders that were somehow connected to Joy, and Greg was ready to declare his own private war. Maybe he could bully Deputy Hawkins into revealing something that would help him identify his enemy.

"MIND TELLING ME why you want to know?" said Amanda Hawkins, eyeing them suspiciously.

"We'd like to find out who paid for that expensive remodeling we saw when we used the phone," Joy answered quickly. "The owner can tell us."

Amanda put her elbows on her desk and leaned toward them. She was wearing round glasses with dark lenses that hid her eyes. They made her look vaguely hostile.

"I'd be glad to give you his name," she said, "but he lives out of town, and there's no reason for you to bother him if the remodeling expenses are all you're interested in."

Joy's eyes widened. For the second time that morning, someone they'd considered uncooperative seemed about to tell them what they wanted.

"If you know who paid for that remodeling, we'd like to hear it." Joy stared at her, eyeball-to-eyeball. "But we'd still like to find out the name of the owner—in case we think of some other questions."

Amanda went to a four-drawer safe against the wall behind her desk, the heels of her boots clumping on the wood floor. She twisted the dial on the top drawer, opened it, and pulled out a file.

"His name is Carl Riker," she said. "His address is on Kenwood Drive in San Francisco."

Joy pulled a pen and notepad from her shoulder bag and wrote down the street address and telephone number. "Did Mr. Riker pay for the remodeling, or did Ms. Cardoza?"

"She did," Amanda said, putting the file back in the safe and twisting the dial. "The whole kit and caboodle."

Greg crossed one leg over his knee and clasped his hands behind his head. "Doesn't that strike you as a little odd, Deputy? We had a chance to walk through the house before you arrived, and those improvements must have cost a bundle."

Amanda sat down again and shrugged her shoulders. "I'm no expert, but the place didn't look all that fancy to me."

"It looked fancy enough for you to check into who paid for the remodeling," Joy said. "Sounds to me as though you're investigating Maria Cardoza's death. What puzzles me is why you're so reluctant to admit it."

Joy knew she was dangerously close to revealing what they'd found out about a cover-up, but the opening was too good to pass up. Staring at Amanda's face, she detected a muscle twitch at the corner of the deputy sheriff's mouth. She looked as if she were hiding something, and it was bothering her.

"Any investigating we've done has been purely routine," Amanda snapped. "In case you people haven't figured it out, that's what we do around here. We ask questions. We investigate. Even accidents like the Cardoza woman's drowning."

"You could have fooled me," Greg said. "How you can consider her drowning—and Airman Tuck's—to be accidental is beyond me."

It was the first time Joy had heard him say the deaths weren't accidental. At last Mohammed had come to the mountain.

"They're accidental until we find out otherwise, Colonel." Amanda shrugged again. "Maybe when we get the autopsy reports..."

"In a month or two?" Greg said.

"We've already gone over that," Amanda said, rising from her chair. "Now, I've got an appointment— I was on my way out when you came in."

Joy didn't stir. Neither did Greg.

"Before you go, I've got one more comment, Deputy," he said. "A few minutes ago you said Ms. Cardoza's place didn't look too fancy. You're right. It doesn't. On the outside it looks like a run-down old shack."

"Mind telling me what you're getting at?" Amanda retrieved her hat from the top of the safe and started toward the door.

"On the inside the place looks like a palace." Greg stood up. "It's as though Ms. Cardoza was deliberately trying to camouflage her luxurious little nest—fool people into thinking she was living in a shack when the opposite was true."

"Are you telling me she was doing something illegal?"

Greg started to answer but Amanda cut him off. "Because if you are, Colonel Weston, I'm warning you right now to get your nose out of police business and back to the Presidio where it belongs. Amateurs meddling in matters that don't concern them are apt to find themselves in a passel of trouble."

Greg opened the door and held it while Amanda strode through to the covered porch outside. "Your threats don't scare me, Deputy," he said, following Joy outside.

"It wasn't meant to be a threat, Colonel. More of a warning. Back off before you screw things up." She twisted a key in the lock. Joy heard a bolt click into place. She felt Greg take her arm as they started down the wooden steps to the narrow tarmac street.

The deputy stared down at them from the porch.

Why did I ever think Amanda Hawkins looked like Smiley? Joy wondered, watching the woman's mouth squeeze to a hard, thin line. Reflected sunlight flashed from the opaque lenses of her glasses.

"There's nothing I can to do stop you, but let me tell you this, Colonel," she spit out. "Break the law in this investigation of yours, and you'll both go to jail. I catch either of you so much as sticking a finger someplace where it doesn't belong and, so help me, I'll guarantee you both a *vacation* you'll not soon forget."

She descended the stairs stoically, like a hooded executioner resigned to the grisly task he'd just performed. The last they saw of her was the back of her head, topped by her sheriff's hat, as her gold-colored police cruiser turned toward the Carmel Valley Road.

In another minute, they were in the Jeep headed back to the Presidio. On the way, they formulated a plan of action for the afternoon. Joy would quiz her training officer about the meeting she'd noticed on Sergeant Philpott's calendar and would take care of other squadron business. Greg would call Maria's landlord to find out more about her remodeling expenses. Then Joy would examine the Cardoza and Ramon personnel files.

"Why don't I go over everybody's file in the Spanish Department while I'm at it?" Joy said. "Somebody murdered her, Greg. Considering what Señora Ramon said—that she was curious about other people's business—she probably wasn't well-liked. Isn't it worth checking out the other instructors?"

He nodded. "Let's both go over them. I'll make the arrangements as soon as I get back to my office." *The sooner we examine those files, the better,* he added grimly to himself.

After their encounter with Deputy Hawkins, Greg was even more convinced something was terribly wrong. The deputy wasn't a very good liar. It was plain to him that she knew the deaths weren't accidental. Did she suspect, as he now did, that a killer was stalking his school?

WHEN JOY GOT BACK to the squadron orderly room at a little before noon, her first sergeant was waiting with a problem.

According to Sergeant Blakeman, the mail was ready for pickup at the main post office half an hour too late for the mail clerk's noon delivery to the troops. Changing the distribution time to afternoon would mean changing the clerk's duty hours. If his hours were changed, he'd lose his off-duty job. When Sergeant Blakeman tried to expedite the pickup time, he was given the runaround.

"I'll call Admin and see what the tie-up is," Joy said. "Until we get this resolved, we'll simply have to make distribution at noon the next day. I don't like to hold the mail that long, but Airman Hanson's mechanic's job is important, too."

"Thanks, Captain." Sergeant Blakeman stood up. "He'll be grateful. He's got a couple of kids to support."

"Just a minute, Sergeant," Joy said, stopping him at her office door. "What's happening to Airman Tuck's mail?"

"I've been holding it since he disappeared, ma'am. Now that we know he's dead, Lieutenant Bowen from Personal Affairs will be over this afternoon to go through it before sending it to his family. I didn't open anything, of course, but from the envelopes there's nothing his parents shouldn't see."

"Let me take a look, would you please, Sergeant Blakeman?" Air force policy prevented Joy from opening the letters and reading them. Since she was in the airman's chain of command, that chore had to be handled by someone outside the squadron. But there wasn't any reason she couldn't examine the envelopes.

A few minutes later she tucked the small packet of mail into her desk drawer. She intended to glance through it after she'd questioned her training officer about Colonel Spellman's scheduled meeting with her airmen—the meeting posted on Sergeant Philpott's appointment calendar.

"Please tell Lieutenant Gwizdak to come in," she told Sergeant Blakeman, as he left her office.

Lieutenant Ted Gwizdak was Joy's training officer. If anybody knew about Colonel Spellman's meeting, he would. Short and well proportioned, Gwizdak had the bouncy look of a male cheerleader. Bursting into Joy's office, he exuded an anxious breathless energy.

"You wanted to see me, ma'am?" he asked, standing stiffly in front of her desk. A second john, fresh from officer training at Lackland, he obviously prided himself on his military courtesy.

"Please sit down, Lieutenant Gwizdak." Joy motioned toward the chair beside her desk. "This morning while I was at headquarters, I learned that Colonel Spellman had scheduled a meeting for this afternoon with some of our students. Do you know anything about it?"

In the three months she'd been at DLI, Joy hadn't heard about any meetings the assistant commandant had had with the enlisted air force students. As Squadron Commander, she should have been told any time Spellman showed special interest in her people.

"I'm sure I briefed you on that when they had the last one," Gwizdak said, obviously disturbed. Something had fallen through the crack, and he appeared to be the one responsible.

"They? Who're *they?*" Interested, Joy leaned toward him.

"Colonel Spellman and that dragon from the front office."

"Colonel Spellman and Sergeant Philpott?" Joy's eyes widened. "Why in heaven's name are they meeting with our students?"

"They've been having these meetings for about a year now," Gwizdak said nervously. "I'm sure I told you about it, ma'am. The colonel talks to everyone being assigned to the National Security Agency a couple of weeks before they graduate."

A red flag waved in Joy's mind. First the "School for Spies" article and now this. Why was Erick Spellman interested in students assigned to the super-secret agency after they graduated? The most hush-hush organization in Washington, NSA was even more secret than the Central Intelligence Agency.

"Have you been to any of these meetings?"

He nodded. "Almost all of them since I've been here. They don't amount to much. The colonel was assigned to NSA before the Presidio. He likes to meet the people going there, press the flesh, tell them what Fort Meade is like." NSA was located at Fort Meade, Maryland, about twenty-five miles from Washington D. C.

"Actually," the training officer continued, "it's a nice thing to do. Everybody appreciates it."

"It sounds like sort of an orientation briefing," Joy said. "What does Sergeant Philpott do at these meetings? Was she assigned to NSA, too, before she came here?"

"The way I understand it, she organized the meetings once she found out Colonel Spellman reported here from NSA. They started with briefings for the army troops and expanded to include us."

"How about the Naval Security Group students?"

"I've never checked into it, but always assumed they met with them, too."

As Ted Gwizdak left her office, Joy jotted a note to remind herself to sit in on this afternoon's NSA briefing.

THE CIVILIAN PERSONNEL OFFICER, Mr. Lester Sumner, was out to lunch when Joy called. Rather than wait until Sumner came back, she asked the office secretary, a man named Cardwell, if his boss had approved her review of the files of the Spanish Department instructors.

Obviously protective of the personnel records, Cardwell's voice exuded disapproval. "Mr. Sumner said Colonel Weston wanted to be notified as soon as you got here. I'm sorry, Captain, I can't pull any files for you until I get his okay."

Impatiently, Joy drummed her fingers on her desk. She was sure Greg had already authorized her examination of the files. Getting a second okay from him sounded like the secretary's idea.

"Then I suggest you start dialing, Mr. Cardwell," she said. "I'll be in your office in ten minutes, and I'll expect those files to be ready for me."

"I'll do what I can, Captain."

When Joy arrived a few minutes later, she found Greg waiting for her. As she'd thought, he wanted to be notified when she got there so that he could go over them with her.

Under Greg's commanding gaze, Cardwell's attitude changed from disapproval to unctuous cooperation. A robust six-footer who seemed as though he'd be more at home behind the wheel of a semi than a Selectric, the secretary ushered them into the personnel chief's private office. On one side of the room was a large desk, on the other, a table. A stack of manila folders was neatly piled near the center of the table.

"If you'd like anything, I'll be right outside, Colonel."

"Thanks," Greg said, shutting the door to the outer office.

With the files between them, they sat down next to each other at the table.

Maria's file had been placed on top. As Greg reached for it, Joy touched his arm to get his attention. It felt so natural to her that she wasn't aware she'd done it until she felt the change in his breathing.

So maybe their investigation wasn't as much all business as he pretended, she thought—and immediately felt guilty for letting her mind stray from the work at hand.

"Before we start on the files, tell me what Mr. Riker said," she asked. Her own breathing had become as ragged as Greg's. She pushed her forearm against the table and leaned away from him.

Greg laid down Maria's file. "He confirmed what the deputy told us. Maria paid for the remodeling expenses herself. She wanted to buy the place. Made him a cash offer he couldn't refuse before she started remodeling."

Joy twisted in her chair so that she could face him. "How could she possibly come up with that much money on her salary?"

"There's more," he said. "According to Riker, the police questioned him for over an hour about it. Compare that to the five minutes the deputy talked to us on the porch."

Joy's excitement mounted. "Why do you suppose they're covering up their investigation?"

He shoved Maria Cardoza's folder toward her. "Maybe they don't want the murderer to know they suspect foul play."

"That's not a good reason, Greg. People need to be told there's a killer on the loose so they can take precautions." With a sigh, Joy opened Maria's folder. She read for a moment, then looked up. "You say you've already checked out these people she's listed as next of kin?"

He nodded. "Yesterday I called a friend in Zaragoza. As far as we could determine from the addresses, there's no wealth in her family."

He picks up the phone and calls a friend in Spain. Probably a beautiful woman friend. Joy pictured a dark Spanish beauty and fought down the uncomfortable feeling that went along with the image.

She scanned the rest of Maria's file.

In accordance with school policy, the instructor's teaching ability had been evaluated in reports signed by her administrative supervisor and endorsed by her department chairman, Julio Ramon. Her supervisor's reports were above average but not outstanding.

Julio Ramon's endorsements, however, were consistently high. Joy noted that the chairman's enthusiasm for Ms. Cardoza's teaching increased significantly as time passed. He'd rated her as outstanding on the past year's reports.

"Did you see this?" she asked Greg, pointing out Ramon's glowing endorsements.

"It didn't register yesterday, but it sure as hell does now. Let's take a look at Ramon's file."

He sorted through the stack until he found the department head's folder. After scanning it quickly, he passed it to Joy.

Julio Ramon had been with DLI for almost fifteen years, so his folder was noticeably fatter than Maria Cardoza's. Skipping over the routine information, Joy noted that Julio, like Maria, came from Zaragoza. Was it possible he'd

known her in Spain? Perhaps she'd been holding some
thing over him that happened there, maybe involving hi
family. Hadn't Señora Ramon mentioned Maria's interes
in relatives in the old country?

Joy nudged Greg. "It might be worth a call to your con
tact in Spain to find out something about Julio's family
He's from the same part of the country Maria was."

Greg passed her more folders. "While you're goin
through these, see if you can spot anybody else from Zara
goza. I'll tell my friend to ask around about them, too."

By the time the civilian personnel officer came back fron
lunch, Joy was halfway through the stack and had writte
two names on her notepad under her notes on Julio Ra
mon. Both were instructors with family ties in the Zara
goza area.

Lester Sumner, a mild-mannered man in his fifties, set
tled himself behind his desk with the wary caution of
wildebeest who's just spotted a couple of lions drinking a
his water hole.

"If there's anything I can do to assist your research
Colonel Weston, Captain Donnelly..." he began.

Greg stopped him with a wave of his hand. "We'll be ou
of your hair in a few minutes, Mr. Sumner. Don't let us in
terfere with your work."

They returned to the stack of folders, hardly aware of th
other man's nervous paper-shuffling at his desk behin
them.

When Joy reached the file on Santos Mueller she exam
ined it with special interest. The big man was from Para
guay, a landlocked South American country with man
citizens of German descent.

Joy nudged Greg again. "Maybe his family had connec
tions to the Nazi movement in Germany in World War II."

"That's ancient history. Asking questions about Naz
connections would be a waste of time." Greg's frown re
flected his disagreement.

"Maybe not, with German reunification and everythin
else that's been going on in Europe lately. I know he's you

friend, Greg, but that's all the more reason we should check him out." Joy kept her voice soft, her manner reasonable.

"You're right, of course." Greg's acquiescence was grudging.

"Since the language school instructors don't need security clearances, they don't get background investigations. No telling what kind of politics they were involved in back home." Joy passed Santos's folder back to Greg. "None of the effectiveness reports or endorsements mention his warehouse job."

Greg placed the folder on top of the stack. "No reason they should, as long as the outside work isn't affecting his teaching."

They stood to go. "I'll be in touch later this afternoon after I've made some calls," he said, as they parted in the hallway outside the personnel office.

When Greg walked into his outer office after his session with Joy in Personnel, the secretaries for the chief of staff and the assistant commandant—middle-aged civilian women—were bent over their Selectrics. Greg suspected their antennae were twisted toward his sergeant's desk.

"Come into my office with your pad," he said to Sergeant Philpott. As usual, her no-iron uniform shirt was not only ironed but stiffly starched.

When she was seated beside his desk, he gave her terse instructions.

"Get in touch with my contact in Spain. After I've talked to him, track down Manuel Garcia in Paraguay." He gave her a telephone number. Garcia was a revolutionary Greg had trained. He'd kept in touch with the man over the years.

"Is that all, sir?" Sergeant Philpott remained seated.

Greg nodded. "You can buzz me when you've reached the first number."

Still she didn't leave. "You must be planning some kind of reunion with your protégés with all these overseas calls. Spain yesterday and again today and now Paraguay."

She made the remark casually, as though she wanted to chat, but it was so unlike her that Greg took special notice. Curiosity wasn't one of Sergeant Philpott's failings. When he grunted noncommittally, he noticed that she seemed vaguely disappointed, almost as though she'd been hoping he would tell her what the calls were about.

Chapter Eleven

"Please leave the door open," Greg told Sergeant Philpott as she walked out of his office.

From her crisp "Yes, sir," he couldn't tell whether she guessed the reason: that he wanted to make sure she didn't listen in on his calls to Spain and Paraguay. Greg wanted nobody but Joy to know that he was conducting his own private investigation into the lives of some of the school instructors. In addition to being counter to the privacy laws, such an activity, if it became known, would cause serious morale problems among the teaching staff. Sergeant Philpott's curiosity about the calls, combined with Joy's suspicion that she might be eavesdropping through the squawk box, made Greg decide to watch her through the open door while he talked to his two sources.

Within an hour, he'd reached both men. Each promised to find out what he could about the people Greg named and to report back to him at his quarters in twenty-four hours.

Then he made two more calls: one to a locksmith to arrange for locks to be installed that afternoon on the doors and windows of Joy's house; the other to Major Easely. It didn't take a mind reader to figure out she didn't like the idea.

"That's an expensive job, sir. Each of the bolt locks is at least seventy-five dollars, and the windows will be even more."

Greg took a deep breath. "I thought I made it clear that I intend to pick up the tab for this, Major Easely."

There was a short silence. "I don't like anybody paying my bills, Colonel. Especially not my commander."

"Humor me on this, Major. Since this is my idea, it's only right that I pay for it."

There was another, longer silence. Greg shook off the feeling that she was trying to think up more objections.

"Oh, all right then, since you insist." Her voice was sharper than usual. "But you'll be wasting your money. We're in a good neighborhood."

Greg sensed she had more to say and drummed his fingers on the desk, waiting.

"Maybe I shouldn't mention this, sir," she went on, finally, "but Captain Donnelly is well able to take care of herself. I know you don't think so, but, believe me, she is."

"I'm sure you both are." Greg tried not to let his irritation show. He hung up the phone with the disturbed feeling that Major Easely was protesting too much. What legitimate objections could she have to the security work he wanted done, work that would only add to the value of her house? Greg couldn't think of one, and it bothered him.

He had a sudden urge to tell Joy about the arrangements he'd made. They also had some things to talk over before they saw Santos in the morning, he told himself. He'd surprise her by dropping in at the squadron orderly room.

As he walked through the outer office, he astonished Barbara Philpott by smiling at her.

JOY HEARD Sergeant Blakeman shout a loud *"Attention!"* and glanced through her open door to see Greg heading her way.

"As you were," he said to the staff of the 3483rd, standing stiffly behind their desks.

"Captain Donnelly is in her office, sir," Sergeant Blakeman said, rather unnecessarily since they could both see her through the open door.

Joy got up to meet him, surprised by her flush of pleasure at the sight of him.

"Good afternoon, sir," she said, for the benefit of her staff, who were hanging on each word. It wasn't every day that the DLI Commandant paid the squadron a personal visit.

As soon as Greg stepped into her office, she shut the door behind him. "To what do we owe this unexpected pleasure?" she asked, the suggestion of a smile on her face.

He pulled the chair in front of her desk around and sat down beside her. She turned hers to face him.

"Just wanted to touch base before we see Santos tomorrow morning," he said. "Since he's meeting us at my quarters at 0645, why don't I pick you up at your place half an hour earlier?"

"That wouldn't be right." Taken by surprise, Joy answered quickly, without thinking.

Scowl lines appeared over his eyebrows. "Why not?"

Joy ignored his frown. "We don't want Santos to feel like a third wheel," she began cautiously. "If you pick me up, he might think you're...ah...interested in me, and he'd be doing you a favor by backing out at the last minute."

Greg's forehead smoothed, and he adjusted the band holding his eye patch. "You're probably right. Santos has just enough Latin chivalry to pull a stunt like that."

"That's the way I've got him sized up, Greg. I'll plan to be at your quarters at 0645, too, if that's okay?"

He nodded. "Fine. Incidentally, the locks are being installed on your house this afternoon. Major Easely should be on her way over there right now to supervise."

The warm, cared-for feeling Joy remembered from this morning swept over her again.

"It really isn't necessary," she said, but smiled to show him she appreciated his concern. "What did Donna say when you asked her about having them put on?"

Greg frowned again as he remembered Major Easely's illogical resistance to his plan. "She said you could take care of yourself very nicely, and implied that I was being a patronizing old fool by suggesting you needed extra locks on the doors.''

Joy couldn't help laughing. "Well, good for Donna. Every so often she makes me realize why we get along so well.''

Greg smiled so she wouldn't see how worried he was about Major Easely's disregard for the house's security. Did she want to make it easy for somebody to break in on one of those many nights she was away from home?

As he stood to go, Joy remembered the mail addressed to Airman Tuck.

"Just a minute," she said. "I've got something to show you." She opened her desk drawer, pulled out the packet of letters, and handed them to him.

"The squadron's been holding these since Airman Tuck disappeared last Wednesday. We've arranged for Lieutenant Bowen from Personal Affairs to stop by this afternoon and go through them before they're sent to his family. He'd probably appreciate it if you'd do the job for him.''

Sitting down again, Greg shuffled through the stack. "Three from his mother in Louisville, two from a Mrs. Wright in Louisville, a couple of bills from a motorcycle repair shop. Which should I open first?"

She handed him a letter opener. "The ones from the married woman, of course.''

Carefully, he slit an envelope along its top seam and took out the letter inside.

"Mrs. Wright's his sister," he said, glancing at it. "She's upset because he's going to marry someone he's met here in Monterey.''

"Maria!" Joy confirmed. "Then the crystal he gave her must have been an engagement present. No wonder he was so sure she always wore it.''

Greg scanned the letter. "She never mentions Maria by name. She's concerned about the age difference. Spends two pages warning him that twelve years is too much.''

"There was at least a fifteen-year difference," Joy said.

Greg opened another envelope. "A couple of years got lost in the shuffle. From this letter it's obvious he intended to marry Maria Cardoza and that she'd said yes."

He skimmed the second letter. "Another one from the sister—a repeat of the first but written the next day."

After glancing at the backs of the envelopes again, he opened another and pulled out the letters inside. "His family was really worried. Two of his mother's letters are postmarked the same day."

Joy watched his eye track down the page.

"Hello there." Greg's voice held a note of triumph. "This one mentions Maria by name and says that just because she's a newspaper columnist and an instructor, doesn't mean she's right for a man almost young enough to be her son. Especially since she's a foreigner who doesn't know quote our ways unquote."

Joy leaned toward him, engrossed in this latest revelation. "If Airman Tuck knew she was a newspaper columnist, he must have known she was Eye. Maybe it wasn't as much of a secret as that editor tried to make us believe."

"We'll find out from Santos tomorrow morning," Greg said, glancing at another letter from the airman's mother.

"More of the same." He put it back in its envelope and handed it to Joy.

As Greg stood to go, she bundled it with the other letters and returned them all to her desk drawer.

A FEW MINUTES after Greg left, Joy slipped into the squadron's downstairs study room to observe Colonel Spellman's National Security Agency briefing. The scheduled period was about halfway over when she arrived, and she seated herself near the door so she wouldn't interrupt.

Let's see what the colonel and sergeant are up to, she thought.

Thirty to forty uniformed men and women—the airmen to be assigned to the top secret National Security Agency— were crowded behind the desks. There weren't enough chairs for everybody and some were standing.

Apparently the formal part of the briefing was over. Colonel Spellman and Sergeant Philpott were mingling with individuals in the group. The sergeant appeared to be collecting a copy of each person's orders.

Joy's training officer, Lieutenant Gwizdak, was sitting nearby. She beckoned him to her.

"Why do they take copies of orders?" she asked, when he had joined her.

"Sergeant Philpott makes appointments for anybody who wants more time with her or the colonel," Gwizdak said. Joy could see he was anxious to make amends for forgetting to tell her about the briefing. "Philpott says the orders help her identify people. She jots down information about each person at the top."

Even as Joy watched, Barbara Philpott made a notation on the sheet of paper she'd just taken from a young man.

"What's the formal part of the briefing like?" Joy asked.

He grinned at her. "It's no dog-and-pony show, I can tell you, Captain. About all he does is say a few words about the Maryland climate and the recreational facilities at Fort Meade. It takes about three minutes."

Joy glanced up to find Sergeant Philpott staring at her. The woman's face was leached of color. Resisting the urge to turn around and look behind herself for the source of such terror, Joy smiled and nodded. Barbara Philpott mouthed the words, "Good afternoon, ma'am," before resuming her conversation with one of the prospective graduates.

During the rest of the briefing period, Joy scrutinized Erick Spellman and Barbara Philpott as best she could without being obvious.

Plainly in his element, the congenial Spellman shook hands and chatted with everybody there. Barbara Philpott continued to collect a copy of the orders of each person she talked to. But Joy noticed that she took no more notes after she saw Joy watching her. The annotated orders were zipped up in a black leather briefcase she never let out of her grasp.

JOY STOPPED BY the library on her way home from work. She wanted to find out something about skeet and trap-shooting before Saturday morning. After she'd scanned an excellent book on the subject, she knew enough about the rules and procedures of the sport so as not to appear a complete novice.

While she was there she glanced through the filmed records of the Eye columns in the *Monterey Tribune,* searching specifically for comments about Santos Mueller. If she read what Maria had written about Santos, maybe it would be easier to find out what he knew about the woman's work as a gossip columnist.

Joy didn't have far to look. Only days before Maria died, she had devoted an entire column to Santos's moral support for a right-wing South American revolutionary movement. Joy wondered how she'd missed the article when she glanced through the folder at Maria's house. Then she realized there had been no Eye columns in the folder. Maria probably kept a file at the *Tribune.*

He Drives By Night, read the caption. The article below, written in Eye's chatty style, explained that DLI instructor Santos Mueller spent his off-duty hours driving refugees from the stricken country to their new homes in the local area and running errands for those without cars. Since U.S. government policy opposed the dictatorial leftist regime in power, the country's political refugees were welcome in the Unites States.

Joy read the article with a great deal of skepticism. Santos Mueller was the last person she'd consider altruistic. Was this a compilation of half-truths, just as the article about Joy herself had been? Before she left the library, she made a copy of the column and slipped it into her handbag.

Saturday Morning

As DLI COMMANDANT, Greg was assigned quarters next to Rasmussen Hall, the headquarters building. A two-story wooden structure painted yellow, the 1920s-vintage house was distinguishable from the ones next to it mainly because its porch was larger and because it had a privacy fence around the backyard.

When Joy arrived, the fog was even thicker than usual. Ordinarily she rather liked the misty stuff, but this morning it seemed heavy and oppressive. Peering through the gray semidarkness, she could see moisture glistening on the late-model Chevrolet station wagon standing in front of Greg's house. Santos was already there, she thought, pulling up behind the Chevrolet.

As soon as she got out, the salty, damp air covered her like a spongy blanket, smothering her. What if Santos Mueller were somehow involved in the murders and suspected the real purpose of their trip to the shooting range? She tried not to think about the guns they'd be using. How easy would it be for a weapon to misfire, for someone to get hurt? She took a deep breath to dispel her anxious feelings.

Greg and Santos came out on the porch as she started up the walk. They were both dressed in jeans, but there the similarity ended.

Greg's were old and unpressed; Santos's had designer's initials on the pockets. Greg wore a plain, worn leather belt; Santos's leather belt had a big silver buckle. The rest of their clothes—from Greg's Sears-catalog plaid shirt to Santos's hand-sewn leather boots, were just as disparate.

Neither was wearing a hat. A cowlick Joy hadn't noticed was sticking up at the back of Greg's head. Santos's straight brown hair was combed to one side in a style designed to flatter his big, square face with its pronounced nose and chin.

Just how friendly are they? she wondered.

Greg came toward her, smiling.

"Miss Texas in person," he said, appreciating her outfit.

His compliment pleased her more than she'd have liked—in spite of the attention she'd given to her clothes that morning. Since Greg had said the skeet range was near Salinas, about twenty miles east of Monterey where it was sunnier and warmer, she'd worn a denim jacket she could take off. In true Texas style, she was also wearing cowboy boots, jeans, and a Western shirt with blue cornflowers on it. A big-brimmed cowboy's hat was on her head. She'd go down looking like a Texan even if she couldn't shoot like one.

Greg turned to Santos, a step behind him. "I've got a feeling we're in for some real competition this morning, amigo."

The big man laughed heartily, but Joy saw no laughter in his bleached, hypnotic eyes. "Never underestimate a woman, *Comandante*. Especially a beautiful woman. Joy will probably destroy both of us."

It was an odd choice of words since she intended to do exactly that to whomever was behind Airman Tuck's murder.

"Unfortunately, you don't have much to worry about," she said, turning quickly so that Greg was between her and the instructor. She wanted no gratuitous bowing and scraping in the name of Latin chivalry. Santos Mueller's courtliness was starting to scare her. His touch was a little too heavy, his eyes too piercing for the congeniality he pretended.

"I've never shot skeet before," she said as they walked the last few steps to Santos's car. "My only experience has been with a carbine on the rifle range at Lackland."

"We'll be shooting at moving targets so this is more interesting than the fixed targets at the standard military firing ranges," Greg said. "Once you get the hang of it, you shouldn't have any problems, since you're an expert marksman."

His hidden challenge made her forget her anxiety. She smiled up at him. "As long as you don't expect a perfect twenty-five the first time 'round, I'll be okay."

Both men glanced quickly at her, and Santos tsked his tongue against the roof of his mouth. "We're going to have trouble with this one, *Comandante*."

"I thought you never shot skeet before," Greg said.

Joy didn't explain about her stop at the library. "I know a little something about the sport," she said noncommittally.

Santos opened the passenger door and held it for her while Greg slid into the backseat. As they pulled away from the curb, Joy sat back, prepared to enjoy Santos's discomfiture when Greg quizzed him about his reasons for asking that Airman Tuck be assigned to his class.

She waited in vain. During their twenty-five minute ride to Salinas, the subject never came up. Joy stepped out of the car with the uncomfortable feeling that she'd underestimated Greg's loyalty to the burly instructor, and overestimated his desire to get at the truth. Apprehension crawled down her spine like a poisonous spider. Was this morning's outing to be a chance to quiz Santos Mueller as she'd thought? Or was it, instead, a heaven-sent opportunity for Greg to vindicate his old friend?

THE SALINAS SPORTSMAN'S Club, located south of the city only a short distance from Fort Ord's eastern perimeter, opened for business shortly after they arrived.

While they were waiting, Joy suggested they try the coffee in the clubhouse, a structure built of logs that, outside, vaguely resembled an old army fort. Inside, a barnlike room housed the registration desk at one end and the coffee bar at the other. Battered wooden tables and chairs filled the center.

Now that they were east of the hills, the fog had disappeared. The rising sun glared through windows streaked with dirt. On the opposite wall, yellow stains dripped from the ceiling down the light-colored paint. It didn't rain often in Salinas, but when it did, apparently the roof of the Sportsmen's Club leaked. There were no pictures or decorations on the walls.

At the coffee bar, the trash container was overflowing. A drip can on the floor underneath the coffee pot spigot held a dark mixture so foul that it changed color while Joy looked at it. She could tell from the rancid smell emanating from the big pot that the coffee had been reheated. She poured herself only half a paper cupful, lightening it with a spoonful of powdered cream. Even so, it was too strong, and she poured it into the drip can after her first swallow.

Greg and Santos seemed to relish the wicked brew and finished their cups while they were walking back to the desk.

Several young men came up. Since they were in a uniform of sorts—dirty white sweats with golf caps and ear protectors—Joy assumed they were part of the staff.

The registrar beckoned to Greg. Whether it was the fellow's stringy straight hair or his insolent manner, to Joy he seemed more adolescent than adult. This was a young man who would profit greatly from six weeks' basic training under a hard-nosed drill sergeant.

"Your puller's ready, Colonel," he said, leering past Greg at Joy. "You can get started soon's you sign in. Just three of you today?"

Greg nodded, signing their names on a numbered list with the date at the top.

"That'll be nine dollars," he said.

Santos laid a ten-dollar bill on the counter and pocketed the dollar change.

They went back to the car to get the shotguns. When Greg handed one to Joy, she took a short step backward. It had been a long time since she'd handled a gun, and she found herself unexpectedly nervous. He didn't seem to notice her hesitation.

Gingerly, she grasped the wood stock and broke the gun open. Then they walked to the trap and skeet fields a short distance from the clubhouse. The fields were cleared areas about the size of a single football field, surrounded by heavy stands of pine. A piece of chain fastened two feet high to upright logs ran along the perimeter, some twenty feet from the road.

Signs hanging on the chain warned spectators to stay behind it. When Joy read them, her apprehension returned. This wasn't tiddledywinks they were playing. This was a dangerous sport involving loaded guns. When she stepped through a break in the chain to the first station, her heart began thudding out of control.

Like the other structures at the club, the two sheds on either side of the semicircular skeet range were painted fire-engine red.

"Do I need to explain skeet to you?" Greg asked.

She shook her head, breathing deeply to steady her voice.

"You and Santos go first. I'll copy. I've never fired a shotgun. Only a carbine. But if I watch you, I'm sure I can manage." She stepped back, as far from Santos and as close to the chain perimeter as she could get. The puller was standing there, operating the skeet traps with an electrically controlled hand device. He wore big earmuffs.

"Same stakes, amigo?" Greg said to Santos.

"Five dollars a station is fine with me," Santos said. Stuffing some earplugs in his ears, he stepped onto the mound at Station One and loaded his shotgun. When he yelled "Pull," a clay, platelike object hurtled out of the high window of the shed or "house" on his left. Santos destroyed it. He yelled "Pull" again, and another clay bird flew from the low window of the house on his right. After it, too, was shattered, he paused to load two more shells. At his third yell, two birds were propelled out, one from each side. Santos knocked both down with two more shots.

"Your turn, Joy," Greg said. "I forgot to get you some earplugs, so take mine." He handed them to her. Unlike the big ear muffs the puller was wearing, these were worn inside the ear to avoid interference when the shooter fired his weapon.

Her heart in her throat, she stepped to the mound. Out of the corner of her eye, she could see Santos, standing off to one side. Thank heaven he wasn't behind her. She loaded her weapon with the two shells Greg handed her.

"Pull," she yelled, just as Santos had, keeping her gun trained on the clay pigeon. To her surprise, when she pulled the trigger, the object splintered into a thousand pieces.

Greg came up behind her, so close she could feel his breath on the back of her neck.

"Well done," he said.

Helpless to resist the spate of impulses jerking up and down her spine at his nearness, Joy forgot about Santos.

Greg stepped backward. Taking a deep breath to quiet her racing pulse, she raised her shotgun.

In the distance she heard a single popping sound, like a firecracker going off. She started to yell "Pull," but the word died in her throat as puffs of dust exploded near her and a series of sharp loud cracks split the early-morning air. At almost the same instant, Greg's big body crashed into her from behind, his arms wrapped tightly around her to cushion the blow when she hit the ground.

"Down, Santos," he shouted, his mouth barely inches from her ear. "Some bastard's firing at us."

Chapter Twelve

Joy's shotgun hurtled from her hands when she hit the ground. Inches from her head, more bullets impacted, raising small puffs of dust. Terrified, she struggled to sit up.

"Stay down!" Greg ordered, his breath hot on her hair.

Beneath him, Joy screwed her eyes shut, the dirt stinging her nostrils. She was barely conscious of him on top of her until he moved, lifting himself with his elbows.

"Are you okay?" he whispered.

"I think so." She spoke into the dirt, without moving her head. "What's going on, Greg?" Through the mists of her terror was a growing awareness of his big body sprawled across her back, covering her like a giant shield.

"Somebody was shooting at us," he said through clenched teeth. "Those rifle bullets were too damned close to be an accident. I saw them hit the dust in front of us right after I heard the pistol shot."

She heard scuffling noises and cautiously opened her eyes. Santos wriggled up to them on his belly. His normally pasty complexion had taken on the gray hue of cold oatmeal.

"They almost got me that time, *Comandante,*" he said, gasping for air. "If you hadn't reacted to that pistol shot just before the rifle fired, I'd be a dead man now."

Santos, like Greg, had identified the shots they'd heard as coming from two different weapons—not a difficult distinction to make since a pistol's retort is different from a rifle's. The instructor seemed convinced the rifle bullets were meant for him. But how could that be, Joy wondered, if he were the murderer?

"The shots landed closer to us than you, amigo." Greg replied, rolling to one side. "If we hadn't dropped when we did, one of us would have been hit for sure."

Greg sounded so positive, Joy's skin prickled. What if he hadn't heard the warning pistol shot and knocked her to the ground? Would they both be dead now, victims of a so-called "tragic accident" at a shooting range?

As for Santos, she noted that his face was quickly losing its gray color. "Nobody has any reason to kill you and Captain Joy, *Comandante,*" he said, coughing nervously.

"Why did you think the shots were meant for you, Santos?" Greg asked.

"I was stupid to make such a statement," Santos answered quickly. "It was the gut reaction of a terrified man."

In the distance a car engine turned over. Greg raised himself to squatting position. Shading his face with his hand, he stared down the gravel road that led to the highway.

"A green sedan's leaving in a big hurry, but there's another car parked farther down the road. Let's take a look, Santos. Joy can wait for us in the clubhouse."

"Is that wise, *Comandante?* Maybe the rifleman is still there, waiting in the pines."

Greg stood up. "I'd be willing to bet my good-conduct medal that our sniper hightailed it out of here in the green sedan. If you don't want to come, wait with Joy."

She scrambled to her feet, barely noticing the pain in her right hip where she'd hit the ground. "I'm coming with you, Greg," she said. "Don't try to talk me out of it. You said yourself the sniper was gone."

Thanks to Greg, Joy's shoulder was remarkably free of bruises, but the front of her fancy Texas shirt was torn and dirty, as much of a mess as Santos's hand embroidered one.

He eyed her up and down. "To be on the safe side, why don't you wait in the clubhouse?"

"I'm coming, no matter what." Her tone brooked no argument.

As if on cue, the youthful puller ran toward them, yanking his ear-protectors off as he came.

"Whatsa matter with you folks?" he asked. It was obvious he hadn't seen the bullets hit the dirt near them.

"Somebody was firing at us," Greg said. "From that direction." He motioned down the access road, toward the stand of pines around the cleared field. "If you insist on coming," he said to Joy, "let's check it out."

"I'll go with you," the puller said. He examined Greg through narrowed eyes. "Safety's our motto around here, mister. There's no such thing as someone shooting at somebody at the Salinas Sportsmen's Club."

Greg didn't bother answering. With Joy beside him, he turned and began walking toward the road. The puller, apparently anxious to prove there was no hidden gunman in the pines, jogged ahead of them.

Faced with the prospect of being left behind, Santos followed.

THE CAR parked off the access road in the shadow of the pine trees was a dark blue Chevrolet sedan less than a year old. From its outward appearance, there was nothing to distinguish it from a million other American-made cars.

When Joy peered through the windows, though, she observed that the inside was noticeably tidier than most cars. There were no stickers on the windows, no Garfields clinging to the dashboard or rear window, no debris of any sort on the seats or floors.

Like a car somebody checked out of the motor pool this morning, she thought. *Or a rental car that's just been scrubbed clean for its next customer.*

The doors were unlocked. She watched Greg open the passenger door and then the glove compartment. Like the rest of the interior, it was remarkably tidy, with nothing inside to identify the owner. All it contained were a couple of area maps and a brown paper bag with two peanut-butter sandwiches, a banana and a couple of Diet Pepsis. Whoever had driven the car this morning must have intended to eat his lunch in the vehicle or near it.

"You were right, Greg," she said. "Whoever fired at us wasn't driving this car."

"Why so?"

She pointed to the paper bag. "Would a killer stick around to eat a sack lunch after a murder?"

"Maybe he intended to eat elsewhere after he did it," Santos said.

"Then where is he?" Joy asked.

"Nobody's here," the puller said. "You can see that for yourself."

Joy ignored him. Walking around the car to the front, she jotted its license number on a pad she took out of her shoulder bag. She tore off the sheet of paper and handed it to Greg.

"When you tell the police somebody's been shooting at us, I'm sure they'll identify this car's owner," she said.

"Nothing's happened here, mister," the puller insisted. "There wasn't no shots. Whoever owns this Chevy's around here someplace. You want to know who, leave your number with us and we'll call you soon's he shows up."

"He's got a point," Greg said. "Whoever was driving this car might still be in the vicinity." He examined Joy's face and saw that she was in full control. "It's a good idea for one of us to stick around to be sure we have a chance to talk to them. It's a long shot—this car probably has nothing to do with our sniper—but it's barely possible the driver may have gotten a look at him."

"I'll stay," Joy said quickly. "Maybe a call from a colonel will get the police here quicker than a captain's would."

Greg's protest died in his throat. She was probably right. Besides, she was less exposed down here in the pines than on the open access road to the clubhouse. He turned and began walking up the hill.

Inside the clubhouse, the stringy-haired registrar took one look at Greg's face and put a telephone on top of the counter within easy reach as soon as he asked for it.

Greg made two calls: one to the Salinas Police Department and one to Deputy Sheriff Amanda Hawkins. The sergeant at the Salinas PD promised to send an officer to the Sportsmen's Club to investigate their complaint.

Greg's call to Deputy Hawkins was equally successful. As Joy had predicted, as soon as the deputy found out what had happened, she was more than willing to run a check on the owner of the Chevrolet. She promised to get in touch with him later that day at his quarters.

At almost the same moment, Greg heard Joy scream. It was a piercing, primordial scream that sliced through the dry air like a machete through a ripe pineapple.

His heart stopped beating when he heard it.

JOY STARED at what she'd tripped over. The blood-spattered body lay face down in the weeds. Dressed in dark blue slacks and a matching long-sleeved shirt, it was virtually invisible in the undergrowth.

The scream that rose in her throat was instinctive, the startled release of three days of pent-up anger, and guilt, and just plain horror. She didn't realize she'd made a sound until the young puller ran up to her, glimpsed the corpse, and turned away, violently ill.

Santos had a stronger stomach. Arriving at her side a few seconds later, he took a spotless white linen handkerchief from the rear pocket of his custom-made blue jeans and wiped his perspiring forehead.

"So we have found our guardian angel," he said softly, pointing toward the ground.

Her mind reeling, Joy followed his finger. Still clutched in the corpse's hand was a snub-nosed revolver. It must have fired the single pistol shot they'd heard a heartbeat before the rifle bullets. It was the warning shot that might have saved their lives.

Who was he and why had he fired the shot? Who had killed him? Why was he lying here now, dead?

She heard shouts behind her and swung around to see Greg crashing through the underbrush like a charging rhinoceros.

"What's going on?" he thundered.

Joy hardly recognized him. In place of his usual cynical expression was a look close to panic.

He grabbed her as though she were being swallowed by quicksand and held her tight against him. "Thank God you're all right! Thank God!" he muttered.

She could feel his heart beating, could smell the warm man's smell of him through his damp shirt. He'd obviously run all the way from the clubhouse. Had her scream inspired such an instantaneous reaction from this cool jungle fighter with nerves of steel? It hardly seemed possible.

"I should never have left you down here alone," he said, hugging her again and pressing his cheek against the top of her head.

"She was hardly alone," Santos said.

At hearing the instructor's voice, Greg released Joy quickly, embarrassed by his show of emotion.

"Why the screaming?" he asked and, in the next instant, took in the small tableau before him: the corpse with the pistol in its hand; the young puller, still retching a few feet away.

"I see you found the Chevy's driver," he said.

SANTOS WAS in remarkably high spirits as he drove them west toward Monterey through the ragged hills. A misty green in February, the hills divided the coast of central California from its interior.

Joy noticed that the oatmealish tone of Santo's complexion began disappearing as soon as Greg suggested that the shots weren't meant for him. His usual pasty color had reestablished itself during their hour at the Salinas police station. It was clear to her that the instructor's fear for his life had diminished significantly with the discovery of their "guardian angel," as Santos had called him. *Why?* Joy wondered.

What did Santos know or suspect about the dead man that had so relieved his mind? Whatever it was, he hadn't let the authorities in on his suspicions during their hour-long debriefing session at the Salinas Police Station. After each of them had told his own version of what happened, they were permitted to leave. Unfortunately, there was no identification on the body, so they were unable to learn anything about him.

"We'll find out who he is in short order," one of the police officers told Joy confidentially as they were leaving the station. "This whole thing smells like another fight over drugs. Too bad you people got caught in the middle. Just watch the news tonight on TV and you'll probably get the whole story." Joy made a mental note to do just that.

"So, *Comandante*," Santos said over his shoulder to Greg in the backseat of the station wagon. "All's well that ends well, eh?"

Greg grunted. "Until I get that sniper, nothing's ended, amigo."

Joy half turned so she could see Greg's face. "Do you think the sniper shot the man with the pistol?"

Greg nodded. "Nothing else makes any sense. The way I see it, our unknown friend spotted the sniper taking aim in our direction. He managed to get one shot off that warned us and probably upset the sniper's aim—and got himself killed for his trouble."

"Our friend probably got a good look at the sniper," Joy said. "I wonder what he was doing there."

"We'll know more about that when we find out who he is," Greg said. "Maybe he was simply an innocent bystander who interrupted a shooting. There's sure no doubt what the sniper was doing there. He was gunning for one or both of us. Period."

Joy's flesh crawled. It was the subject she'd been avoiding. When Greg said it out loud, she knew she had to face it.

"Do you honestly think he was trying to kill us?" she asked, her voice trembling. As long as she lived, any sharp noise sounding like the crack of a rifle, would turn her blood to ice.

Greg leaned forward and put a hand on her shoulder. "That's the way I see it. We'll have to be damned careful from now on."

Santos glanced over his shoulder. Joy caught the alert questioning look in his faded blue eyes.

Greg did, too. "I've had a colorful career, as you know," he told the instructor. "It seems I've made an enemy who wants to get even."

Joy knew he was diverting Santos's attention from the most likely reason for the attempt on their lives: their investigation into the two drownings. They were getting too close for somebody's comfort. But how could anybody know what they had found out? Joy asked herself, fear knotting her stomach.

To get her mind off her vivid memories of the bloody corpse, she forced herself to concentrate on the purpose of this trip. They were supposed to be finding out how much Santos knew about Maria Cardoza's job as a gossip columnist and why he'd asked for Airman Tuck to be assigned to his class after she died.

"Did you see that awful article about me in Thursday's paper, Santos?" she asked, to get the conversation started.

He turned toward her, his eyes narrowed. "Everybody saw that article, Captain. Its message came through loud and clear."

In the backseat, Greg leaned forward. "Of course you know it was a complete fabrication."

"That's what I heard, *Comandante*." Santos wasn't smiling. His facade of bubbly good spirits had vanished. To Joy he looked mad, mad and dangerous. Why had mention of the article inspired such a change in his attitude?

"What do you mean 'the message came through loud and clear'?" she asked. "What message?"

He turned toward her, his bleached-blue eyes staring at her through tiny slits. "No one could miss the message in a headline that big," he said.

He hadn't answered her question, but Joy wanted to talk about him not her so she dropped it. "The article made me curious about the Eye columns. I asked a few questions, and somebody told me Maria Cardoza wrote them."

"I'm sure she did."

It was another of Santos Mueller's heart-stopping pronouncements.

For half a second after he spoke, there was complete silence. Greg found his voice first. "My God, man. Did everybody but me know that woman wrote a gossip column?"

Santos shrugged. "I knew and I'm sure there were others, but we didn't talk about it in the department."

Joy reached in her handbag and pulled out the copy of the Eye column that she'd taken from the library last night. "When I was looking through some of her columns, I found one about you, Santos. It was written only a few days before she died."

"Ah, yes, the refugee item." He snorted, obviously disgusted.

Joy watched him closely and could spot no other physical reaction. "Was it as full of lies as the one about me?"

He kept his eyes trained on the road. "Exaggerations, yes. Lies, no. The information was old—something I did years ago—and the article made a big thing about my few little errands."

"But essentially, it's true?"

He didn't turn toward her. "You could say that."

They reached Greg's quarters a few minutes later. Santos left the motor running when he got out to hand Greg his shotguns from the back of the station wagon.

"Sure you won't come inside for some chow, amigo?" Greg asked. He'd issued the invitation the first time as they entered the Presidio's Lighthouse Avenue entrance, and Santos had been quick to refuse.

"My houseboy makes great steak sandwiches. When you eat as early in the morning as I do, you're hungry again by eleven hundred hours."

"Not today, *Comandante*. I've got some things to attend to. Next time I'll take you up on it."

When the station wagon swung around the corner at the bottom of the hill, Greg turned to Joy. She was standing next to him, holding one of the shotguns zipped up in its case. "Come inside. We need to talk."

He saw her quick glance at her dirty shirt. The pocket on the left side was half ripped off and hanging loose. The thought of possible bruises to the tender flesh beneath made Greg clench his fists. Somebody was going to pay for what had happened this morning if it was the last thing he did on this earth.

"I'm not in very good shape," she said. "I should go home and get cleaned up before we check out the Iberian Market this afternoon."

"Not before we talk," he insisted. "You can use the guest bathroom in my quarters to wash up."

She handed the shotgun to him. He could see that she was about to start for her car.

"Somebody tried to kill us this morning. It's urgent that we compare notes before you leave here, Joy."

He hated to bring the shooting up again. In the car, he'd seen how much it bothered her. Hell, being the target of an unknown killer would bother anybody. It did him. But he had to talk to her.

The blood drained from her face. He wanted to reach out and hold her, to reassure her with his touch. But he couldn't, not in front of his quarters on the post.

"Before we go to the market this afternoon, we need to talk about Santos," he urged. "I thought he acted guilty as hell."

That convinced her. Without further argument she went to the house with him.

"I thought so, too," she said, when they were inside.

"We'll talk about him later, after we've cleaned up."

A short Oriental man came down the hallway to meet them. His muscles bulged beneath his uniform, a white shirt that fell below his hips and dark, pajamalike trousers.

"Joy, this is Phong, my houseman," Greg said. "He's been with me for more than ten years now."

When Greg announced his guest would be staying for lunch, Phong grinned from ear to ear. He bowed deeply to Joy, and then hurried toward the kitchen at the back of the house.

"I don't have many lady guests," Greg explained, unexpectedly flustered by his employee's enthusiastic greeting. "Living next to my own headquarters has its disadvantages."

"It must be terrible," Joy said. "Like living in a glass house. You've got no privacy at all."

"I haven't especially missed it," he said. Not until now, he added to himself. Until now he'd been more than content to find his privacy elsewhere. Joy Donnelly was different from the other women he'd known. He wanted her to see where and how he lived.

He examined her face. There was a raw place on her cheek he hadn't noticed under its layer of dirt. He put his hand under her chin and twisted her head toward the light from the living room to see it better.

"You've skinned yourself," he said. "You'd better wash up so it doesn't get infected. The bathroom's to your right at the top of the stairs. Use the tub if you want and take as long as you like. If you need anything, poke around in the cabinet, and if you still can't find it, yell and Phong will be up to help."

Joy took Greg at his word and luxuriated in the old-fashioned claw-footed tub for a good half hour, letting the dirt in her pores dissolve in the warm water along with her aches and pains.

The bathroom smelled faintly of paint, an omnipresent odor in the bathrooms of old military houses, which are coated with hard, shiny oil-based enamel every few years.

Even though a new washbasin and countertop had been installed, there was no disguising the place's ancient origins.

She washed her hair in the sink and dried it with a man's hair dryer she found in a linen closet at the foot of the tub. Then she rummaged through the drawers hunting for antiseptic and finally found a bottle of peroxide near the back of the bottom drawer. She soaked a Kleenex with the sizzling liquid, wincing at its sting when she patted it on her face.

By the time she'd reapplied her makeup and dressed, it was close to noon, and the houseboy had two places set at the end of the big wood table in the dining room. Bright with hazy sunlight now that the fog had lifted, the room seemed to sparkle in spite of its austere straight-backed chairs and drab pottery dinnerware.

As Greg pulled out a chair for her, she realized she was famished.

"Thank goodness you talked me into this," she said, taking a generous helping from the big bowl of salad he placed before her. "I'm absolutely starving."

When she passed the bowl to him, she caught him staring at her as though he'd never seen her before.

"It's very likely that somebody tried to kill you this morning," he said, "and you don't seem at all bothered."

"As soon as I walk out of here, I'll be scared to death," she admitted. "But nobody's going to try anything here in your house, and I've got no intention of letting something that might happen tomorrow spoil my appetite today." To prove her point she took a big bite of salad.

He nodded with approval. "Most people can't help worrying."

"Worrying isn't practical." She reached for more salad.

His expression of approval turned vaguely troubled. "Practical as in wanting to be a general? You're on track now that you've made major below the zone. Keep in touch with the right people, and you just might make it."

Joy put down her fork. "You must know me well enough by now to realize I'd never fawn on anybody for anything under any circumstances."

"That's not what I meant," he protested, as Phong served them steak sandwiches hot off the charcoal broiler.

Joy leaned back in her chair and folded her arms across her chest. "You're right. That's not what you meant." Her voice was deceptively soft. "What you meant was that I'd never amount to anything without help."

Greg stopped eating, too. "That's not what I meant either, but you've got to admit it doesn't hurt to have a friend or two in high places."

She took a deep breath to hide her pain. Of all the officers in the military service, why did she have to fall for one who so consistently underrated her? "So you are saying that I need help to get along in the military service, that I'd never have been selected for major below the promotion zone if somebody hadn't given me a shove in the right direction."

From his expression, she could tell that he was about to deny it. Incredibly, he seemed unaware of what he was doing. Before he could say anything, she plunged on.

"You know, Greg, right from the very first you've undervalued me. You've consistently..."

"Undervalued you! You don't know what you're saying, Joy." His shock showed in his voice.

"Yes, I do. You may not even be aware of it, but you're constantly underrating my capabilities. You don't think I can do anything right. From the way I handle my squadron, to the way I manage my career, to the way I deal with the press, you're continually undervaluing my judgment and ability."

He pulled his chair closer to hers. "But I value you, Joy. I care about what happens to you. Doesn't that count for anything? Why do you think I had those locks put on your house? Why do you think I've spent so much time with you the past few days?"

Joy swallowed hard to keep her voice from quivering. He looked so earnest, leaning toward her with his eye patch a little crooked, that she felt like swatting him. Couldn't he see what he was doing to her?

"You value me because I'm one of your troops, Greg. There's a big difference between that and valuing me as a capable individual you care about personally. The reason you're spending so much time with me is that our lives may depend on finding out what's going on."

He leaned toward her and took her hands in his strong fingers. A current of raw tension arced between them.

"I never meant to undervalue you in any way, Joy. If that's what you think I'm doing, I'm sorry. You've become much more important to me than one of my troops." His voice was husky. "If you can't see that, maybe it's because you don't want to."

Joy didn't want him to notice how confused she was by his admission. Could he be right about her? Could she be as blind about him as he was about her? Slowly she withdrew her hands and picked up her fork. "The only thing I can see right now is that our food is getting cold. I shouldn't have brought this up at the dinner table, Greg. I'm sorry."

"We needed to clear the air," he responded softly. But Joy noticed that his face didn't lose its troubled expression, even after they'd finished their sandwiches, and Phong had served coffee and lemon meringue pie.

Chapter Thirteen

"Amanda Hawkins has had plenty of time to find out who owns that car, Greg," Joy said, taking a bite of pie. "Since she hasn't called us, I think we should put some pressure on her."

When Greg saw Joy's enthusiasm, he felt his spirits lifting. "The deputy's not going to tell us anything until she's good and ready, but if you think you can get something out of her, be my guest."

"Where's the phone?" Joy asked, glancing around the room.

"Aren't you going to finish your pie?" He pushed his chair away from the table.

"It'll still be here when I get back." She followed him through the living room, past the staircase, to the den.

Unlike the almost cell-like spareness of the rest of the house, this room had a lived-in, comfortable warmth to it. On the walls were black-and-white photographs of soldiers in uniform. Covering part of the floor was a brightly colored rug that Joy recognized as handmade by native Americans. A bookcase crammed full of books lined one wall. The faint smell of old leather mingled pleasantly with the almost imperceptible aroma of pipe tobacco. She'd never seen Greg smoke, but perhaps he had, sometime in the past.

The phone was on the big desk in one corner.

He motioned for her to sit down in the high-backed executive chair behind the desk and then settled himself in the leather recliner opposite the sofa.

"Deputy Hawkins here," a familiar voice said curtly after Joy had dialed the number.

"This is Joy Donnelly, Amanda." Joy could feel her heart thudding and concentrated on keeping her voice steady.

"Colonel Weston and I are still pretty shook up over what happened this morning. We were wondering if you've been able to find out who owns that car?"

"I thought the colonel said shots were fired at you people?" Amanda answered.

"That's right." Joy wondered why the deputy sheriff sounded skeptical. "If we hadn't dropped to the ground when we did, we'd have been hit. The bullets were inches from our heads."

There was a moment of silence. Joy could hear Amanda Hawkins breathing.

"Are you sure about that, Joy?" she asked softly. "Our people in Salinas tell me the incident was part of an ongoing government operation against drug dealers. It had nothing to do with you or Colonel Weston or the man who was with you. If some of the shots impacted near you, it was just a coincidence."

Joy couldn't believe what she was hearing. "Are you telling me it was just a coincidence that we were nearly killed this morning?" She heard her voice rising and was powerless to control it. "This sounds like some kind of runaround to me, Amanda."

Across from her, Greg lurched out of his recliner.

"It's no runaround," Amanda Hawkins said. "Listen to your evening news tonight, and you'll hear all about it."

This can't be true, Joy felt like screaming into the telephone receiver. *You're lying again.* She lowered her voice with an effort. "You still haven't told me who owns the car."

Greg had come around the desk and was kneeling next to her, his head close to hers. She held the receiver out, so he could hear Amanda's response.

"I just did, Joy. You weren't listening." The words came out slowly, as though the woman were forcing herself to say them. "The government owned that Chevrolet. The dead man was a government agent involved in the antidrug operation."

Joy looked at Greg's face, only inches from hers, to be sure he'd heard. It reflected the same confusion she was feeling.

Why had the authorities made up a cover story about a drug operation? And how did a government agent get mixed up in this?

"Did you hear me, Joy?" There was an odd urgency in Amanda's query.

Joy cleared her throat. "I heard you, Amanda."

"Let me know if I can be of further assistance."

Joy thanked her. As she hung up the phone, she got the weird feeling that her world was slowly slipping sideways, off its axis. Judging from Greg's expression, he felt the same way.

"Judas Priest!" he said, returning to his recliner. "It's obvious when somebody's shooting at you. I know it. She knows it. A killer's gunning for us, and the police are covering up. They seem to want us to stay fat, dumb and happy, like lambs being led to the slaughterhouse."

"Do you suppose the government agent was keeping an eye on us on purpose?" Joy's puzzlement showed on her face.

"You mean to protect us from whoever killed Airman Tuck and Maria Cardoza?"

She nodded.

He considered her notion for a couple of seconds. "Not possible, Joy. Even if the authorities acknowledge a killer's running loose around here, they have no way of knowing who his targets are. Besides, Washington doesn't get called in on local murder cases."

"By firing a warning shot, that agent may have saved our lives, Greg," she persisted, not wanting to let the idea go. "Santos knew it right away. You should have seen the relief on his face when he saw the pistol. Maybe that agent wasn't protecting us, but Santos sure thought he was."

Greg's brow furrowed. "Maybe Santos knows something we don't. Let's go to the living room and see if we can figure out what it is while we're finishing our pie and coffee."

When they were settled on the western-style sofa, Joy let herself dwell on the scene she'd been trying to forget. In her mind she saw the corpse dressed in dark clothing, bloodied, with a pistol in its hand; the anonymous car that looked as if it came from a motor pool. Her pie, placed on the coffee table by Phong, no longer looked good to her.

"Do you suppose Santos recognized the man was a government agent?" she asked, unconsciously moving closer to Greg.

"He just might have." Greg's answer was slow, thoughtful. He was having difficulty keeping his mind on the subject with Joy so close to him. "All the indicators were there: the car, clothes, weapon. If Santos had some reason to think the Feds were in the vicinity, there's no doubt of it." He wanted to reach out and touch her.

"But why would he think that?"

Close up, when she leaned toward him, Greg could see that the scrape on her cheek was worse than he'd thought. It had to be painful.

Looking at it, his throat got tight and thick-feeling. He reached out and cupped her face in his hands. Her skin felt warm to his fingers, soft and warm. She didn't back away from him.

"We're going to know a lot more about Santos Mueller and his family later this afternoon after I talk to my source in Paraguay." His voice had gotten huskier. He stared at the raw place on her cheek. "Until then, your guess is as good as mine."

Noticing his stare, she smiled. "That little scrape doesn't amount to anything." When Greg touched her cheek with one finger, she didn't flinch.

"Does it hurt?"

"A little. I'll live." Her voice sounded husky, like his. In spite of her efforts to control it, her breath was coming in short, quick gasps.

"I don't want to hurt you," he murmured. His face was only inches from hers.

"You could never hurt me, Greg," she said, suddenly aware that it was so. Closing her eyes, she waited breathlessly for what she knew was coming.

With his hands still cradling her face, he kissed her, his lips exploring hers with the gentle reverence of new discovery. He sensed her trust. It made this afternoon totally different from last Thursday night. Through a veil of tenderness, he felt a strange sense of pride that she was here in his quarters with him, sharing the essence of what he was.

Resisting the pressure building inside him, he forced himself to savor the sweet taste of her mouth slowly, without hurrying.

The tension inside him mounted. Wrapping both arms around her, he moved her backward, his mouth harder now, his tongue probing. Joy didn't resist, not even when she was on her back on the sofa, and he was bending over her, almost on top of her. Suddenly a vivid picture of leaning over her to protect her from the rifle bullets flashed across the screen of his mind.

My God! Joy Donnelly is the most loyal woman you've ever known. This morning you saved her life. Now that she trusts you, you're on the verge of taking advantage of her. What kind of a man are you?

Pulling himself away from her, Greg sat up and took her hands in his. He struggled to get control of himself before it was too late.

"Oh, Joy." He whispered the words hoarsely, hardly able to talk. "If we don't stop right now, I won't be able to."

She sat up, her eyes slumberous with desire. "Do you want to stop?" she asked, her voice trembling.

"My God, no!" he growled, his voice still thick. "I want you the way I've never wanted any woman in my whole life."

She shook her head, dumbfounded, yet thrilled by his confession.

"I want you, too, Greg." Her body ached for his warmth and the hardness of his chest against her. "More than anybody I've ever known."

Gently Greg squeezed her hands. "I know. That's what makes it so tough." He saw the desire in her eyes, and it was all he could do to keep from clutching her to him and finishing what he'd started. What the hell was happening to him? Why didn't he take her right now and make them both happy?

"If we'd gone ahead I'd have been using you." Greg stared straight into her clear green eyes. "You're too good for that, Joy Donnelly."

Joy gazed back, her heart jumping at his words. He really cared, and oh, how she wanted him to.

"Why not let me judge whether or not I'm getting used?" Her voice was low but brimming with certainty.

Her trust in him was so sincere it hurt him to witness it. "There's something you don't know, Joy," Greg said. "I've been doing my damndest to get reassigned from this mothball job. I could get orders any day now."

He couldn't bear to see the glazed brightness in her eyes or hear her quick gasp. Could he be wrong about her career being all-important to her? Suddenly it became vitally important that she know his thoughts about intimate relationships.

"Regardless of whether I stay or go, I'm not a man who can be tied to a woman's apron strings. With me, the service has got to come first." He stared at her, hoping for some sign her career goals weren't as important to her as he'd thought. His heart sank when he saw her eyes narrow.

"I know that, Greg." There was resignation in her voice. "Since you're Army and I'm Air Force there's not much chance we could both arrange good assignments in the same area."

By "good assignments," he knew she meant jobs that would advance their careers. He stood and crossed to the window to regain his composure. "So that's it, then," he said, his back to her. "We'll take each day as it comes."

He heard her follow him to the window.

"Now is the important time, Greg," she said softly. "Tomorrow can take care of itself." They were brave words, designed to lighten their mood, but Joy knew in her heart that she didn't believe what she was saying. Without the hope of shared tomorrows, today lost something of its fullness.

Reaching up, she brushed her lips against his smooth cheek and realized he'd shaved—and probably showered—while she was in the guest bathroom. He was still wearing the same plaid shirt and jeans from this morning, probably to keep her dirty clothes company. The small gesture was another indication of the sensitivity hidden under his tough, jungle-fighter's hide.

"It's about time for me to get home and into something clean before we check out the Iberian Market," she said, turning toward the door.

He moved alongside her. "I'll follow you. Make sure everything's okay at your place."

"What about your phone calls?" She struggled to control her rebellious emotions. "They're important. Shouldn't you stay here and wait for them?"

"If I'm not here, they'll call back," he said. "You're the Number One priority around here right now. I almost lost you this morning. I'm not about to let that happen again."

She returned to the sofa. "Since you want to get rid of me, I've decided not to go." She grinned at him and was relieved to see a trace of a smile on his face. She patted the sofa beside her. "Sit down and tell me about these two sources of yours and what you hope to find out from them."

The first phone call came before Greg had finished. She went with him to the den.

He was frowning when he hung up the receiver. "That was Manuel Garcia in Paraguay," he said, getting up from the edge of his desk where he'd been sitting. "It seems Santos's family has no political connections."

Her face fell. "Then that couldn't be what Maria was holding over him."

"No, but there may be something else. Garcia claims the Mueller family was part of a small middle class until a couple of years ago when they acquired an estate and raised their standard of living significantly. The locals think they're involved in the drug business. It's just a guess, of course, but Santos could be sending them money. Their good fortune coincides with his arrival in this country."

Joy took a deep breath. "Drugs again. Maybe Santos *is* involved in drugs. Maybe Maria Cardoza found out what he was doing and was blackmailing him and that's why he killed her. If he's importing drugs, it's logical for our government to be trying to catch him. Maybe that agent *was* involved in an antidrug operation, just the way Amanda says."

He shook his head. "I can't buy it, Joy. You're not involved in drugs. Neither am I. There's no reason for drug dealers to be gunning for us. But somebody tried to kill us this morning. I'd stake my life on it."

Obviously frustrated, Greg stood up and paced back and forth a couple of times before sitting down behind his desk. "Another thing—if the government knows Santos is bringing drugs into the country, why haven't they arrested him? From what you told me about his reaction to finding that agent's body, it sounded like he thought the agent had been protecting him rather than trying to arrest him."

Joy shrugged. "Maybe Santos thought wrong. No matter what the agent was doing, you've got to admit Santos Mueller is a suspicious character."

Greg leaned back, his expression thoughtful. "He sure acted afraid of somebody when he insisted those shots were meant for him. And now we learn his family's come into sudden wealth. I think it's time for a little eyeball-to-eyeball chat with my old *amigo.*"

Joy couldn't believe she'd heard him right. "He'll never tell you the truth, Greg. If you confront him, you'll scare him off. He'll be out of the Peninsula faster than a jackrabbit with a coyote on his tail."

"You really think he'd take off?"

"Sure. If he's guilty. He's probably renting. All he'll have to do is pack a suitcase and he's on his way."

"I'm not saying I think he's our killer, Joy. I'm just saying he's got some explaining to do."

The phone rang again before Joy could protest further.

"If it's my man in Spain, this may take awhile," Greg said. Picking up the receiver, he settled himself in the chair behind his desk.

From the snatches of conversation Joy heard, she realized that the families of the two instructors from Zaragoza were close to Julio Ramon's and that all three had been identified with the Fascist movement in Spain before their moves to the United States. Since security clearances weren't required for instructors at the language school, no background investigations had been done on the three men.

There was a grim look on Greg's face when he'd finished talking. "Did you get the gist of what he said?"

Joy nodded. "If they kept their Fascist connections in this country, and Maria Cardoza found out about it, they would have wanted to keep her quiet."

Greg leaned back. "It depends on how involved they were in the movement. One thing for sure—if they *were* involved, it would be worth something to them to keep her from writing about their activities."

"Do you suppose that's what Julio was looking for at her house? Pictures of him at a white supremacist gathering or something of the sort?" Joy wracked her brain searching for a connection between what they'd just found out and what they already knew about the Spanish Department head.

"Probably." Greg's brow was as furrowed as Joy's. "But it's not likely she kept anything like that. She didn't need to. Just the threat of exposure in her column was probably enough to get him to cough up."

"Maria Cardoza didn't even keep copies of her column at the house, Greg." Joy visualized the woman's den with its writer's library and word-processing equipment. "Judging from what the city editor told us, she wrote them there, though, and used a modem to send them to her editor."

Joy sat quietly, concentrating on the picture in her mind. Suddenly she leaped to her feet. "I know how that article about me got to that editor's computer, Greg."

He leaned toward her, his face animated. "Shoot."

With a broad smile, she sat down down on the corner of his desk. "You said Julio Ramon was a computer nut, right? When he searched Maria Cardoza's den, he found the article in her computer. He's the one who sent it to the *Tribune*. She must have written the item the night she died. Maybe she'd even left the machine turned on so he spotted it as soon as he came in the room."

"Hold on," Greg cautioned. "Assuming you're right, why was Julio so interested in seeing the article published?"

"To deflect attention from himself, of course." Joy slid off the desk and started toward the door, suddenly eager to investigate the Iberian Market where Santos Mueller worked as a "favor to friends."

"Not good enough." Greg came around his desk. "The police probably went through Maria's computer files. The column didn't have to be published to deflect attention from Julio."

"Then he had another reason. Maybe it had something to do with why she wrote the column in the first place. I still haven't figured that out. But one thing I'm sure of, is that he's the one who sent that article to her editor."

She headed toward her Firebird, parked at the curb outside, with the satisfying feeling that they were finally getting somewhere.

THE IBERIAN MARKET was located on a wide street in an old residential neighborhood with a mix of modest wooden and stucco houses around it. Vans and campers were in some of the yards, and there were cars parked along the curbs.

As they drove up, the market looked closed. They spotted a sign in the window, but the ink was so faint they couldn't read it from the car. At Greg's suggestion, Joy parked the Firebird halfway down the newly blacktopped parking area running the length of the building so they'd get a feel for the store's size. A one-lane driveway with a four-foot-high stucco wall on its far side ran from the street at the store's front to the one behind it.

Leaving the car, they went to take a closer look at the sign. CLOSED FOR WEDDING. OPEN TOMORROW AT NOON, read the hand-printed words. From the look of it, the sign had been used before. In addition to the fading ink, the corners of the cardboard were curling. Apparently a fictitious wedding was a handy excuse for closing the store.

"We'll have to come back tomorrow," Joy said. "But as long as we're here, we might as well take a look around."

With the approach of evening, the fog had drifted in from the ocean, and the streetlights blinked on in response to the gathering darkness. Standing on the sidewalk in front of the store, they peered through its slanting front windows into the interior. Some of the lights had been left on inside. They could see rows of shelves stocked with packaged foods. There were narrow aisles and what seemed to be a butcher counter at the rear.

Joy shaded her eyes with her hand to see better. "There's a meat locker in back," she said. "And swinging doors next to it. There must be an office and storage rooms back there somewhere. Too bad we can't get in and rummage around."

He put a hand on her arm. "See that mirror they use to spot shoplifters? It's on the far side of the store, opposite the cash register. When cars swing around the corner to our left, you can see them in the mirror."

Joy's heart stopped beating. She could tell by his voice that he'd seen something frightening. "Is it the green sedan?"

"I can't tell, but don't turn around," he warned. "There's not much traffic on this street. The same green car turned that corner twice."

"Then he's following us," she said, hardly breathing. "Greg, he's going to try again."

He put his arm around her waist and moved behind her, shielding her from the street. "He's not going to shoot us, or he'd have fired already. Let's turn slowly and head for your car."

They paused at the corner of the building. The Firebird looked a million miles away. Parking halfway down the long lot had seemed like a good idea at the time. What a big mistake that had been.

For a long minute they examined the street. The green sedan was nowhere in sight.

"Run!" Greg commanded, grabbing her hand to be sure he didn't outdistance her. The quicker they got out of this parking area, the better.

Slowed by the heavy boots they'd worn for the morning's skeet shooting, they were only three-quarters of the way to the Firebird when a car turned into the empty parking area and doused its headlights.

Without looking, Joy knew the green sedan was behind them. She felt Greg yanking her hand.

"Hang on," he yelled across his shoulder.

Joy's stylish cowboy boots seemed to weigh at least a ton, but the clatter her steps made on the blacktop wasn't enough to drown out the roar of the monster engine coming at them from behind. She couldn't breathe, couldn't see clearly—could only hear the roaring behind her and Greg's voice yelling "Faster!"

They reached the sanctuary of the Firebird. Joy's knees trembled. Now that they'd made it, she wasn't sure she could stand up long enough to crawl inside.

"Don't get in," Greg yelled again. He jerked her hand. "Run, Joy, run!"

From behind them came the whining screech of braked tires on the blacktop. Greg pulled Joy with him around the Firebird. A heartbeat later, she heard the explosive crash of metal on metal and the sickening rasp of breaking glass. The green sedan had rammed the side of her car where they'd been standing a second before.

Still holding her hand, Greg took off toward the back of the building. Joy's rubbery legs responded with a new burst of energy. Her feet hit the blacktop like lumps of clay, but she kept running. The effort consumed every shred of feeling until she was conscious of nothing but Greg's tight hold on her hand, of his big body beside her, so close he was almost touching her.

"Keep running," he yelled. They'd reached the back of the building, were heading for the street beyond. Across from them, a porch light flicked on.

Behind, there was the scream of tires burning rubber.

They reached the street behind the store. Across from them, an elderly man came out on his porch. Still running, they crossed toward him.

The roaring engine behind them shifted out of reverse. The car's tires screeched again as it started down the street in front of the store. Then the sound of its motor became fainter. In a few seconds, it had disappeared.

Chapter Fourteen

The Firebird's left side was caved in and its front wheel twisted. They arranged for it to be towed to the local Pontiac body shop. After filing the required report with the police, they called a taxi.

In the back of the cab, Greg put his arm around Joy's shoulder and hugged her close. He felt a sensual tug at her nearness and suppressed it with a conscious effort. This was a time for comfort, not passion.

"Do you think the police will be able to find out who owns that green car from the license number you gave them?" she asked.

He shook his head. "Probably not, even if I got it right reading it backwards in the market's mirror. I imagine the car was stolen. As soon as we get to your place, I'll call the deputy. Since she's got a personal interest in us, maybe she'll be more motivated than the Monterey police to do a fast job tracing the number." He kept his arm around Joy's shoulder.

"It won't hurt to let her know what happened, either," Joy said. "It might convince her that somebody's trying to kill us."

"I'm betting she's already convinced," Greg muttered. "She's just not admitting it. The question is why."

"That seems pretty obvious, now that we know a federal agent's involved," Joy declared. "Much as I hate to say it, it looks to me like Big Brother's ordered her to keep the lid on. I thought the U.S. Government was supposed to protect its citizens, not deliberately expose them to attacks by murderous criminals.''

It was a provocative idea. Greg was on the verge of answering when he glanced up and caught the brown eyes of the taxi driver watching them intently in the rearview mirror. Who was he?

All Greg's alarm systems flashed red. Until they knew what was going on here, they'd have to watch every word they said, every step they took.

He hugged Joy's shoulder again. ''We'll talk about it at your place,'' he said, pointing an index finger toward the back of the driver, who was now concentrating intently on the traffic on Lighthouse Avenue.

With a subtle nod of her head, Joy changed the subject.

THEY HAD THE HOUSE to themselves that evening. As usual, Donna was out.

Joy offered to warm up some frozen Mexican dinners in the microwave and Greg took her up on her offer with considerably more enthusiasm for her company than for the proposed bill of fare.

''Do you honestly think the cabdriver was spying on us, Greg?'' Joy asked, leading the way to the kitchen. If their situation hadn't been so deadly serious, she would have laughed at the notion.

''He was listening, no doubt about that. Whether he's got some connection to this mess is something else again. Maybe he was just being nosy, but that notion you had about the government being involved set me to thinking.''

Joy took their dinners out of the freezer while Greg set the table. Then she began slicing lettuce and carrots for the salad.

''If Washington wants the investigation hushed up, that's sure a good reason for the local authorities to keep this whole thing under wraps,'' Greg went on. ''There's been almost nothing in the news about Airman Tuck's and Maria Cardoza's deaths.''

Joy put down her vegetable peeler. "That reminds me..." She headed for the living room. "There should be something on the TV about the shooting. Let's see what the police told our friendly neighborhood reporters about the man who got shot."

A few minutes later, disappointed, they returned to the kitchen.

"At least we know Amanda gave us the approved party line," Joy said. Bending over the sink, she resumed her salad preparations. "The police in Salinas told the press exactly what she told us—that the agent was killed in an antidrug operation."

"They didn't even mention us," Greg said. "Only that some people shooting skeet at the Sportsmen's Club found the body."

"Did you expect them to?" Joy didn't try to keep the bitterness from her voice. "As soon as the police admit we were the intended victims they shoot down their drug story. I wonder how they're going to blame what happened to us this afternoon on drugs? Any fool can see whoever was driving that car meant to kill us."

"They'll say it was an accident," Greg predicted grimly. "That the driver was under the influence." He scowled at the thought.

Joy agreed. Going to the telephone on the wall near the table, she handed him the receiver. "Weren't you going to call Amanda?" she said. "I want to hear her tell you it was an accident."

Greg dialed. Deputy Sheriff Hawkins answered on the sixth ring.

Yes, she'd already heard what happened and was glad they hadn't been hurt. Yes, she knew the car's license number had been reported to the Monterey police. It was being traced.

"One thing I can tell you right now, Colonel. It was a rented car."

"A rented car!" Greg couldn't believe their good fortune. He gave Joy the A-okay sign, a circle formed with his curved thumb and forefinger, as he spoke into the phone. "Then you should have no trouble finding out who rented it."

"The home address and driver's license he used were phony, but there are other ways to trace him."

"Explain, please." Greg's brows drew together.

"He was an odd-looking little man," the deputy sheriff went on. "The clerk who rented him the car remembers him. A police artist is drawing his picture from her recollection. There's also a chance there might be fingerprints on the paperwork."

Greg felt like shouting with relief. Instead, he grinned at Joy who was standing at his elbow, listening, while he held the receiver away from his head.

"Then you're sure to get him, Deputy."

"Not for a while," she said. "The people in Monterey think the whole thing was accidental—that the driver was drunk or drugged. They want to locate him, of course—so does the company who rented that car to him—but it may take time. The investigation doesn't have a high priority since only property damage was involved, and nobody was hurt."

"Of course," Greg's voice was full of sarcasm. "Another accident." He clenched his fist and pounded it on his desk. "Could you keep me informed, please, Deputy? Accident or not, I'd like to know who was driving that car as soon as you have his name."

"Be glad to, Colonel."

After he'd hung up, Greg turned to Joy. "Well, I'm sure you heard what she said about the so-called accident. What the hell's going on around here, anyhow?"

Joy was so excited she was pacing up and down. "I also gathered they've probably got enough evidence to trace the driver. So he's an odd-looking little man, is he? He's behind all this evil business, Greg, I just know he is. Once we find out who he is, we'll have our answers."

"A lot can happen between now and the time it takes to run an investigation like that," he cautioned, well aware that they weren't home free yet. Watching her green eyes sparkle, he couldn't bear the thought that somebody was trying to snuff out that blazing spirit.

"We can't afford to sit here like rabbits waiting for a fox, while the authorities pursue their 'low priority investigation'," he said. "Tonight after I leave you're going to lock this house up tighter than Fort Knox, and you're not going to open the door for anybody."

Joy felt an unexpected warmth at the intensity of his words. "What about Donna?" she asked quietly, lowering her eyes to hide her feelings. "She does live here, you know."

"She won't be home tonight."

"You sound awfully sure of that."

Greg took her to the table and sat her down on one of the chairs. Then he seated himself opposite her. "I'm sure because I know she's staying with her elderly father tonight. He can't be left alone."

"You can't be serious!" Joy was so shocked she couldn't move. "She told me she had a hot date tonight."

"Major Easely doesn't want anybody to know about her dad," Greg explained.

"I can't believe it!" Joy's mind refused to accept what she was hearing. "You mean that's where she spends all her time when she's not here or at the Presidio? With her father?"

He nodded. "Most of it, anyhow. The old man's got Alzheimer's and requires full-time care. She doesn't want to put him in a nursing home."

Joy's confusion showed on her face. "Why does she go to so much trouble to make me think she's having an affair? What possible reason can she have to hide what she's doing?"

He eyed her thoughtfully. "Maybe she doesn't want people to feel sorry for her or to think she needs special favors. The only reason she told me about her father is that the male nurses she hires to take care of him aren't always reliable. Once in a while she has to take off during duty hours to stand in for them. She always makes up the time. It was necessary for me to know since I'm her commander."

Male nurses, Joy thought. *So they're the men who call her at all hours.*

She took a deep breath. "I owe that lady an apology."

He took both hands and cradled them in his. "No you don't, Joy. You thought exactly what she wanted you to think. As a matter of fact, I'm sure she won't appreciate my letting you in on her little secret. But from now on, you need to know when she's going to be gone all night. If you hear somebody at your door on those nights, you'll know it's not Donna Easely."

Greg purposely said nothing about his fears that Major Easely had seemed to want the house left insecure. She'd probably resisted his demand for the locks because she was so damned independent. Suggesting otherwise, he decided, would create unnecessary friction.

For a long moment, Joy sat without speaking, letting the warmth of his hands flow through her. His story had shaken her—not only because of the news about Donna, but also because it revealed how deeply concerned he was for her own safety. She knew intuitively that he would never have revealed another officer's confidence unless it was a matter of life and death.

Her awareness of his concern added a poignant sweetness to the simple dinner they shared a short time later. Joy put a single candle at the center of the table and opened a bottle of California red wine. When Greg made a toast to endings and beginnings, she knew what he meant. Somehow the horrors of that remarkable day had been balanced by its pleasures, enabling them to turn a corner of sorts. During the past twelve hours, the curtain had been drawn on what had been and the way cleared for what was to come.

It was only after he'd left in a cab, his good-night kiss still burning her lips, that Joy forced herself to remember that Gregory Weston had no place in her future. Much as she was torn by the thought, their goals were so different that there was no way they could be together after this assignment. As far as they were concerned, the future was limited to one day: tomorrow.

Sunday Morning

ON THE WAY to the Iberian Market, Joy suggested a plan of action. If the place was staffed with several clerks who had nothing to do but keep an eye on the place, they'd buy an item and come back later. If they got lucky and only one or two clerks were on duty, Greg would create a diversion, allowing Joy to slip through the swinging doors and search the area beyond.

"I don't like it," he said, as soon as she'd finished describing her plan. "If there's any searching to be done, I'm going to do it."

By now she knew him well enough to realize the success of the mission was of paramount importance to him. Since her plan was better than his, she didn't doubt he'd see things her way.

"You can create a bigger diversion than I can," she said logically. "Besides, with you out front keeping an eye on things, what can happen to me? If anybody sees me, I'll tell them I'm looking for the bathroom. Nobody can deny a stricken woman use of the facilities. I'll be able to slip around in back easier than you since I'm not as noticeable."

"That depends on who's doing the noticing," he said.

She smiled at his compliment but didn't say anything, letting him mull over what she'd said. In anticipation of her role she'd worn jeans, dark-colored Reeboks, and a navy-blue turtleneck sweater. By contrast, his bright yellow shirt and black eye patch stuck out like a sore thumb.

He eyed her dark clothes as they pulled into the familiar parking lot. "All right, you do the search," he agreed reluctantly. "But if you see anybody back there, get out fast. I'll make sure nobody comes down that hallway from the store."

Greg parked as close to the front door as he could get. Even though it was only a few minutes after noon when they arrived, several other cars were already in the spaces between the freshly painted diagonal lines in the market's lot.

"Customers," Greg said. "The busier they are, the better." He put a hand on her arm as she started to open her door. "You're sure you want to go through with this, Joy?"

He was going to leave her behind because their scheme might be dangerous. She started to protest. He didn't let her finish.

"There's some danger involved, of course," he said, "but that's not the only problem. The thing that concerns me is that this is illegal. You heard the deputy. She said she'd throw the book at us if she got the chance."

Greg studied her face before adding, "When amateurs fool around like this, there's always the outside possibility they'll get caught."

Incredibly, during the past few days, their positions had reversed. Now he was the one worrying about the consequences of an illegal act. *Because it might hurt me,* she realized, with a melting feeling. And here she was, the one eager to take the risk.

She stuck her chin out. "I'm sick and tired of some creep taking potshots at us. In case you hadn't noticed, I like my life very much. I don't intend to let somebody grab it away from me without a fight. This market may have something to do with what's been going on. Let's get in there and find out what it is."

His broad smile, wide enough to reveal a gold-capped molar in the back of his mouth, lit up his entire face. It was the first time Joy had seen him smile like that.

FOR THE REST of her life Joy would remember that Sunday afternoon whenever she smelled the pungent aroma of hot cider. As soon as Greg opened the door to the Iberian Market, the scent of boiling cinnamon and apples wafted around them. She breathed deeply, enjoying the spicy odor.

Inside, the smell was even more pervasive. It emanated from a pot at the rear of the long counter.

At the other end of the counter, near the store's front, a heavy girl in her late teens sat near an old-fashioned cash register. "Try some of our cider," she said. "It's really good."

She had straight black hair, a prominent nose and the confidence of a congenial Queen Isabella. "There's paper cups back there." A pause. Then, when Greg and Joy remained motionless, she added, "It's free."

"Thanks, we'll have some," Joy said, after a quick glance at Greg. From his pleased look she could tell he thought the setup was perfect for what they'd planned. The teenager was the only clerk on duty. Several customers were hidden in the narrow aisles behind tall shelves containing every kind of packaged and canned Spanish food imaginable. By their very presence in the store, the other customers would be a help, not a hindrance.

Using the spigot on the big pot, Joy poured two tiny paper cups full of the steaming hot liquid. It tasted as good as it smelled, its biting flavor highlighted by the spicy cinnamon.

"We're in luck," Greg said. "There's only one clerk, but somebody else could show up any time. The quicker we move, the better."

From where they were standing, the swinging doors to the rear of the store were only a few steps away. A sign printed in red block letters warned: DO NOT ENTER. EMPLOYEES ONLY.

Joy glanced at the teenager, still seated behind the counter at the other end of the store. She was staring out the front window at the sunny street, oblivious to her customers.

"This is as good a time as any," Joy whispered, finishing her cider. She tossed her cup in a trash basket beside the counter.

"Don't forget your bathroom excuse." He was gripping her arm so tightly she could feel the strength of his fingers through her wool sweater.

"I'll use it if I get caught." She removed his fingers with her other hand. "Greg, it's time for your diversion."

He was staring at her so intently that she reached up and touched his cheek. "I'll be fine," she whispered. "Wish me luck." Then she slipped away from him and eased through the swinging doors.

For half a second, she remained motionless, her heart pounding in her throat, her breath tight in her lungs, half expecting a loud screech from the retail part of the store.

But there were no sounds from behind her, nothing to indicate that anyone was alarmed by her intrusion. Slowly, she released her breath.

Ahead of her stretched a long metallic-looking hallway lighted by a bare bulb suspended from a cord. There were three doors on the hall's left side, one at the end, and a fifth on the right side. The doors had handles, not knobs.

Remembering the market's inside layout, Joy figured the long expanse of wall on the hall's right formed one of the sides of the meat locker. The small room on the right near the end of the hall must also share a common wall with the locker.

From the market came the crash of breaking glass and the excited babble of voices. Among them, she recognized Greg's raspy baritone and the wails of the teenage clerk.

Joy smiled to herself. He'd done a good job. She should have ten or fifteen minutes to look around.

Carefully counting her steps so that she'd have an idea how long the hall was, she reached the door at its end. It wasn't locked. She stepped inside and, locating the light switch, turned it on. She'd barely closed the door behind her, when she heard the teenager's voice in the hallway. The sound froze her to the floor. What if the girl noticed the light was on in the room at the end of the hall?

"My father's going to kill me when he sees this! You're going to have to pay, mister. I hope you realize that." Disgust had replaced the shrillness in her voice.

A door opened and slammed shut. It was probably the door nearest the retail area, Joy thought, identifying that room as a maintenance or cleaning closet.

She heard Greg's voice. He'd obviously followed the clerk into the hall. "Don't worry, miss. You just figure out what all that stuff cost, and I'll give you the cash before I leave. Here. Let me carry that trash basket. I'll help you clean up."

The voices faded. Joy took a deep breath. She was safe so far, but it had been a close call.

She glanced around her.

Lined with boxes and smelling of cardboard, this appeared to be a storage room. Some of the boxes, lying helter-skelter on the floor, were open. She poked around inside several of them to find canned goods, packaged rices and pastas, bottles of pickles. Gunnysacks full of potatoes were piled in one corner, partly blocking a door to the back of the building.

Joy stepped off the distance from front to back as best she could to see how long the room was. Doing some quick mental calculations, she could tell that there was a large area—perhaps as much as half the building—behind the room she was searching. This must be the warehouse Santos Mueller managed as a favor to the market's owners. If so, it seemed unusually large to house supplies for a small family store.

Since this entrance was blocked, Joy decided there must be another somewhere in the market's retail area. On a hunch, she twisted the doorknob. It turned easily. Working quickly, she tossed some of the gunnysacks on the floor and pushed the rest a few inches from the door so she could force it open. Peering through the crack, she saw a huge warehouse piled high with wooden and cardboard boxes.

A distinctive odor assailed her nostrils. Wrinkling her nose, she took a deep breath. A faint oil smell mingled with the more pervasive cardboard odor. Whatever Santos was managing in the warehouse, it wasn't groceries. Annoyed that she didn't have more time to look around, she closed the door and pushed the sacks back in place.

In the hallway again, she turned to the closest door next to the meat locker.

Slowly she pushed it open.

The room, hardly more than a cubbyhole, housed the market's latrine facilities. Without turning the light on, she could see that the sink was dirty and the toilet seat broken.

From the retail part of the store came the muted rattle of glass and metal. *Still cleaning up,* she thought, telling herself to hurry. She had to be back in the store before the clerk returned the mop and brooms to the hallway closet.

She ran across the hall, afraid she was taking too long. Her breath came in shallow gasps. She could hear her pulse pounding in her ears.

The nearest door on the other side of the hall also led to a storeroom. Joy turned the light on, took a quick look, and closed the door.

There was one more room to investigate. It had to be the office.

Bingo! she thought, pushing the hall's center door open and then closing it carefully behind her. Against one wall was a battered metal desk flanked by a couple of file cabinets. Along another wall was a table with a small photocopying machine on top. A video monitor with a plastic cover over it sat on top of the desk.

Quickly Joy leafed through a small stack of manila folders piled near the center of the desk. Most of them concerned taxes. Whoever handled the market's accounts had been working on last year's tax return.

Joy spent a couple of minutes scanning the tax information. She saw nothing that seemed unusual. The Iberian Market appeared to be exactly what it seemed: a small ethnic grocery store.

Near the bottom of the stack, however, she found a folder that had nothing to do with taxes. It contained a slim sheaf of Eye gossip columns clipped from the *Monterey Tribune,* the columns Joy knew had been written by Maria Cardoza until her death. With one shocking exception, each column mentioned Santos Mueller's name at least once.

The one exception set Joy to trembling. On top of the pile, her own picture smiled back at her. It was Thursday's horrid "School for Spies" article. Across her face someone had penciled a big, red question mark.

She returned the folder to its place and put her shaky fingers on the top desk drawer. Struggling to control her shock, she yanked the drawer open.

The room's stillness was shattered by the piercing screech of an alarm. Paralyzed by the screaming assault on her eardrums, Joy stood rooted to the floor.

Chapter Fifteen

Joy barely had time to slam the desk drawer shut before the office door burst open.

A stocky man stormed into the room.

"What the hell you doin' here, lady?" he shouted, above the scream of the siren. Then, turning to the teenager, who was right behind him, "Call the police, Rosa. Our booby trap's just caught us a thief."

Before the girl could reach the phone on the desk, Greg stepped in front of her, next to Joy.

"You all right, honey?" he said.

She nodded, her mind searching frantically for a good excuse to be in the office, going through the desk.

"Judas Priest, turn off that damned alarm," Greg demanded. "My wife's pregnant, and that racket's going to make her sick again. Anything happens to her, and you've got a lawsuit on your hands."

He's said the magic words.

The proprietor hurried toward Joy, flicked a switch near the drawer, and turned off the blaring alarm. Joy sagged against the desk in trembling relief.

Close up, the stocky man examined Joy's face. She didn't realize she looked as shaky as she felt until he pulled out a chair and motioned for her to sit down. She sank into it, letting the blessed silence enfold her.

"Go back and watch the store, Rosa," he said. "I can take care of things here."

"Weren't you able to find the bathroom, sweetheart?" Greg asked, his voice tender.

"It's at the end of the hall, but there wasn't any paper." Joy's voice was quivering. She wasn't acting. The heart-stopping blare of the alarm had been the ultimate shock to her overwrought nervous system. Nausea was rising in her throat.

"And you thought they might keep the paper here in the desk." Greg prompted.

Nodding again, she crossed her arms in front of her and put her head down.

"*Madre de Díos!!*" the proprietor exclaimed. "A moron knows you keep toilet paper in the cabinet under the sink. She's not going to be sick, is she?"

"I don't know," Greg said. "She's had a hard time since we've been in California. I've been terribly worried about her. That's why I was so clumsy out front."

He bent over Joy. "Feel okay to walk, sweetheart?" he said.

Now that the screaming alarm was quiet, she was feeling stronger, but she let herself lean against him, acting her part.

He took her arm.

"I can put out some paper for her in the bathroom," the proprietor offered nervously.

"That won't be necessary," Greg said. "Since she's so upset, we'll have to go back to the motel." They walked slowly down the metallic hallway and through the swinging doors.

The proprietor didn't follow.

As they passed the teenage clerk behind the cash register, Greg asked if they were squared away for the damage.

She said yes, they were, and smiled congenially. "Need any help getting her to your car, mister?"

Greg told her no, he could manage.

Joy was certain their story had been believed.

But when they drove out of the parking lot, she saw the proprietor run out the front door. He had a pencil and a piece of paper, and he was writing down their license number.

OVER DINNER on Cannery Row in Monterey, Joy told Greg about the big warehouse in back of the Iberian Market and about the folder of clippings, each mentioning Santos Mueller.

"Bull's-eye!" Greg exclaimed. "If he's keeping files there, it means he's more than a friend doing the owners a favor by managing their warehouse." He put his fork down and leaned toward her. "Tell me more about the place. You say it was filled with wooden crates and cardboard cartons?"

Joy nodded. An excellent salmon dinner lay half-eaten on the plate in front of her. She was having trouble keeping her mind on either their conversation or her food. Her thoughts kept turning to the tender words she'd heard Greg say and his concerned attention in the market. How much was acting and how much real?

Her voice quivered when she answered. "The place didn't smell like the other storerooms, Greg."

"Well, what did it smell like?"

His curious look brought her attention back where it belonged. She concentrated on the scene in the warehouse.

"Like oil." Remembering, she wrinkled her nose. "Like machine tools. Like a sewing machine when it's being serviced."

Greg leaned closer. "Or like your carbine while you're cleaning it?" His voice vibrated with controlled excitement.

"Yes! That's it!" Joy regarded him thoughtfully. "So that's how Maria Cardoza was blackmailing Santos. Your old amigo is an arms smuggler. I wonder where he's sending them."

"Probably to those right-wing revolutionaries she wrote about in her column." He spoke with quiet determination. "As soon as I drop you off, Mr. Mueller and I are going to have a little talk, eyeball-to-eyeball."

A nasty shiver rippled down Joy's spine. She couldn't let him confront Santos alone. It was too dangerous.

"There's more, Greg," she added, to get his mind off an immediate meeting. "Santos wasn't the only one in that clipping file. A copy of that awful article about me was right on top. There was a red question mark across the picture."

Greg tensed. Anger radiated from his face like heat from a red-hot coal.

"That clinches it." His words were slow, deliberate. "The weapons are bad enough, but this is the last straw. Santos has some explaining to do."

Joy wished she hadn't said anything. Fear for Greg made her throat ache. "Not today, Greg. You can't see him on Sunday."

"What's wrong with today?" His words were quick, his manner impatient.

"You'll be alone with him and whoever works for him. Why not wait until tomorrow morning at your office?" She finished her coffee, swallowing it with an effort.

With a tolerant smile, Greg signaled for the check. "Santos isn't going to hurt me, Joy."

Joy saw that he was humoring her but didn't let that stop her. "We don't know what the man's capable of. Let's not do anything hasty."

"We'll talk about it on the way home." He stood to go.

It wasn't until they were almost to the Presidio that Joy realized they were headed to his quarters.

"Phong will be there if you need anything while I'm gone," he said, over her protests. "So you won't be alone. Maybe we can take in a movie when I get back."

Joy started to insist he take her home but the words died on her tongue. When Greg returned to his quarters, she wanted to be there, to assure herself that nothing dreadful had happened to him. She refused to dwell on her fear that he might not come back.

Inside the house, he led her to the sofa in his living room but didn't sit down beside her. "I'll be home in about an hour." There was an air of finality to his tone. The set of his jaw defied her to challenge him.

"I'm coming with you." Joy stood up in a last-ditch effort to convince him. "My God, Greg, you can't go to his house alone. Now that we know he's smuggling arms, he's a more suspicious character than Julio Ramon."

This time Greg didn't make light of her fears. "That's all the more reason for you to stay here."

Joy turned, intending to brush past him toward the door, but he moved in front of her so that she couldn't pass between him and the coffee table.

"Don't give me a hard time about this, Joy." He grasped her shoulders and looked into her eyes.

Joy stared back at him, her chin thrust out. "Don't *you* give *me* a hard time, Greg Weston."

He was only inches away, so close she could feel the heat of his body. His closeness and the touch of his hands aroused yearnings she couldn't control. Upsetting thoughts raced through her head, thoughts about his tenderness at the market this afternoon, about the way his arms felt when they were wrapped around her.

Greg felt Joy's arm go limp and heard her breathing change. His own heart pounded like heavy artillery as he gazed at her face. She exuded a special warmth that drew him nearer. Every part of him pulled toward her.

This isn't right! He started to step back but couldn't. Not now. Once again, he'd moved close to the flame. But this time he was burning up inside. He gathered her to him, until their bodies were touching. As he felt her breasts against his chest an involuntary groan escaped his lips. It was too much for any man to bear.

He caught his breath as he watched her eyes close, and saw her long chestnut-colored lashes lying dark against her rosy skin. She was the most vitally intelligent woman he'd ever known, and he wanted her with a longing that was beyond all controlling. He put both arms around her and luxuriated in the feel of her softness molded against him.

She responded eagerly, intensifying a desire that he'd believed couldn't be heightened. Her lips tasted sweet, sweeter than the most luscious tropical fruit. Her mouth was warm fire, a refuge from the most biting winter day. With his mouth on hers, he felt her pulsing magnetism and could think of nothing else. Her lips moved under his, adding fuel to the flame of his desire.

After a breathless moment, he pulled himself away so that he could gaze at her face. What he saw made him catch his breath in a confusing mixture of tenderness and self-reproach. Somehow he'd managed to rub the scrape on her cheek raw again. The sight of it brought him back to the real world.

Struggling for control, he examined the scrape with his finger. "You need to put some antiseptic on that. This damn beard of mine..."

As soon as Greg drew back, Joy opened her eyes. On his face she saw such a look of remorse and longing that her heart was torn. She put her fingers over his mouth. "Ssh. I love your beard."

In that instant her desire deepened into something more than a physical need. She felt a fathomless yearning—almost a compulsion—to comfort and protect him.

Joy knew what she had to do. Maybe she couldn't stop him from confronting Santos Mueller this afternoon. But she could sure keep him from going alone.

"Why don't you shave while I dab on some antiseptic before we go visit your old amigo?" She kept her tone light.

"Let's not start on that again." His scowl didn't scare her in the slightest.

"You might as well take me, Greg." There was no pleading to her voice; only total assurance. "Because if you don't, I'll come on my own, and that will be much more dangerous than being with you."

Joy knew she'd backed him into a corner again—the way she'd had to do in the old days to get him to wake up and see the sunshine when they disagreed on some policy or other.

He took an exasperated breath. "We'll talk about it after you take care of that scrape."

"Fine." Joy was careful not to smile.

AFTER THE WARMTH of Greg's embrace, the upstairs hallway seemed cold and drafty to Joy. She could feel the draft until she closed the bathroom door behind her.

The room had been cleaned since she used it yesterday. There were fresh towels on the rack. Bath oil, deodorant, body lotion, and a woman's shampoo were lined up neatly on the counter. She smiled when she saw the toiletries. It looked as if she'd been expected.

Examining her face in the mirror, she noticed that Greg was right: the raw place on her cheek needed more antiseptic. She pulled out the bottom drawer of the linen closet where she'd found the peroxide yesterday.

As she reached for the bottle, her gaze focused on an object lying in a back corner. Had it been there yesterday? She wasn't sure. She'd been so shaken after finding the body at the Sportsmen's Club that she might have missed it.

Joy knelt beside the drawer to get a better look. Then, flabbergasted, she took it out and examined it.

A transparent, polished quartz crystal, it hung on a slender gold chain. When Joy held it up to the light, she could make out the phantom image of a six-pointed star.

It was Maria Cardoza's crystal, the one Chris Tuck had given her as an engagement present.

Stunned, Joy crouched in front of the open drawer, the crystal in her hand. There was a hard, sour feeling in the pit of her stomach.

Where did Greg get the crystal? From Santos Mueller? What was his true connection to the burly instructor?

Maybe the reason Greg didn't want Joy around when he confronted his good old amigo was that he didn't want her to hear what they talked about. Maybe he'd been involved with Santos right from the beginning. Maybe he'd been sticking to her like glue for the past few days to keep an eye on her.

Angrily, she shook her head. How could she think such things? Greg couldn't possibly have had anything to do with the deaths of Maria Cardoza and Chris Tuck. Hadn't he saved Joy's life twice yesterday? Hadn't his life been as much at risk as her own both times?

As for deliberately deceiving her, why had he hidden the crystal in a bathroom he obviously expected her to use? Hadn't he just told her she needed more antiseptic when he must have known the bottle was kept in that drawer?

Had he deliberately left the pendant there for her to find?

Joy put the crystal back in the drawer and shoved it closed.

Then she returned to the living room.

Greg had already shaved. He was sitting on the sofa, waiting for her. There was a fresh scent of Irish Spring in the air. Joy hardened her heart against the warmth radiating from his face when he saw her. Without moving from the doorway, she said, "There's something you should see in the hall bathroom, Greg."

Staring at her from the sofa, he looked so puzzled his expression couldn't possibly be feigned. Or could it?

"Don't tell me we need to get the post roach-chasers over here again?" He got up and strode toward her.

"I wish it were that simple," she said, preceding him up the stairs to the bathroom. Without another word, she pulled the bottom drawer open and motioned for him to look.

He bent down and peered inside.

"Judas Priest!" he thundered, scooping the crystal up in one hand. "How did this thing get in my house?"

"You mean you didn't know it was here?" Her astonishment showed in her voice.

The familiar old cynical expression crossed his face. "This is a big house, Joy. If I wanted to hide something, I could find a hell of a better place than that."

She backed through the doorway. "Then how did it get there?"

His frown disappeared. "I'm sure going to find out." He went to the head of the stairs and yelled for his houseman. Phong appeared quickly, as though he'd been waiting for a summons.

Greg showed him the crystal. A rapid-fire conversation ensued.

Whoever broke in here was real lucky they didn't get caught, Joy thought, noting Phong's squat, muscular build.

After a quick look around upstairs, Greg and Joy went back to the living room.

"Phong will search the downstairs, but I'm sure the bastard's gone. He must have put the crystal in the drawer last night. Phong says he went through all of them thoroughly when he cleaned yesterday afternoon, and it wasn't there then."

"How did they get in?" she asked.

"Probably through the fire door."

From the outside of the house Joy had seen the long flight of wide wooden steps in back leading to the second story. The stairs, with their triple rows of white railings on both sides, were the most noticeable feature behind the old two-story houses on the Presidio. Dormers had been built into the roofs to provide short hallways and exits from the second floor. Significantly, the hallway in the commandant's house ran alongside the bathroom wall, making that room the closest to the exit.

"Don't you keep the fire door locked?"

Greg grunted. "It's always locked. I just checked it. There's no sign of forced entry, but that's probably how he got in."

"Greg, those fire stairs are in plain sight of the road in back of the house. Somebody would have seen him."

"It's been dark and foggy the past few nights. A whole division of troops could have been marching by on that street and not seen him."

Greg motioned for Joy to sit down. "Whoever it was must have been a real expert at picking locks. There's a good one on that door. Either that, or he had a key."

"Had a key!" Joy plopped down on the sofa. "That means it was somebody from the front office! Have Colonel Spellman or Sergeant Philpott got keys to your house?"

"They both have access to the keys," Greg said dryly, sitting down beside her. "And so do a lot of other people. The military police, the sergeant major, chief of staff...shall I go on? I doubt either Colonel Spellman or Sergeant Philpott broke into my house last night."

"The reason I mentioned those two was that they've arranged briefings for all language school graduates assigned to the National Security Agency. The more I think about it, the more those briefings strike me as sort of odd." Joy's eyes narrowed.

"Odd in what way?"

She sensed that he was humoring her again. "Why should two busy staff members—one a full colonel and one a top sergeant—spend valuable time glad-handing people assigned to a hush-hush government agency?"

Greg put an arm around her and squeezed. "We've been through a lot the past few days, Joy. It's only natural to be suspicious of everything and everybody. During the next few days I'll do some checking on the NSA briefings. But right now, we've got two prime suspects in our sights. Let's concentrate on Santos Mueller and Julio Ramon."

He stood up. "Get Phong to fix you some supper while I'm gone," he said.

Joy stood up, too. "This is my fight, too. I meant what I said, Greg. If you won't take me, I'll come on my own."

He grasped her shoulders. "Finding that crystal has brought this whole thing to a head, Joy. Lord knows how much other 'evidence' has been hidden around here. It looks to me like somebody's doing their damnedest to get rid of both of us—by killing you and framing me for the Cardoza woman's murder and who knows what else. I want some answers, and I want them now. If I know Santos Mueller, he'll be much more inclined to open up to me alone."

"I'll wait in the car while you talk to him," Joy offered quickly. "That way I can go for help if anything happens."

Even though Greg didn't actually smile, his expression lightened. "You'll be like the cavalry riding to the rescue? Is that it?"

She didn't care whether he made fun of her or not as long as he took her along. And she hadn't missed the tender, knowing look on his face in spite of his teasing.

"More like the ready reserves," she said, sensing victory. "Out of the way and no special bother, but there if needed."

This time he did smile. "I don't honestly think Santos is going to gun us down on his front lawn, so I guess it won't hurt anything if you wait for me in the car."

"You won't be sorry," Joy promised.

Chapter Sixteen

Greg pulled into the cul-de-sac and parked in front of Santos Mueller's house in Monterey. Squinting through the foggy darkness, Joy made out a small structure designed in the Mediterranean style, with light stucco walls and a red tile roof.

"You may have a long wait," he warned, turning to her. "I'll leave the keys so you can turn on the heater."

As Greg was getting out of the car, she rolled her window down to see and hear better.

The front door was off to one side of a brick patio. Santos opened it himself shortly after Greg knocked. He was wearing an electric-blue satin robe over a white shirt and tie.

"Ah, *Comandante*," he said. "Come in, I've been expecting you."

Instead of stepping aside to let Greg enter, he stared down the walk toward the Cherokee. Joy waved at him through the open window, hoping he'd insist she come inside. If he did, there was no way Greg could object without arousing suspicion.

"Surely you don't intend to leave the captain in the car, *Comandante*?"

Still staring in Joy's direction, Santos joined Greg outside on the entryway. "I demand that she join us. You may not know it, but she is much more involved in this than you are, my friend."

At his words, Joy's stomach twisted into knots. *Involved in what?*

Apprehension swept over her as she watched him come down the walk. With his blue robe flowing behind him, he seemed a dark vision of evil. The robe parted as he walked to reveal immaculate black trousers. Even in the faint illumination provided by a nearby streetlight, Joy could see the sharp creases in his pants.

He opened her door. "Won't you join us, Captain Inquirer?"

He spoke so softly that Joy was certain Greg, by the front door, couldn't hear him. Anger tinged her fear, made it less paralyzing. This man was trying to intimidate her. She wasn't going to let him get away with it.

Ignoring his proffered hand, she climbed out of the car. "What's that supposed to mean, Santos?" There was a decided chill to her voice.

He faced her, undisturbed. "I'm sure you know, Captain. What I'm wondering is whether the *Comandante* knows." His stare was unnerving. "Since you've gotten him so interested in my affairs, the time has come to inform him of yours."

Joy suddenly felt threatened. Obviously Santos knew about their visit to the Iberian Market this afternoon. That must be what he meant by their interest in his "affairs." But she hadn't the faintest clue what he thought Greg needed to be told.

"Colonel Weston knows all about my 'affairs,' as you put it," she said, to egg him on.

He rubbed his hands together. "We shall see about that." An odd expression of curiosity and loathing crossed his face. She felt as though she'd been struck, his dislike was so tangible.

He hates me because I've found him out! Spurred by a jolt of pure fright, she hurried up the walk to Greg.

When she reached him, he put his arm around her. "You're trembling, darling. What's wrong?"

"Let's go, Greg," she gasped, "Right now. Before anything terrible happens."

Greg's arm tightened around her. "What did you say to her at the car, Santos?"

Joy heard no hint of good-buddy camaraderie in his voice.

The instructor chuckled congenially. "Relax, *Comandante*." He put a hamlike hand on Greg's shoulder. "The captain is afraid I will reveal to you her special little secret. That is why she wants to leave."

Joy caught Greg's questioning glance, and her heart sank. Surely he wouldn't believe Santos's lie, whatever it was.

"WOULD EITHER OF YOU like something to drink?" Santos leaned toward them, the perfect host.

His living room, although too glittery with crystal and mirrors for Joy's taste, was surprisingly comfortable. The sofa they were sitting on was positioned opposite a couple of easy chairs with a table in between. Her fear abating, she let herself relax against the sofa's soft cushions.

"Nothing for me," she told Santos.

"I'll pass, too," Greg said from his position next to Joy on the sofa.

The big man seated himself in a chair opposite them. "First, let me tell you that I know you were snooping around at the Iberian Market this afternoon. I've guessed why you were there, but I would like to hear your explanation, *Comandante*."

"To find out what you're up to, of course," Greg said.

"Then she didn't tell you?" He inclined his head toward Joy.

Greg caught Joy's hand and squeezed it. "What makes you think Captain Donnelly knows any more than I do?"

"Because Maria knew what I was 'up to,' as you put it. The captain was collaborating with Maria."

Joy caught her breath. So that's why he had called her "Captain Inquirer." He thought she was working with Maria Cardoza on the Eye column. How could an intelligent man like Santos Mueller make such a gross mistake?

When Santos spoke, Joy was watching Greg's face. She had to admire his self-control. He didn't flick an eyelash at the instructor's outlandish statement.

"Maria was blackmailing you, wasn't she, Santos?" Greg asked.

Santos nodded. "When she was snooping around for the gossip column she found out something about my personal life that could have caused me much trouble. She threatened to write about it if I didn't pay her."

"What did she find out, Santos?" Greg's voice was deceptively quiet.

He's giving Santos a chance to explain about the arms stored in the warehouse, Joy thought.

"Why not let the captain tell you, *Comandante?*"

"Because she knows no more than I do."

Santos winked at Joy. It was a hard, spiteful signal without any humor. "You've done a good job of fooling him, Captain."

Beside her, she felt Greg squeeze her hand again. It gave her courage. She stared straight at the instructor's bleached-blue eyes. "What makes you think I was collaborating with Maria Cardoza, Santos?"

He winked again. "She as good as said so, within a week or two of your arrival. Then, when I saw your picture and that article in the newspaper on Thursday, more than a week after she drowned, I knew she hadn't lied. You had to be the one she was working with. Someday you will have to tell me why you used that particular subject for your story. Was it, perhaps, a warning to another of your victims?"

Greg stiffened. Joy felt the tension in his hand, still holding hers. "What do you mean by 'victims'?"

The instructor shrugged. "I'm sure Maria was black-mailing others, not just me. She liked to brag. She hinted at that, too, the way she did about you." He glanced toward Joy, suddenly not quite as sure of himself as he'd been.

How many others? Joy wondered, remembering Julio Ramon.

"It doesn't matter how many people she was blackmailing," Greg said. "We're going to have to tell the police you were one of them."

Santos blanched. His already pasty complexion turned the color of cottage cheese.

"You can't do that, amigo," Santos said. "Not to the local police. It would ruin everything."

Greg stood up. "There's no way I can cover up evidence like this, Santos. You're going to have to tell the whole story to the authorities—what she was blackmailing you for, everything. If you didn't kill her, I'm sure they'll find who did."

Santos leaped to his feet. "Kill her! Holy Mother in Heaven, I had nothing to do with it. I thought you understood that."

"Then why don't you tell us why she was blackmailing you, Santos?" Greg asked. He was still standing in front of the couch. Joy stood up and began edging toward the door.

"I can't do that, *Comandante*," he said. "And I'm sorry, but I can't permit you to go to the police, either."

With his right hand, he reached into the voluminous pocket of his robe. When he withdrew it, he was holding a snub-nosed revolver. He pointed it straight at Greg's heart.

IT WAS WORSE than the night terrors of Joy's childhood. *This can't be happening,* she thought. *Any minute I'm going to wake up and find out this is a horrid dream.*

But it wasn't a dream. With her heart in her throat, she watched Greg edge toward the big man.

"You're not going to shoot me, amigo." Greg stretched out his hand. "Give me the weapon, and we'll forget this ever happened."

Joy saw the resolve in Santos's faded blue eyes and her heart turned to stone. With cold deliberation, he turned the gun toward her. Joy found herself looking down the barrel of a snub-nosed revolver.

"Don't come closer, *Comandante,* or the captain gets shot."

Greg stopped moving. "Let's sit back down and talk this over, Mueller. There must be a better way to solve your problem."

Santos waved his weapon toward the door. "The time for talk passed when you insisted on going to the police with that stupid story. Now turn around and start walking. Both of you."

When Greg didn't move, Joy stood her ground. "Where are we going?" she asked, fighting to keep her voice steady.

He pulled back the hammer on the revolver with his thumb. "Don't give me an excuse to pay you back for all the trouble you've caused me, Captain." There was a nasty gleam in his eyes. Joy didn't doubt he'd shoot her. Her mind searched frantically for some way to escape.

Across the room, Greg started slowly for the door. "You're a fool, Mueller."

"You won't think so when you know the truth," Santos said.

Without taking off his blue satin robe, he followed them outside, down the walk to the Jeep.

"In back, Captain," he said, waving the revolver at her.

Dumbly, Joy climbed in the backseat.

"Where the hell are we going?" Greg growled. "You won't get away with this, Mueller." The way he said it, the name was laced with poison.

Santos sat down in the passenger seat and pointed his weapon at Joy. "Get inside, please, *Comandante.* Don't make it necessary for me to do something unpleasant."

Slamming the door, Greg started the engine.

"We're going to the market," Santos said. "You know the way."

Greg headed out of the cul-de-sac. "While we're there, why don't you show us what you've got hidden in that warehouse at the back of the building? That's what Maria was blackmailing you about, wasn't it?"

Joy listened intently, expecting Santos to tell Greg to shut up.

Instead he smiled agreeably. "The warehouse contains nothing but groceries. Ask the captain. She knows all about it."

"Why not tell us your story right now, Mueller, and save us the trip?" Greg's words were clipped, harsh.

"Because you wouldn't believe me. It will take someone in authority to convince you."

So there's more to Santos's story than smuggling arms, Joy thought, stunned by what she'd heard. *And it involves someone in authority!*

Could Santos be working with the federal government on some secret project? Could a government agency be the "authority" he was referring to? It couldn't be the local police. He'd pulled his weapon only after Greg mentioned contacting them. Had the murdered agent been protecting him?

Almost without knowing it, Joy edged forward.

Santos waved the revolver at her. "Sit back in the seat, Captain."

Shivering with nerves, Joy slid back, her mind seething with unanswered questions.

"Why do you think I won't believe you?" Greg asked. "I'm a reasonable man. Try me, Santos."

"Telling you and telling the captain are two different things, *Comandante*. Since she was working with that witch, Maria Cardoza we'll have to figure out what to do about her after you've talked to my...ah...sponsor."

"The way you decided what to do with Maria? Try anything like that with Captain Donnelly and I swear, I'll get you, Mueller, if I have to throttle you with my bare hands."

The tone of Greg's voice lifted the fine hairs on Joy's neck. If words could kill, Santos Mueller would be a dead man.

"I've told you I had nothing to do with Maria Cardoza's death, *Comandante*," Santos protested. "Since you won't believe me, further talk is useless."

They drove the rest of the way to the market in silence.

Santos told Greg to park near the front of the building. Then, holding the weapon with one hand, he fished a key out of his pocket with the other.

When the market's front door opened, Joy heard the warning buzz of a security alarm about to go off. Unlike the desk alarm this afternoon, the main alarm was probably hooked into a security-service answering system. The thought gave her a new hope. Maybe Greg would have a chance to grab Santos's revolver while the instructor turned the alarm off.

She watched carefully as the beefy instructor herded them to a panel hidden behind boxes of produce along a side wall. Maybe she could divert his attention long enough for Greg to take action.

When Santos reached to open the panel, Joy knocked some cans off a shelf. They hit the wood floor with a hollow thudding sound. At the same moment Greg leaped in front of her. She sensed rather than saw the flash of the revolver as it fired.

Greg whirled and took her in his arms. "Are you all right, darling?"

"I don't know...I guess so." She shook her head to clear it and a bolt of fear shot through her. Greg had been standing in front of her. What if he'd taken the bullet meant for her? Frantically she wriggled away from him. "What about you? Did he get you?"

Santos's voice jarred her concentration. "Nobody got hurt—this time. Try something else and it'll be a different story."

Greg was still facing her with his back to Santos. She saw fear in his eyes and realized it was for her. "Don't cross him," he mouthed.

Joy felt cold drops of perspiration dripping down her back under her wool sweater. What if Greg had been killed protecting her? What if her foolish action had caused his death? She couldn't bear the thought. *You must be more careful,* she warned herself. *Always consider what Greg's doing and how he'll react.*

The alarm's warning buzz went silent. Motioning toward the back of the store, Santos followed them down a narrow aisle to the meat locker, switching on lights as he went.

So that was how they were getting into the warehouse from the store, Joy thought, watching the instructor swing the heavy refrigerator door open.

Inside, the low temperature pressed against her, a frigid barrier to be crossed. Santos yanked the door shut behind them and twisted the lever into place. Big pieces of meat hung on hooks along one wall. On the opposite side were floor-to-ceiling shelves containing smaller cuts of packaged meat.

Opposite them was a metal hatchway, resembling the doors of naval vessels. Santos opened it and waved them through. They stepped into the warehouse Joy had glimpsed this afternoon. Santos turned on a bank of overhead lights by flicking a switch near the door.

"When are you going to tell us what you've got stored in here, Mueller?" Greg asked. "It sure as hell doesn't look like groceries."

"The lady knows all about it, don't you, Captain Inquirer?" The man's eyes were accusing.

She shook her head, meeting Greg's questioning glance straight on. He had to believe her. She knew no more than he did about what was stored here. Just because they'd guessed it was weapons didn't mean they were right.

Santos turned to Greg and his tone changed from harsh command to congenial amiability, "These boxes may not look like groceries, but that's what they contain, *Comandante.* Foodstuffs from overseas must be carefully packaged." He winked at Joy as though she shared some nasty secret with him. "Now, there's somebody waiting to talk to us."

He motioned for Greg to turn around and go through the door to the meat locker.

When Joy tried to follow, Santos blocked her way.

"Not you, Captain," he said. "You stay here. This conversation is not for your ears." He smiled. "I suspect the *Comandante* will be easier to manage with you locked up tight inside my warehouse."

"Now look here, Santos." Greg's voice rang with command. "Anything you've got to say to me privately can be said right here, out of Captain Donnelly's hearing."

"You won't believe what I tell you unless you talk to my sponsor." There was a bitter edge of resignation to his voice.

"I'll believe you. And things will go easier for you later if you cooperate with me now."

Santos stuck the gun in Greg's back. "Move, *Comandante*."

Joy saw Greg stiffen. There was a dangerous stillness to him. "You're going to be damn sorry you did this, Mueller."

Santos jabbed Greg's back again. Reluctantly, as though he had weights on his feet, Greg moved out of the warehouse.

When the metal door of the meat locker clanged shut, Joy heard a sharp click, probably a bolt on the other side being jammed into place. She stood for a breathless moment, listening and waiting, half expecting Greg to work some kind of miracle and come charging back after her.

Surely he wouldn't let her stay here alone, locked up in a warehouse that might hold untold tons of weapons, while he and Santos went to talk to Santos's "sponsor."

There's nothing he can do about it, she told herself angrily. When Greg walked out of here, he was Santos's prisoner. As long as she, too, was a prisoner, Greg's ability to maneuver was limited.

Maybe there was something she could do about that.

Her first minutes of petrified fear gave way to frantic activity. She dashed to the meat-locker door and rattled the handle on the slim chance she might be wrong about the click she'd heard. Of course, she wasn't. The door was bolted. The one to the storeroom she'd been in yesterday was locked.

Most of the wall area was hidden by tall stacks of boxes and crates piled nearly to the ceiling. There were narrow aisles through the stacks, and she ran to the back of the building.

A huge garage-style door that opened on a track was securely locked. A standard door on the opposite side of the back wall wouldn't budge.

Looking up, she studied the row of windows near the ceiling on both sides of the room. The boxes were stacked just below the windows.

At first glance, it seemed preposterous even to consider escaping that way. The crates were piled straight up. Even though the stack was only about ten feet high, it would take somebody a lot more skilled than she to work her way to the top.

She took off her running shoes and tried slipping a toe in between the crates. When she grabbed the one above for balance, it shifted under her weight, and she jumped backward, afraid she was going to pull the whole pile down on top of herself.

Pull the whole pile down... It was an interesting idea. She considered it while she laced her shoes.

If there was some way to make the boxes fall and not get herself crushed in the process, she could use them to climb to the windows. Outside, the windows weren't that high off the ground. Once she got one open, she could crawl through, and hang by her hands on the edge of the building. It wouldn't be more than a six-or eight-foot drop to the ground.

Joy threaded her way through the aisles between the stacked crates, looking for the easiest route. Her window had to be on the dark side of the building where Santos couldn't see her if he should come back too soon. The crates were stacked closer to the wall in the area nearest the meat locker. That meant there would be a barrier on that side, preventing the tumbling boxes from knocking her down or falling too far. She examined the crates on that side. Different sizes, some were set in wood frames that would give her fingers something to grip.

For an intense moment she studied the stacks of crates, hunting for exactly the right one to make the others fall the way she wanted. Finally she settled on one medium-sized crate. It appeared to be a key block that, if removed, would disassemble the whole pile under the end window nearest the meat locker.

She gave the crate an exploratory tug. It didn't budge. Putting a hand on either side, she pulled, hard. The crates above it swayed ominously, but her crate remained stubbornly in position.

Next she tried wiggling it. There was a slight movement, and she inched it back and forth until an edge stuck out beyond the pile. Bracing one foot against the crate beneath it, she threw her entire weight behind her next yank.

The crate tumbled to the floor, barely missing Joy's head. She landed on her backside and instantly rolled to her right, as far from the stack of crates as she could get.

For a breathless instant nothing happened. Then a couple of lower crates fell in toward the center and—with hollow, pounding sounds like artillery fire—the entire pile collapsed, the way an old building drops under demolition explosives.

It was an awesome sight. Scrambling to her feet, Joy stood watching until the last crate had fallen, the last box had crashed to the floor.

What remained wasn't an orderly pile, but with any luck she'd be able to claw her way up to the window. After a quick survey of the jumbled mess, she located the easiest route to the top. Then, crossing to the light switch, she turned off the overhead lights. There was no sense being framed in the window like a sitting duck when she made her escape.

Some illumination was provided from the lighted parking lot on the other side of the building. In a minute or two, her eyes had adjusted to the darkness. She returned to her starting point.

Her first step, to the top of the bottom row of crates, was easy, but when she reached for the crate above to pull herself up, it teetered with her weight. She pushed it instead, and it fell away from her, settling into a lopsided position. At least it was solid. Needlelike slivers of wood tore into her hands as she struggled to pull herself onto it. She ignored the stinging pain.

Thank heaven for running shoes, she thought, balancing on the box's slanted wooden side. Above were two stacked crates, leaning against more crates on their wall side. She got a toehold on one and pulled herself to a kneeling position on the one next to it. From there she was able to make it to the top. The window she hoped to climb out of was within easy reach.

Cautiously she ran her hand along the frame around the heavy pane of glass. It was metal, solidly constructed. The window opened by swinging out and down on sturdy metal hinges. When open all the way, she saw that the glass would be perpendicular to the side of the building and parallel to the ground. There was no bar on it, no way to keep it from being opened from the inside.

She twisted the handle at the bottom of the frame. Then she pulled up until the window slid noiselessly out and down to a horizontal position. The salty, foggy air from the ocean enveloped her like some wonderful magic blanket. The neighborhood around the warehouse was noticeably still this Sunday night, as though the fog had trapped the houses and their occupants in misty cocoons. She took a deep breath, planning her next move.

There was very little space under the open pane of glass so she couldn't crawl beneath it. She'd have to get on top.

Praying that it was strong enough to support her weight, she scrambled off the top crate and onto the flat surface of the glass, crouching as close to the building as she could. Holding her breath, she waited for the window assembly to collapse beneath her.

In the silence she heard a snorting, blowing noise.

It sounded human and was undeniably near by.

She froze, her senses jolted by a massive dose of adrenaline.

There it was again. The same sound. Above her. On the roof. Slowly, using the side of the building for support, she rose until her eyes were level with the rooftop.

Perched across from her on the far corner sat a creature straight out of hell. It was a little man with the face of a gargoyle, and he was staring right at her.

Chapter Seventeen

"Be reasonable, *Comandante*. If you give me your word you won't jump me until after we've met with my sponsor, I'll put my weapon away."

Greg kept his gaze on the road, and his fears for Joy out of his voice. "Not until you tell me what you're up to."

"I can't do that," said Santos, but Greg noticed that he put the revolver in the pocket of his blue satin robe. "It will be explained to you very soon. Turn here, onto Del Monte."

Greg made the turn. Santos hadn't told him their destination, only that it was in the northern part of Monterey, near its border with Seaside. Greg decided he had nothing to gain and much to lose by challenging the burly instructor.

"If you can't tell me what you're up to, how about what you suspect about Captain Donnelly? You claim she was collaborating with Maria Cardoza in some kind of extortion racket. Where's your proof and what does that newspaper story have to do with it?"

When Greg changed the subject to Joy, Santos's sigh of relief was audible.

"About three weeks after the captain arrived," Santos said, "Maria began hinting that someone in authority at the school would take over the column if anything happened to her."

"Hints are mighty slim evidence, Santos." Greg kept his voice congenial while he waited for a chance to grab Santos's revolver.

"There were other clues, *Comandante.*" He seemed eager to convince Greg he wasn't lying. "Maria said that her collaborator was a woman, and that she also wrote for the paper. How many women are there on your staff who arrived in Monterey the same time as the captain?"

Greg stopped at a red light. "Did it occur to you that Maria was lying to protect herself? You said she had other victims. Maybe they'd threatened her, and she wanted them to know that the extortion would continue, even if something happened to her."

Greg believed Santos capable of making such a threat himself. But would he admit it?

Surprisingly, he did. "Three months ago she raised her demands," he said. "I warned her not to do it again or there would be trouble. That's when she started talking about a collaborator."

Greg snorted. "There you are, Santos. It was all a bluff."

The light changed, and the traffic moved ahead.

"In spite of your warning, did she increase her demands again?" Greg asked. "Just before she was killed?"

Santos nodded. "She went too far." He was silent for a moment and then added, almost as an afterthought, "Her accident seemed too good to be true, *Comandante.* But I didn't kill her."

"How about the airman?" Greg asked. "How did he end up in your class?"

For a bare instant, Santos hesitated.

Deciding whether to tell me the truth or not, Greg thought grimly.

"I confess that I had Airman Tuck assigned to my class so that I could keep an eye on him," Santos admitted. "I wanted to find out more about her accident."

"Did it work?" Greg glanced at the man beside him. "Did you learn anything from him?"

Santos threw up his hands. "God only knows why, but the foolish young puppy was obsessed with that witch. He was ready to sacrifice everything for her. He knew about her column and suspected she was using it to her own advantage. In fact..."

Greg tensed behind the wheel. "Did he tell you that?"

Santos nodded. "The stupid fool talked more than he should have when he'd been drinking. We had dinner together one night soon after she died. He made no secret of the fact that he thought she'd been murdered, and he intended to find out who and why."

"Evidently Maria's killer thought he was getting too close." Greg glanced at Santos. The instructor was sitting with one hand near each hip. *He can easily grab his revolver,* Greg thought. *This isn't the right time to make my move.* Holding his frustration in check, he turned back toward the road. "Did Tuck know about her blackmail scheme?"

Santos shrugged. "Who can say? He knew she was pressuring Julio Ramon to raise her instructor's rating. I found that much out."

"What about the article about Captain Donnelly in Thursday's *Tribune*, Santos? What possible connection does it have to Maria's extortion racket? She wasn't blackmailing Captain Donnelly."

"Turn left at the next light, *Comandante*." He frowned and his eyes narrowed. "I thought you understood. That's how Maria put on pressure. Through the newspaper. First she'd write a warning article to show she meant business. Then, if you didn't pay up, she'd print the real thing."

Greg remembered Eye's column about Santos's support for the right-wing guerrillas and the refugees from their stricken country—now being ruled by a Marxist dictator. Maria had probably written the item to pressure Santos for more money. Instead of giving the guerrillas moral support as Eye alleged, Maria knew Santos was smuggling arms to them. But Greg could see no connection between Santos and the column about Joy. He glanced questioningly at the instructor.

"But the 'School for Spies' article has nothing to do with you." Greg thought he was stating a simple fact.

"Yes, it does, *Comandante.*"

Greg heard his blood pounding in his temples. He didn't try to control his voice. "My God, man, tell me what."

"My sponsor will do that." Santos's tone was mild. "He's going to be very unhappy when he finds out what those two witches were up to."

Greg seethed with anger and frustration. First Santos caught him off guard with another of his heart-stopping, enigmatic statements. Now he was calling Joy a witch. Greg felt like knocking his block off.

"Damn it all, man, don't be an ass. Maria Cardoza wrote that article before she died. The city editor told us it was published as a sentimental gesture because it was Eye's last column. Captain Donnelly had nothing to do with it."

"Are you sure of that, *Comandante?*" The instructor's astonishment was evident. "I wondered why the captain made no extortion demand before it was printed."

Greg frowned. Something wasn't adding up. "Then the Cardoza woman made no demand, either, that could be connected to the 'School for Spies' article?"

"She was blackmailing me for something else, *Comandante.* Something of a very sensitive personal nature."

A cold, disturbing suspicion surfaced in Greg's mind. "She must have written the article to pressure somebody else."

"Of course," Santos murmured, as though that explained everything. "So, somebody reasoned as I did. It was the captain they were after yesterday..."

Santos's sudden insight shook Greg to the core. "We've got to go back..." He moved to the right-hand lane, intending to turn the corner and reverse direction.

With a motion as quick as a snake's, Santos yanked his revolver out of his pocket. "She's as safe there as anywhere," he said. "When we've had our talk, we'll go back."

Greg slammed on the brakes. The car skidded sideways in he sandy gravel by the side of the road.

Santos must have expected Greg's move. When the car stopped and Greg turned to look at him, he was smiling.

"Enough theatrics, *Comandante*." He pointed the revolver at Greg's thigh. "You will be of little use to her with a bullet in your leg."

A few minutes later they parked in a space in front of Room Six at the Seashell Motel. Prodding Greg toward the door with his revolver, Santos knocked. A man's voice said "Come in."

As soon as Greg caught sight of the room's occupant, he knew what the score was. The man had Government Agent written all over him. From his plain dark brown suit, to the revolver in a holster hanging from his shoulder, to his name—"Ed Jones," obviously a pseudonym—everything about him spelled Spook.

He was a big, rangy man a few years younger than Greg with an unsmiling, unreadable face. He closed the door and shook hands with Santos, and then with Greg.

"I understood you're about to expose Mr. Mueller to the local authorities, Colonel," he said. "I hope I can convince you not to."

Greg didn't try to contain the anger boiling inside him. "What the hell do you think you're doing, Jones? First your boy Mueller locks up one of my staff officers, and then he brings me here at gunpoint. I don't know what government outfit you're hooked up with and honestly can't say I give a damn, but I do know something about..."

"What's the story, Mueller?" Jones interrupted, before Greg could finish. "If we can trust anybody, it's the colonel."

Santos smiled his big, congenial smile, but with a little less confidence than usual. "After he threatened to go to the local police, I had to hold Captain Donnelly to insure his cooperation."

The agent frowned at Santos. "You should have brought her along. I'm sure both of them would have come willingly."

Santos has said nothing to the Feds about the blackmail scheme, Greg thought with sudden insight. *Otherwise the agent would know Santos thought Joy was collaborating with Maria.*

Santos's face blanched. "I thought she might be the spy we've been after, Ed."

"Captain Donnelly? A spy?" Greg thundered. "What the hell are you talking about?"

"Keep it down, Colonel," the agent cautioned. "These motels have thin walls. If you'll sit down," he motioned toward the room's two chairs, "I'll explain everything."

Greg turned toward the door. "Let's have our discussion after we get Captain Donnelly out of that warehouse, Jones."

The agent didn't get up. "I won't be going back with you so we either have our discussion now or we don't have it at all."

Greg flung the door open. Agent Jones's voice followed him outside. "You'll be doing your country a great disservice if you leave before you hear what I have to say, Colonel. It will take less than five minutes."

Reluctantly Greg returned to the room and closed the door.

"She's perfectly safe, *Comandante,*" Santos said.

"The way Maria Cardoza was safe? The way Chris Tuck was safe?" Greg turned to the agent. "I'm sure you realize both of them were murdered. Now that I know the Feds are involved, I've got a pretty good idea why the local authorities are yelling 'accident' in spite of overwhelming evidence to the contrary."

Agent Jones focused on Santos. "We hushed up the investigation because we thought Mueller was behind the murders. We thought we could nail him on the Q.T. without revealing our operation."

Santos's face was the picture of pained surprise. "How could you think that, Ed, after the years we've worked together?"

"Knock it off, Mueller. We knew the Cardoza woman was blackmailing you about the arms you've been smuggling to those right-wing revolutionaries in South America. We figured you killed her to shut her up."

Greg watched Santos's face turn albino white. Worried as Greg was, he couldn't help enjoying the instructor's discomfort.

"So you knew about the arms all along," Santos said, sighing. "Why didn't you arrest me?"

"You were doing us a favor," the agent replied. "Our country supports those revolutionaries. We want to see them overthrow the Marxist government in power down there. It's the last leftist regime on the continent. By using you in our informer program, we were killing two birds with one stone: monitoring your arms operation and getting useful information about the Defense Language Institute at the same time."

Greg leaned forward, his eye riveted on the agent. "Santos Mueller is a paid government informer? What the hell's going on at my school that you need a paid infiltrator?"

Jones smiled. "Not at your school, exactly, Colonel. In the business of military intelligence. That's where the trouble is. Did you know that every serviceperson caught selling secrets to foreign powers during the past few years was trained at your language school? We thought there might be a connection."

"Why didn't you come to me?" Greg asked. "I know more about what's going on at the school than Santos Mueller."

The agent shook his head. "Not so, Colonel. An instructor's privy to inside information you never hear." He paused, searching Greg's face. "Besides, from what Mueller tells us, you're about to get reassigned. We needed somebody permanent, on the civilian staff."

Greg didn't argue. He could see where the agent was coming from. "Somebody's trying to frame me for the Cardoza woman's murder," he said, starting for the door. "They broke into my house last night and planted some of her jewelry."

"It fits," the agent replied, studying Greg's face. "The murderer probably thought our man was following you Saturday, not Mueller. He got the notion we were after you for the murders and decided to give our investigation a little positive reinforcement. How did they break into your place?"

Before Greg could answer, the telephone rang. Agent Jones went around the bed to answer it.

He listened without saying anything, his face impassive. After he'd hung up the receiver, he turned to Greg.

"We've got a special setup for monitoring Mueller's warehouse when he's got arms stored inside. They report that somebody's just cut the outside phone lines. Barring a hell of a coincidence, there's only one reason to do that. Unless we get there in time to stop him, our murderer's going to claim another victim."

IT TOOK JOY an instant to realize that the ugly little man perched on the edge of the roof opposite her couldn't possibly see her. She was in almost total darkness, and, with her long bangs covering most of her forehead, very little of her skin was showing.

Her heart pounding wildly in her throat, she clung to the edge of the roof, watching his every move. He was clearly visible to her. The illumination from the parking lot below that side of the building reflected on his face, defining it in detail.

With his pointed chin, angular nose and sunken forehead, his visage was remarkably like the grotesque carving on some Gothic cathedral. Without bothering to use a handkerchief, he blew his nose again—the snorting sound Joy had heard—and turned toward the edge of the building, leaning far out with a tool of some sort in his hand.

Joy had seen enough. Amanda Hawkins had mentioned an odd-looking little man who'd rented the car that crashed into Joy's Firebird yesterday. This could be no one else. She shuddered. His presence here meant only one thing. He's seen her go inside the warehouse, had watched Greg and Santos leave, and now he was coming for her. She was shaking all over when she lowered herself to the flat surface of the window and knelt there, struggling to regain control of herself.

His ladder was propped against the opposite end of the building. She had to get out of here or he'd be sure to spot her when he climbed down off the roof. Keeping her knees in one spot she flattened herself to her stomach.

So far so good. The window seemed solid enough to support her—at least when she was lying flat.

She peered over the edge to the ground, about twelve feet below. It looked a long way down, but at least she wouldn't be dropping on concrete. Weedy grasses bordered this side of the building. A hedge of oleander about five feet away marked the property perimeter. Even though its foliage was skimpy, it would have to provide the cover she needed.

Pushing herself around, she gripped an edge of the window near the wall and pulled herself to it with her hands. The closer she stayed to the building, she reasoned, the less likely that the weight of her hanging body would cause the frame to collapse.

Awkwardly she moved to a sitting position at the edge of the window. Then, without giving herself a chance to think about what she was doing, she swung herself around, grabbed the metal frame and dropped into empty space.

Her hands, pierced with wood splinters and bleeding, screamed with pain. Her shoulders felt as though they were being yanked from their sockets.

But her hands held and so did the window. She hung suspended for a breathless instant and then dropped, falling to her side as soon as her feet touched ground to let her hip absorb some of the shock.

He was coming.

Even as she lay there gasping for breath, she heard the scrape of his shoes on the loose rock on the roof. It was a raspy, irregular sound made all the more terrifying by its proximity and speed. He was moving very quickly, almost running, across the roof to his ladder.

A neighborhood dog heard the sound and started barking, a loud German shepherd's bark. Almost immediately a door slammed, a voice yelled into the night, and the barking stopped.

Struggling for breath, Joy managed to get her feet under her. Bent in a half crouch, she bounded to the oleander hedge, tore her way through it, and flung herself down on her stomach on its far side, resting her face on her arm.

She didn't dare raise her head to watch him. In a moment the muffled noises of his metal ladder scraping against stucco told her he was on the ground. There was a subdued rattle of metal parts when he laid the thing out flat in the weeds.

A minute later he loped past her, not two feet from her terrified eyes. If he saw the open window, he gave no sign of it.

Hidden behind the oleander hedge, Joy had a clear view of the street in front of the market but not of its facade. Frozen by a mixture of horror and fascination, she watched the little man turn toward the door. When he didn't reappear, she guessed that he'd somehow gotten inside.

What to do now?

She could run to a neighbor's house and call the police, but who knew how Santos would react when he saw them? Hadn't he said it would "ruin everything" if the local authorities found out what he was up to? Maybe he'd vent his anger on Greg, a possibility she couldn't risk.

She could hail a cab, go home, and lock herself in. But that would leave Greg in limbo when he and Santos returned. If he thought she was still locked up, he'd be at the mercy of both Santos and the fiend inside.

Greg. He had to be her primary consideration. Both those alternatives were out because they threatened him. She had to find some way to let him know she was free without alerting Santos. That was the answer. Perhaps she could arrange a diversion that would give him a chance to get Santos's weapon . . .

Without warning, light flooded the area around the oleander hedge. She shrank into the dirt, hiding her face in her arms, certain that she'd been seen. But no one appeared. She turned her head toward the building.

The windows inside the warehouse were bright with light strong enough to reveal her hiding place. Through the open warehouse window, she heard a man's voice . . . oily, threatening, loathsome.

"You can't hide from me, missy. No use trying."

He was hunting for her inside the warehouse. That meant he hadn't yet noticed the open window.

A terrifying but strangely exciting thought struck her. If she could lock him inside, there was a chance he might still be there when Greg arrived. And even if he wasn't—if he discovered her escape route and dropped from the open window just as she had—she doubted he'd stick around. For all he knew, after she locked him in, she'd gone straight to a phone and called the police.

With adrenaline pumping madly through her, she scrambled to her feet and headed for the street, bursting through the market's front entrance as soon as she reached it. Across the big room, the door to the meat locker was half open, its lights turned off. She ran down the nearest aisle, circled the meat counter, and paused at one side of the metal door, where he couldn't see her if he'd left the entrance to the warehouse open.

Cautiously she peered around the heavy metal frame.

There was a crack of light in the darkness at the far end. That meant the door was ajar, but just barely.

Joy took a deep breath. If he thought she was hiding in the warehouse, he'd have to stay near the door to be certain she didn't escape while he was searching for her. But he'd probably have his back to the refrigerator. Maybe she could close the door without his noticing.

She slipped inside, moving next to the wall beside the half carcasses of beef on their meat hooks. By staying behind them, she avoided framing herself in the light from the market. As she neared the door, she paused, holding her breath, listening.

It was too quiet. A stab of pure terror shot through Joy. What if he'd gotten out the open window, circled around, and was even now behind her, hidden near one of the hanging carcasses?

Then she heard a snorting noise from inside the warehouse, the same sound he'd made on the roof. As she'd guessed, he was near the door. She let her breath out slowly, with infinite care.

Reaching for the handle, she pushed the door the last couple of inches until it closed. Just as carefully she swung the handle down. She didn't want him to hear her. The longer it took him to figure out that he was locked in, the better the chances that he'd still be there when Greg came back.

The bolt was hanging on a chain near the handle. She thrust it through the two rings, pushing with all her strength. For good measure, she stood behind it and shoved with her full weight, ignoring the pain in her hands.

It was done.

If Mr. Gargoyle came out, he'd have to exit through the window. And if he came through the window, she wanted to watch him flee in a panic, the way creepy things always fled when somebody turned over their rocks.

Closing the meat-locker door behind her, she ran through the market and took up her position flat on her stomach behind the oleanders. He'd probably turn the lights off, the same way she had, before he began climbing the crates. In the darkness, hidden behind the hedge, she would be virtually invisible.

His voice floated to her through the open window.

"We've played enough games, missy. Since you won't come out on your own, let's see how you like a little smoke."

Smoke! Joy couldn't believe what she'd heard. Nobody would be so stupid as to set a fire in a warehouse piled high with arms and ammunition.

He doesn't know, Joy thought, stunned. *That means he isn't Santos Mueller's man. But if he isn't working with Santos, whose man is he?*

Chapter Eighteen

A tendril of smoke curled from the open window. The little man inside the warehouse must have set fire to the tumbled crates beneath the window, unknowingly cutting off his only escape route. Before Joy's horrified eyes, the glow of light intensified, began dancing. More smoke poured out.

She trembled as panicky doubts assailed her.

Something was going on here that made no sense. What if she were wrong? What if he wasn't the murderer?

And even if her worst suspicions were true, there was no way she was going to lie quietly behind an oleander hedge and watch a human being burn to death, not if there was anything she could do about it. She'd locked him in and, by heaven, she'd open the door and let him out.

For the second time in the past ten minutes, she leaped to her feet and began running toward the street. As soon as she hit the market's front door, she could smell the smoke. The trashy odor of burning cardboard filled the air around her.

She pounded down the narrow aisle, barely conscious of the cans she knocked off the shelves in her frenzied dash for the meat locker. The butcher-shop counter loomed before her and she scrambled around it. When she reached the meat locker, she flung the door open, leaving it gaping wide behind her.

Gasping for breath, she slid to a stop at the end of the refrigerated room. The handle on the door to the warehouse was jerking up and down, a frantic signal that the man on its other side had finally figured out that he was locked in his own fiery prison.

She grabbed the bolt and yanked it. Nothing happened. She yanked again. It didn't move. The man on the other side was putting pressure against the door, tightening the bolt.

Her hands felt like pieces of raw meat. Her fingers couldn't find purchase on the stubborn metal.

The smell of smoke was getting much stronger. Joy's nose and eyes began watering. In the distance she heard the wail of a siren.

The frantic jerking of the handle slowed and stopped.

She pulled harder on the bolt, then glanced wildly around, searching for something solid to pound against it. There was nothing.

She ran to the market. It was beginning to fill with puffs of smoke. She gasped for breath. Taking in air became a painful ordeal. She yanked her sweater up so that it covered her nose and mouth, but could do nothing about her burning eyes. Crouching close to the floor, she grabbed a can from the nearest shelf.

Outside, the scream of sirens, much closer now, slashed through the foggy night.

Bending low, Joy dashed through the locker to the warehouse door. She shoved the can against the bolt. It didn't move. Then she put the sole of her shoe flat against the bottom of the can and, bracing herself, shoved with her entire weight. The can burst open, its top pierced by the bolt. Tomatoes from inside the can splattered all over her jeans as she tumbled backwards.

But there's been some movement in the blasted thing. She leaped to her feet and clawed at it, trying desperately to yank it out. Dimly aware of the sirens outside, she didn't notice anybody behind her until she heard Greg's shout.

"Joy! Thank God you're safe!" He grabbed her arm, forcing her to turn, "We've got to get out of here."

"No!" Joy twisted back, grabbed the bolt and yanked it free. "There's a man inside. He may still be alive."

Greg didn't stop to ask questions. Jerking the handle, he swung the door open. Clouds of smoke billowed out of the room. Crumpled on the floor behind the door was the pathetic body of a little man with a gargoyle's face.

Greg threw him over his shoulder, like a gunnysack full of potatoes, and yanked the door shut behind them.

"Run like hell," he yelled. "This place is going to blow any second."

They made the street before the explosions started. A series of sharp bursts shook the ground. Sparks shot skyward, turning the foggy night into a giant fourth-of-July display. Two fire trucks stood on the street in front of the market, their hoses gushing streams of water.

When Greg and Joy were well away from the fire, he lowered his burden to the sidewalk and leaned forward to begin mouth-to-mouth resuscitation.

A man appeared behind him. "I'll take over," he said. Then Joy saw that an emergency vehicle, its lights flashing, had pulled up at the curb.

Santos, still in his blue bathrobe, materialized out of the orange brightness. He was followed by a stranger in a dark brown suit. Terrified, Joy gripped Greg's arm. He hugged her, holding her close.

Everything's going to be all right, she thought, her mind swimming. *It's all over and everything's going to be all right.* She felt dizzy and would have fallen but for Greg's arm behind her.

"I owe you one, Colonel," said the man in the brown suit. Joy eyed him, perceiving instantly that he was a government agent.

"Between the two of you, you've managed to save the life of your would-be killer," he said. "Tomorrow I want to hear the whole story." He checked the paramedic's progress.

The figure on the sidewalk was breathing regularly.

The agent bent down and nudged his shoulder. "You've got a lot of talking to do, haven't you, bud?"

The little man opened his bloodshot eyes. "Screw you," he said, his voice scratchy.

The medics put him on a stretcher. The agent climbed in the ambulance with him, and the vehicle took off, its siren wailing.

Santos turned toward Joy. "I must apologize for my incorrect assumption about you, Captain, and for the indignity of locking you up."

"That was more than an indignity, Mueller," Greg said harshly. "What you did nearly cost her her life."

From the tone of Greg's voice, Joy doubted he would ever call Santos amigo again.

"I also detect a certain method in your studied friendship for me as the DLI Commandant," Greg went on, his good eye fixed on the instructor in a cold stare.

"I was an FBI informant," Santos replied softly. "Can you suggest a better way to keep informed, *Comandante?*"

Joy's ears pricked up. FBI informant? Santos Mueller? She blinked. Amanda Hawkins was striding toward them.

"Word travels quickly, Deputy," Greg said.

"Mr. Jones called the local police from his car right after you and Mueller left the motel," she said. "Since I've got a primary interest in this case—meaning you and Captain Donnelly and the two Carmel Valley murders—they let me know right away."

She handed something to Joy. "We found the suspect's van parked on the street in back. This was in it."

Joy stared down. In her hand was a single enlisted air force service insignia, the duplicate of the one Joy had found on the hill across from Maria Cardoza's house.

"The suspect had your airman's clothes in his van at some time or other," Amanda explained, "and the insignia dropped out of a pocket. I'm guessing he chloroformed Ms. Cardoza and your airmen, using the minimum amount of gas to prevent detection in the autopsy. He drowned them in the pool as soon as possible afterward—that means with their clothes on—dressed them in their swimming suits after they were dead, and threw their bodies back in the pool.

He couldn't leave the wet clothes in the house, so he took them with him.''

"But why did he do it, Amanda? There had to be a reason.''

"Because he was getting paid, of course." Amanda flashed her wide grin. "Don't worry, Joy. No matter how tough he is, he'll talk to save his skin. The money won't do him much good where he's going."

BEFORE GREG TOOK Joy home, he insisted on stopping at the Fort Ord hospital so that she could get her hands treated and bandaged. While they waited for the doctor, they shared the evening's war stories.

"What's going to happen to Santos?" Joy asked, after Greg told her about the instructor's role as an informant and arms shipper.

"As we were leaving the motel, Agent Jones told him he'd outlived his usefulness—said he'd have to leave the country in forty-eight hours. Knowing Santos, I imagine he'll devote the next few years to spending that pile of money he made."

Joy leaned back in her chair in the hospital's well-lighted emergency-room reception area. Across from her a young woman with a small child drank coffee from a plastic cup.

"So Santos gets off scot-free, a rich man. It doesn't seem fair, Greg."

"Prosecuting him for arms smuggling would have opened up a nasty can of worms worse than the Contra scandal," Greg replied thoughtfully. "Since the government knew about it and didn't arrest him, putting him on trial would raise all sorts of questions. Plus that, he was a paid informer, and a trial might have revealed classified information about the program. I'm sure there are people in Washington who will sleep a lot easier when he's safely tucked aboard a plane for Paraguay."

Joy sighed. "Well, it's pretty obvious he's not behind the murders. Do you suppose the murderer was that spy he and Agent Jones were after?"

"It's sure possible. Actually, the murderer could be anybody Maria Cardoza was blackmailing."

"We're almost positive she was after Julio Ramon," Joy went on. "And we think he used her modem to send the 'School for Spies' article to the *Tribune* editor. You don't suppose Julio's the spy?"

Before Greg could answer, a nurse called Joy into a small room where a young female doctor treated her wounded hands. Joy tried to ignore the stinging pain by concentrating on Julio and the embarrassing article.

"Julio Ramon couldn't be the spy," she said, after the doctor had finished and they were leaving the hospital. "According to what Agent Jones told you, there were a number of traitors, each selling secrets to a different country. That means they were each fluent in a different language, not just Spanish."

"Then the spy must be somebody who has a legitimate reason to come in contact with a lot of students."

Joy stopped dead in her tracks. "And who's been overly interested in all the language school graduates assigned to our super-secret National Security Agency?"

Greg's eye narrowed. "Colonel Spellman and Sergeant Philpott." He shook his head. "I can't believe either one of them . . . but they both have access to the keys to my house. Either could have paid someone to plant Maria's crystal in my bathroom."

"One of them's running an espionage ring and Maria knew it." Joy started across the parking lot, her pace much quicker now. "That's why she wrote the 'School for Spies' column. To pressure the spy to cough up more money. I'll bet she never intended to publish it. Just to show it to whomever she was blackmailing."

They reached the Cherokee and got in.

"We're going to get to the bottom of this right now," Greg said grimly. He turned out of the parking lot. "Philpott and Spellman have some explaining to do. So does Julio Ramon. He may not be the spy we're after, but he's involved in this up to his ears." He glanced at Joy. "How long will it take you to change into your uniform?"

Joy saw the determined look on his face. "At least half an hour."

The Jeep's speed increased noticeably after they swung off the post. "Make it ten minutes. We don't want to give our spy time to find out what's happened to his or her hired killer."

"Greg, I've got to shower. I've got tomato sauce all over me."

She saw his gaze drop to her bandaged hands. His grim expression melted.

"Okay." His voice was gruff. "Half an hour it is, but sooner if you can. Pretend you're back in basic and the squadron's got to be on the drill field in five minutes. I'll make the telephone calls from your place while you're dressing."

"What are you going to tell them?"

"That I want to see them in my office at ten o'clock tonight." The authority in his voice was unmistakable.

JOY SHUDDERED when she saw Greg slide a service revolver into his desk drawer. He'd picked up the weapon at his quarters when he'd changed into his green service uniform.

"I doubt I'll need this, but nobody's going to catch me off guard again." He didn't sit down. Instead, he pulled a straight-backed chair across the room to a place near the door and motioned Joy toward it. "This is for you. Sitting here, you'll be out of the line of fire if one of them pulls anything."

She'd hardly be able to see their faces. Joy started to protest and swallowed her words. Stationed near the big mahogany door with its old-fashioned brass knob, she'd be behind their three suspects. That might be an advantage. Besides, this was no time for foolish bravado. She could have gotten Greg killed this afternoon by causing Santos to fire his weapon. It mustn't happen again. She couldn't let herself forget she was part of a team.

Erick Spellman, who lived on post, was the first to arrive. He was dressed in civilian clothes—a blue knitted shirt with a well-worn tan sweater over Bermuda shorts that exposed slightly bowed, hairy legs. As soon as he spotted Joy in her air force blues, he said hello and started apologizing to Greg.

"Sorry about the civvies, Colonel Weston. I thought this was going to be an informal chat between the two of us. Didn't realize there'd be anybody else around, or that you'd be in uniform."

Greg glanced at his watch. "The others should be here shortly.

"Others?" Erick Spellman turned toward the door. "Maybe I should go home and change."

"Sit down on the sofa, Colonel," Greg said shortly.

Spellman did so. "What's this all about, sir? Who else is coming?"

"I'll explain when they arrive." Without further explanation, Greg seated himself behind his desk.

An expectant silence filled the room. It was broken by Sergeant Philpott's entrance a few minutes later. As usual, her uniform was freshly pressed, her brass gleaming, her shoes spit-polished. Joy had never seen her any other way.

Greg stood when she approached his desk. "Sergeant Philpott reporting as ordered, sir," she said, saluting.

He returned her salute. "Sit beside Colonel Spellman on the couch, please."

As she sat down, Joy caught the assistant commandant's don't-ask-me-what's-going-on shrug. Sergeant Philpott made no answering move that Joy could see. Instead, she pulled a notebook and pen from her bag, put them in her lap, and folded her hands. Only the nervous squeezing of her fingers revealed her nervousness.

Julio Ramon came in at exactly ten o'clock. He was dressed in a dark blue business suit with a light blue shirt and red bow tie. Joy caught a whiff of bourbon as he nodded and said good evening to her. Quietly she closed the door behind him.

When Julio was seated next to Sergeant Philpott, Greg came around his desk and stood in front of it, his arms folded, facing the sofa. Joy leaned forward expectantly. For what seemed an eternity, he said nothing.

Finally, he spoke. "You three are here because you were being blackmailed by Maria Cardoza. One of you murdered her. I want to know who."

A kind of horrified quiet engulfed the room. The shock waves coming from the sofa were palpable. If Greg intended to shake up his listeners, he'd certainly succeeded.

Then Erick Spellman shot to his feet. "She sure as hell wasn't blackmailing me, Weston. Murder! My God! You'd better get your facts straight before you make accusations like that...er, sir."

"Sit down, Colonel." Greg's voice was like a splash of cold water on Spellman's angry face. Slowly the balding little man returned to his seat.

"Thank you," Greg said when his command had been obeyed. "Now will you please explain why you organized those briefings for our students being assigned to the National Security Agency."

"As a favor to them, of course. Whatsamatter? There's something wrong with trying to make things a little smoother for them?" Joy heard the puzzlement in his voice.

"You'd been assigned there. Sergeant Philpott hadn't. Why bring her along?"

Barbara Philpott answered for Spellman. "He wanted me to take notes, sir."

Joy watched Spellman's head jerk toward the noncom. "Tell him the whole story, Sergeant. The briefings were your idea. You're the one who organized them. I just came along for the ride."

Greg focused on his secretary. "Is that right, Sergeant Philpott?"

"No, sir, it isn't." She didn't look at Spellman. "The colonel must have forgotten. I made the arrangements only after he suggested it."

"I can't imagine why—but she's lying, sir." Spellman sounded flabbergasted. Joy couldn't tell whether or not he was acting.

Suddenly Joy remembered what her training officer had said—that Barbara Philpott was the one who got the briefings going. Did that mean Erick Spellman was right and Sergeant Philpott was lying? Or did it mean that the officer had believed a lie told to him by Erick Spellman?

"Don't worry, Colonel." Greg's expression was grim. "If somebody's lying, we'll find out who and why." Greg turned his attention to Julio Ramon, who'd been sitting as one petrified, ever since Greg's first words.

"Julio, please tell me why you sent the 'School for Spies' article you found in Maria's computer to the *Tribune*?"

The Spanish Department head's voice was so low, Joy could barely hear him. "What makes you think I would do something like that, *Comandante*?"

"That's what I'm asking you, Julio. Why you did it. We know Maria was blackmailing you about your Fascist..."

"You don't have to go on." The man's voice was trembling. "Maria had hinted that Captain Donnelly was her collaborator. When I saw the captain's name and picture in the column, I assumed it was true. Maria must have written the article to persuade someone. They'd probably threatened her, and she wanted to remind them that the blackmail could continue even if something happened to her." He fell silent, as though afraid he'd said too much.

"We're waiting," Greg said, his face threatening.

He knows what's coming, Joy thought, wondering what Julio could say that would make Greg look so angry.

"When I found the body, I was sure Maria had been murdered. I wanted to be certain nobody connected me with her. The column had nothing to do with me. If it were published, I knew it would put attention elsewhere."

Greg stepped toward him. The department head shrank back against the sofa cushions.

"It would put attention on Captain Donnelly. Right, Ramon? Didn't you hope the murderer would see the article, believe—as you did—that Captain Donnelly was Maria's collaborator, and get rid of her, too?''

Joy couldn't believe what she was hearing. Had Julio Ramon set out to have her killed? Was that the real reason he had sent Eye's "School for Spies" column to the *Monterey Tribune*?

Chapter Nineteen

Julio Ramon had wanted her dead! Joy's knees turned to water as she forced herself to accept the fact. She was glad she was sitting off to the side where the three people on the couch couldn't see her face.

Suddenly he twisted toward her. "I'm sorry, Captain. I was convinced you were collaborating with that evil woman."

"No matter what you thought, there was no excuse for what you did." Greg's voice brimmed with disgust. "Trying to get Captain Donnelly murdered!" His scowl darkened the room. "You're damned lucky she's alive. Damned lucky. I'd better have your resignation on my desk at 0800 tomorrow morning, or the authorities are going to hear how you tampered with evidence in a murder case."

"The police believe it was an accident..." Julio protested.

"Not any more they don't." Greg spit the words out. "Before you decide to fight my order, think about a trial and what it entails."

"But the language school is my life, *Comandante*." Pulling a handkerchief from his pocket, he coughed into it.

Even though Julio Ramon had almost gotten Joy killed by sending Eye's column to the *Tribune*, Joy felt a twinge of sympathy for the man. He seemed on the verge of breaking down.

"You should have thought of that sooner, señor." Greg's voice was harsh. "Your plan worked, you know. Maria's murderer tried to kill Captain Donnelly three times since that article was published. It's only by the grace of God that they've failed."

Julio turned toward Joy again. She could see the glassiness in his eyes, could hear the pleading in his words. "You must forgive me, Captain. I am truly sorry."

Joy searched her soul and couldn't find the words he wanted to hear. "I can't do that, Julio. Maybe later—when this is behind us."

Like a shadow diminishing before the nooning sun, he seemed to sag into himself when he turned toward Greg. "You'll have my resignation in the morning, *Comandante.*" He struggled awkwardly to his feet.

"Sit down," Greg commanded. "We're not through here, yet."

Beaten, Ramon fell back on the sofa.

Greg focused on Barbara Philpott. "Why don't you tell us about the espionage ring you've organized, Sergeant?"

Shocked silence greeted Greg's question. Nobody moved or breathed.

When Sergeant Philpott finally spoke, her voice was low but clear. "I beg your pardon, sir?"

"You heard me, Sergeant."

"You'd better be careful whom you're accusing, Colonel." Her tone sharpened. "I agree with Colonel Spellman. You start spreading nasty rumors about us, and we'll take action against you."

"Hey, leave me out of this," Spellman mumbled, shrinking away from her.

"I haven't done anything." Sergeant Philpott's voice was growing more strident. "If you think I have, where's your proof?"

Joy knew there was no proof.

So did Barbara Philpott. Joy sensed that the woman was even then making plans to disappear as soon as she left Greg's office. She probably had a pile of cash stashed in some foreign bank account.

"The servicepeople you picked to be traitors didn't know you were behind it, did they, Sergeant?" Greg asked. "It was strictly between you and the countries that used them. You supplied the names and the backgrounds. Their agents did the one-on-one recruiting."

The woman's position on the sofa changed subtly. More erect, she seemed to be gathering strength. "I don't know what you're talking about, sir."

She was trying to get away with murder! Joy could see it in her confident bearing, could hear it in the contemptuous tone of her voice. Joy wasn't going to let her.

"You know exactly what he's talking about, Sergeant Philpott," she said clearly, from her chair by the door.

Startled, the three people on the sofa turned toward her. Greg looked as startled as they did, but Joy didn't let that stop her.

"You suspected all along that I was the gray eminence behind Maria Cardoza," she began. "I'm sure she hinted as much to you, just as she did to Señor Ramon. That's why you were so hostile to me."

Sergeant Philpott's expression was smug. "I didn't even know the woman, Captain."

"Of course you did. When her fiancé, Airman Tuck, came to me right after he'd spent an evening with the Carmel Valley deputy sheriff, you were even more positive Maria and I had been in cahoots. That's when you started having me followed, the way you did him."

"If you were being followed, I had nothing to do with it, ma'am."

Joy detected a shade less confidence in the noncom's tone. The woman was guilty. By now, Joy was certain of it, but she wanted to hear Barbara Philpott admit it. She bored in with the persistence of a yellow jacket after a picnic lunch.

"As Colonel Weston said, you weren't completely convinced until you saw that Eye column in last Thursday's paper. That's when you sicked your paid assassin on me. You were the only one, outside of the commandant, Santos Mueller, and me, who knew we were going to the Sportsmen's Club on Saturday. You had plenty of time to make the arrangements. When we got there, your man was waiting for us with his high-powered rifle.''

"I don't know what you're talking about, ma'am." Although the noncom spoke in the same contemptuous tone, Joy detected a shrill edge that hadn't been there before. She sensed that the woman's defenses were crumbling.

"You're starting to sound like a broken record, Barbara." Joy used the woman's first name to remove the respect implicit in her military rank. What she'd done made her unfit to wear her stripes.

"You might as well tell us the whole story," Joy went on. "Your assassin—an odd little man with a face like a gargoyle—is in custody. Colonel Weston and I caught him burning down a warehouse in another attempt to kill me. The police say he's very willing to talk to save his skin."

Barbara Philpott's face drained of color when she heard Joy's description. She gagged. For an instant, Joy thought she was going to be sick all over Greg's army-blue carpet. Then she lurched to her feet. "That ugly little man has nothing to do with me. He's lying if he says different."

"Sit down, Sergeant," Greg commanded, moving toward her. He grabbed her arm.

She tried to yank herself away. "You can't hold me here against my will. It's against the Code."

"The hell with the Code. Don't give me a hard time or I'll flatten you, so help me."

In spite of Greg's harsh words, Joy doubted that he'd actually hit the woman. Barbara Philpott must have doubted it, too. For an instant she remained motionless. Then, striking quickly on Greg's blind side, she rammed a heel across his instep. At the same time, she punched the fist of her free hand into his Adam's apple.

Gasping for breath, he relaxed his grip on her arm. She jerked free and sprinted toward the door.

Joy knew she had only a fraction of a second to act. Leaping from her chair, she twisted the shiny brass key below the old-fashioned knob and yanked it out of the lock. The woman grabbed Joy's arm, but she was too late by the time of a heartbeat. Joy had already tossed the key. It made a tinkling sound as it hit the wall on the far side of Greg's desk.

Frantically, Barbara Philpott released Joy's arm. Like a woman gone crazy, she yanked at the doorknob, twisting and jerking with the mad strength of a platoon of Furies. The door refused to open.

Still gasping, Greg caught up with her. He grabbed both her wrists and held them behind her back. "You're going to sit down on that sofa until the MPs get here, Sergeant. And don't try pulling another stunt like that. You won't get away with it again, I promise you."

He forced her to the sofa. "Hang onto her, Spellman, so she doesn't try something before the MPs get here."

Instead of doing as Greg asked, the assistant commandant leaned away from the sergeant. "She's right, Colonel. Holding an enlisted person against their will is against the Uniform Code of Military Justice."

Unexpectedly, Julio Ramon locked bony fingers around the sergeant's wrist. "It's not against my code, *Comandante*. Let me do the honors. An unemployed department head isn't bound by your military rules." From the way Barbara Philpott flinched, Joy suspected Julio's grip was less than gentle.

Greg went to his desk, dialed a number, and said a few terse words into the receiver. "The police are on their way," he said, after he'd hung up.

Joy was still standing near the door. As she watched the three people on the sofa, she was engulfed by a grief almost as deep as that she'd felt for Airman Tuck. Why had Barbara Philpott, a career non-commisioned officer dedicated to the Army, committed such heinous crimes as espionage and murder?

Joy came around the sofa where she could see the woman. Although her face was pale, it still wore a defiant contemptuous expression.

"How much money did it take to get you to betray your country, Barbara?" she asked softly. Folding her arms, she stared down at the woman in front of her.

There was no remorse on the sergeant's face. "You're wrong when you say it was betrayal, Captain. The United States isn't at war."

Joy couldn't believe what she'd heard. "*Not at war!* Does that mean there's no need for us to protect ourselves as long as we're not at war?"

"None of the countries I worked with was going to attack us." She made the statement flatly, as though it were obvious and Joy were being dense by questioning her about it. "I was simply doing a favor for Third-World people who needed a little information."

"Information about our national defenses? About the defenses of their neighbors so they can start ruthless little border wars to grab more territory? The way Iraq grabbed Kuwait? C'mon, Barbara. Why don't you admit you did it for the money." Joy studied the woman's face.

Sergeant Philpott shrugged. "Because that makes me sound like a traitor and I'm not. The money was important, but it didn't mean I betrayed anybody."

Joy felt Greg beside her. "If it wasn't betrayal, then what the hell was it?"

Joy could hear the anger in his voice. And the pain. With sudden insight, she realized that Greg must feel hurt and deceived himself—even more than Joy did. He'd trusted Sergeant Philpott and she had betrayed his trust.

"Like I said, Colonel, it was a way to help the Third World."

"What a stupid thing to say!" Joy forgot about Greg and the two men on the couch. She forgot that she was a captain and the other woman was a sergeant. The only thing that mattered was that this was someone who had defiled the military uniform, and who was making incredibly dumb excuses for what she'd done.

"Don't you realize that Third World countries are behind most of the terrorist operations in the world?" Joy's eyes blazed as she warmed to her subject. "How can you sit there and make excuses for helping them?"

The woman's expression turned self-righteous. "The United States meddles too much. What other countries do is their own business. We should just let them alone."

"Even if their own business—as you put it—is manufacturing chemical and biological weapons that can wipe out whole populations? Or using food as a bargaining chip to stay in power while hundreds of thousands of their people starve to death?"

Sergeant Philpott shrugged. "None of that has anything to do with a so-called betrayal of the United States."

"Then how about Airman Tuck's murder? How can you justify that?"

"Maria Cardoza was an evil woman who deserved to die."

"You didn't answer my question. What about poor Airman Tuck? Did he deserve to die, too, because he was her fiancé?"

The sergeant looked away from Joy's penetrating gaze. "He was a nosy young man who didn't know when he was well-off."

"And because of that, he had to die." Joy fought her feeling of grief and revulsion. "I can't look at you any more, Barbara Philpott. The sight of your face is making me sick."

Swallowing her angry tears, Joy returned to her chair.

LATER, after two military policemen had led a recalcitrant Barbara Philpott away, Greg took Joy home.

"Come in for some coffee," she urged, too keyed-up to let the night end.

"Sure you're not tired?"

"Heavens, no. Just the opposite. If you don't come in I'll end up talking to myself about all that's happened."

He laughed. "We sure can't have that."

In the kitchen, Joy put a kettle on the stove and measured instant coffee into two cups. When it was ready, they sat down across from each other at the table.

Inevitably, the conversation started with Barbara Philpott. Joy was too grieved by the woman's crimes to refer to her by her military rank. "Can you believe the excuses she—

Barbara—used to rationalize what she did, Greg? Imagine. Do you think she believed what she said about helping Third World countries?''

Greg nodded thoughtfully. "If criminals didn't rationalize, they wouldn't be able to live with themselves."

"What about Julio Ramon, Greg? Are you really going to fire him?" Joy took a sip of her coffee. It was too hot and she put more milk in it. "He seemed awfully sorry for what he did."

"He got off easy." Greg's face darkened, the way it had in his office when he'd learned Julio was indirectly responsible for the attempts to kill Joy. "As long as I'm commandant of the Defense Language Institute, Señor Julio Ramon will not be on the staff."

"Will he be able to get his job back when the new commandant comes on board? Joy felt sorry for the man in spite of what he'd done.

"It may be awhile before there's a new DLI Commandant, Joy. I wasn't going to tell you this tonight, but since it's come up— I've decided to extend my tour here."

Joy stared at him wide-eyed, hardly daring to hope she was reading him right.

"Are you sure you want to extend, Greg?" She leaned across the table toward him. "You hate this job."

He reached out and took her hand in both of his. "When I thought you were inside that burning warehouse, I wanted to kill Santos Mueller. I would have torn him apart if anything happened to you. Then, tonight, when Julio admitted he'd gotten that article published for only one reason— to get you killed— I had the same reaction. It set me to thinking about what's important and what isn't."

"I know." She spoke quickly so she wouldn't lose her nerve. "More and more over the past few days I've felt like we were a team—like the two of us working together had a much better chance of success than the two of us working separately. It's made me change an idea I've had all my life—that she travels farthest who travels alone."

He caressed her bandaged hand. "My goals are different, now, too. When I saw you standing inside that meat locker, I knew a year here with you was worth ten anywhere else." Just touching Joy's hand made him dizzy with longing. A woman's apron strings had never before looked so good.

"If you find a slot you like better than the one here as commandant, I'll arrange a transfer to an air force base as close to your army post as I can get." Joy half stood from her chair and reached for him with her free hand. "If we can come up with a compassionate reason for the transfer, it shouldn't be any problem."

Greg leaned toward her, and she sat down again. "The only compassionate reason I can think of is marriage." His pulse was pounding so hard he was sure she could hear it. "But if you marry me, you'll never make general. And it's a cinch you'll never be married to one."

Greg had to give her a chance to refuse. He knew how much her military service career meant to her. It would be virtually impossible for her to arrange career-enhancing assignments if her first priority were being stationed near him. "Do you think you could stand being married to a one-eyed mustang colonel for the rest of your life?"

Freeing the hand he was holding, Joy cupped his face with her fingers and stared straight across the table at him. "For a man who sees better with one eye than most people with two, you've got a serious blind spot, Greg Weston."

"What is it?" He saw the sparkle in her eyes. It belied the serious look on her face.

"You're underestimating my abilities again. Only this time you're underestimating yours, too." She grinned, the wide Irish grin he loved so much. "Wouldn't care to make a little wager on which of us makes O-7 first, would you, Colonel? Or does the idea of being married to a general scare you too much to risk a bet?"

Greg grinned back at her. His beloved adversary was in as good form as ever. "I can't think of anything I'd like better than being married to a general—as long as the general is you."

He meant every word, and she knew it.

"The feeling's mutual," she replied.

my VALENTINE 1992

Celebrate the most romantic day of the year with
MY VALENTINE 1992—a sexy new collection of four
romantic stories written by our famous Temptation
authors:

> GINA WILKINS
> KRISTINE ROLOFSON
> JOANN ROSS
> VICKI LEWIS THOMPSON

My Valentine 1992—an exquisite escape into a romantic
and sensuous world.

 Harlequin Books

VAL-92-R

Take 4 bestselling love stories FREE

Plus get a FREE surprise gift!